I0666403

# Incoming

Prudence MacLeod

Published by Prudence MacLeod, 2024.

# Incoming

(second edition)

by

## Prudence MacLeod

Copyright: Prudence MacLeod / April 15/2008

INCOMING

**First edition. April 9, 2024.**

ISBN: 978-1927478844

Written by Prudence MacLeod.

# Instinct

Did you ever notice that, sometimes, something small will catch your attention? A thing that seems so insignificant it should be unworthy of your notice, but somehow it sends shivers up your spine and tells you, beyond a shadow of a doubt, that your world has just changed forever.

That's how it was for Heather MacKay, one hot summer night. It was just a small flicker of light but, when pointed out, it caught her attention. A second later it flickered again and she sat up straighter in her chair. The third time it flickered a shiver of cold fear ran down her spine, for she knew then that the burning question which had shaped her life was about to be answered and she would finally be vindicated.

QULLAR, NINETEENTH Emperor of the Minaor Dynasty, gazed down from the raised dais upon which his throne rested. Before him stood a creature vastly different from his own people. She was a hybrid of two species that had, out of necessity, united to create an entirely new race; a warrior people like no other in the empire. In truth, he owed his empire to their sacrifice, but now he had to find a way to be rid of them. They were far too popular now, and he feared they might turn against him if they had no other wars to fight.

Their leader knew this of course, and he knew that she knew. Ah well, he had timed it as best he could. The page was waiting in the wings for the signal, her enemies had been set in motion, and all he could do now was put a happy face on it and hope that it would work.

"Long ago," Qullar, began, "the last battleship of Nylass warriors brought down a Gray Raider transport. Both ships crashed on a nearly barren planet, unable to rise again. After the Greys were dispatched, the captives of the Greys and the last of the Nylass warriors melded themselves into a new people, the Nymen. Somehow this new folk managed to repair the aging battleship and return to the empire. It took them many long age cycles, but return they did.

"For the past five generations, your people have fought to protect the empire." Qullar stepped down to stand looking up into the fierce blue eyes of the tall, battle-scarred woman. "I am told that it was your leadership and courage that has not only prevented us from being overrun, but has actually granted us the victory."

She smiled in return, but the smile did not reach her eyes. "My lord is too kind."

"We are all in your debt, as is the entire empire. Name your reward, Freydis Pull-Karr. If it exists at all in the four quadrants of the galaxy of my empire, you shall have it."

"The home world of the Nylass was destroyed by the Greys, Great Lord, but we believe the home world of our human ancestors may still exist, at the rim of the fourth quadrant of the galaxy. The wars are over now, and there is little room for retired warriors in polite society. We ask for ships large enough to carry those of us who would seek out that place, and we beg permission to go."

"You shall have it, Freydis. I am told it was your ship and two others who broke through the enemy lines and set them into disarray. That is your ship, Captain, and the two who followed you. Take as many transports as you need. The empire will miss you, but you have earned your reward."

Suddenly, Qullar pretended to notice a page trying to get his attention. "Come!" The small one skidded to a halt, kneeling before the emperor. "Speak."

"The home world of Lord Freydis has been found, Sire. A small armada of Grey ships seems to be heading that way."

"Why?"

"The great minds believe that, since the last defeat at the hands of the empire, the Greys need slaves, captives for breeders and warriors, and food for their carrion fighters. The last of their great fleet is heading that way."

Nodding his huge head, Qullar turned back to the woman. "You have no time to lose, Freydis Pull-Karr. Take your ships, your people, and go. May your gods be with you."

# Flicker

Heather MacKay stretched her tall, lean frame as she rose from her chair. This was a completely boring job, but she had requested it and she embraced it. Everyone thought she was a bit crazy, but she knew the truth. There was something out there and Heather meant to prove it. She shook out her long golden hair and made a few graceful martial arts moves before sinking back into her chair.

No one ever truly believes a story about alien abduction, at least not unless you personally have experienced it. Heather had, or so she believed. The first time had been as a child, then again as a young teenager, and the last time as a young adult. That was ten years past, but it still haunted her mind.

These abductions, and the humiliating abuses she believed she had been subjected to, were very real to Heather, that is why she chose astronomy as a career. It was also why she had studied karate for so many years. She had vowed that, the next time, she would kill her attackers, or die in the attempt.

Heather sighed deeply and returned her gaze to the computer screen before her. True, there was a huge telescope in the gigantic room she occupied with her two colleagues, but they rarely looked through it. The information being beamed back to earth from the scope out in space was far more detailed and of greater interest.

"See anything earth shattering?" asked a small man as, smiling, he approached and offered her a coffee. He was in his sixties and nearing retirement age, although he often swore he'd rather die than retire.

"SSDD," she replied, as she accepted the cup from his hand.

"So why don't you run away with some young buck and live a life of complete decadence on the beach somewhere?"

"Love to, Jimmy my sweet, but there are none such out here on this godforsaken mountain."

Suddenly the room was filled with a blinding light and a soft humming noise. "Run, Jim!" She pushed him aside and swept up a chair which she hurled into the light.

"Whoooo, whooo, come to me, earth woman." A soft male voice oozed from behind the light. "I want you to bear my children."

The voice was cut short by bellowing laughter as the light dropped to the floor and a young man stood holding his sides as he shook with mirth. Gasping for breath, he pointed at Heather and made the 'whooo' sound again.

"Frank Hunter, you stupid son of a bitch." Heather was trembling as her emotions shifted from fear to rage. "This time you've gone too far. You clean up this mess then get your sorry ass off the premises. You're fired."

"Aw, Heather, come on girl, I was just having a bit of fun with you. Where's your sense of humour?"

"I don't have one, now clean this mess up."

"So I see. Alright, I'll clean it up. You can't fire me though. My father helps funds this operation and you need me."

"I don't need you at all, Frank, I already have an asshole. Tell your father to screw himself."

"I did," he muttered, as he started sopping up the coffee she'd spilled. "That's why I'm here being tortured."

"You have no idea what torture is, Frank, but try that again and you'll learn the hard way." With that she stormed off to the washroom to clean herself up as best she could.

"Tortured, Frank?" Jim asked the young man softly.

"I'm stuck out here in the desert with a man who just stares at the sky all night, and the world's most beautiful woman. A woman who is as crazy as a loon and who hates my guts. A woman I am absolutely mad for. I swear, I'd sell my soul just to see her smile at me, but..."

"One man's madness is another man's genius." Jim grinned at the hapless young man. "Heather may or may not be crazy, Frank, but you're the reason she hates you. Those experiences you read about on the internet are real to her. What the hell possessed you to do such a fool thing like this anyway?"

He sighed as he cleaned up the last of the broken mug. "Aw, I dunno, Jim. I guess I just wanted to get her attention so badly, I cracked."

"Well, you sure accomplished your aim." Jim chuckled as he passed Frank more paper towels.

"Okay, so I blew it all to hell. What do I do now?"

"Apologize to her, and mean it. Give her time to cool down first, and then apologize. Oh yeah, if you really want to get on Heather's good side, start acting like an adult and taking your work seriously."

"I do take my work seriously." He paused, then sighed. "Yeah, I guess you're right, Jim." Frank righted the chair she'd thrown at him. He pulled it over to the computer desk and sat down just as Heather returned from the washroom.

"You okay, honey?" asked Jim as he stepped into her path.

"Sure, fine." Heather didn't meet his eyes. She was still trembling from the effects of the adrenaline rush.

"Liar, lair, pants on fire." He gently took her in his arms.

Heather had never known her real father, and Jim was both a mentor and a father figure to her. She melted into his arms for a moment and let the tension subside. "He knows he crossed the line, sweetie. Be merciful."

"Can I torture him a bit first?"

"Sure, he's got that much coming." Jim grinned as he released her.

Heather approached the contrite young man in the chair at the computer. Frank Hunter was six years her junior. He truly was a devoted astronomer, but he had been so smitten by the first sight of Heather MacKay, he'd completely reverted to the behaviours of an awkward teenager. However, seeing the effect his practical joke had on her seemed to have snapped him out of it. "Now what the hell are you doing?"

"Taking the first of a thousand steps."

"Explain."

Frank rose and turned to gaze into those fierce blue eyes, and under that withering gaze, Frank the Joker died. "A journey of a thousand miles begins with a single step," he said softly as he met her eyes. "Heather MacKay, I have behaved like an ass since I first met you. I apologize for that, and especially for what I did here tonight.

"I know it'll take forever to make it up to you, but I swear I'm going to give it my best shot. I thought I'd start by keeping an eye on this monitor while you go home and change the clothes I ruined. I will pay all your cleaning bills, as well as replace whatever needs replacing.

"If I swear an oath in blood to behave like an adult, can I keep my job? If I am truly fired I will go, but I'm begging you for another chance."

Heather gazed into his eyes for a long moment, seeking the betrayal but finding none. "Alright, but I warn you, the next time you truly will shed blood. Now get to work."

"Yes, ma'am, I hear and obey. Thank you, Heather." He returned to the screen before him, then suddenly winced as her strong fingers dug into his neck muscles with a painful pinch hold. She bent over his shoulder to whisper fiercely in his ear.

"Listen carefully, Mr. Hunter. I've had three terrifying and emotionally crippling experiences. I know you don't believe that, and I am not asking you to. All I am asking for is respectful tolerance. It would be even nicer if you could manage to keep an open mind to the possibility, no matter how remote the likelihood."

"I will, I swear."

"Find those little grey bastards for me so I can avenge myself, and I swear I'll marry you and bear your children." She straightened up and relaxed her grip on his neck.

To Heather's great surprise, he turned to gaze into her eyes. She was startled by the emotion she saw there. "Just like in the old myths, eh Heather? If I can fulfill the task you set me, I get the reward?"

He was trying to lighten the mood and she relented. "You got it, Frank, my boy. Find me those little grey buggers and you get the girl."

"If they exist at all, Heather, I will find them."

"Fair enough, but you're still taking me shopping for new underwear the next time we get a few days off."

Frank Hunter sighed with relief. He'd been given a reprieve and her anger had dissipated. "Yes ma'am, I hear and obey. Any city on the planet you choose, Heather. Just name it and away we go."

"Just shut up and get to work; I have to go home and change."

"Thank you, sweetie," Jim said, as she passed him on the way out. "That was well done. The man has a serious crush on you, you know, and he's really not a bad guy."

"Yeah, he's like a puppy I once had. It wouldn't behave, but you couldn't stay mad at it either. Don't tell him I said that."

"Lips are sealed." He grinned as she headed for the parking lot.

"WHAT THE HELL IS GOING on here, Heather MacKay?" she asked the mirror, as she changed her shirt. "You forgave him pretty damned easy. You'd have killed anyone else for less than that." Heather sighed and gazed at the mirror for a long moment before she answered her own question.

"I guess I did at that. Ah well, why lie, I actually like the guy. I just wish he'd stop being such a clown. Just once, I wish a guy would like me for who I am, issues and all. Most just want to get laid then get far away from the nut job as fast as they can. Just once I would like to look a man in the eye and see some sincerity there."

"Actually though, I think I did," she mused, as she returned to the car. "I believe he really meant that apology. Ah hell, he's young, he's cute, and he's rich. I'm old, poor, and crazy. I guess you can't make much out of that." Heather sighed deeply, then started the car and returned to the observatory on the top of what passed for a mountain in those parts.

Frank Hunter remained on best behaviour after that. Three months later, Heather had actually begun to enjoy his company. In point of fact, Frank was a good astronomer, and she was beginning to appreciate that. One hot summer's night she took a short stroll to work out the kinks. She had a surprise waiting for her upon her return.

"Did the galaxy explode while I was gone?" she asked as she approached the two men bent intently over a computer screen.

"No, it just flickered." Frank replied to her question without taking his eyes off the screen.

"Flickered?"

"Yeah, you know, switched off then back on again really quick."

"The entire galaxy?"

"Yeah, well, not this galaxy, but three of them did."

"Frank, for the love of god will you..."

"He telling you the truth, honey," muttered Jim. He hadn't taken his eyes off the screen either. "Show her, Frank. I'll watch this."

"Sure, check this out, Heather." Frank excitedly led her to another computer. His fingers flew for a moment then the screen came to life with a view of deep space. "Sit down here and tell me what you see." He held the chair for her.

"So, what am I looking for?" she asked, as she lowered herself gracefully into the chair.

"Keep your eyes on sector 967, then tell me what you see. This was recorded just after you left. I have shortened the timeline a bit for effect, but that's all."

"Okay, I don't get it, Frank. I don't see anything..."

"Please trust me, Heather. Watch sector 967 and start planning the wedding."

"Jesus Christ, Frank, I..." Heather's voice trailed off as she saw the small flicker on the screen, a moment later there was another and then a third.

She was still staring at the screen when Jim's voice broke the silence. "It's changing course."

Heather and Frank were instantly leaning over his shoulder. "Whatever it is, it just changed course," breathed Jim. "Why the hell can't we see it if it is that big?"

"Oh, dear sweet mother of god." Heather gripped Frank's arm tightly. He was suddenly very aware of her touch.

"What is it, Heather?"

"Take a hard look at the objects that have flickered, Frank. What can you tell me about them?"

Frank gazed at the screen for a long moment before he spoke. "They're really big and very far apart. Really far apart. That means that the object is moving..."

"At ten times the speed of light or more. That's why we can't see it, just the effects of its passage."

"Good Jesus Christ..."

"Course correction again," said Jim.

"My sweet lord," breathed Heather, as she gripped Frank's arm tightly once again. "How many kids did you say you wanted, Frank?"

"At least a half dozen, but don't start planning the wedding yet."

"Why not? You chickening out of the deal already?" There was a note of pain in Heather's voice. Jim caught it and glanced up, but Frank missed it completely.

"No way, lady, a deal is a deal, and you will be all mine once I fulfill the quest," he replied, still looking intently at the view screen. "However, we do seem to have a small problem."

"Oh?"

"Yes, Miss MacKay, my betrothed, we do. Whatever, or whoever, that is out there, they are too damned far away. Whatever attacked you is already in the neighbourhood. I still have some little grey bastards to find before I can claim my prize."

"Really?" She arched an eyebrow at him. "Are you saying you suddenly believe me now?"

Frank's gaze was torn from the screen by the note in her voice. He turned and met her eyes squarely. "Yes I do, Heather. At first I believed you were just having a bit of fun with the world at large. After your reaction to my bad practical joke, I came to believe that you had experienced something so traumatic, that your mind had devised the alien abduction story as a way of coping with an horrific experience."

"And now?"

"And now I can see irrefutable evidence of extraterrestrial life, life far more advanced than we are. If such a thing can exist so far away, then it follows that it could exist close by as well. We've worked together for over a year now, and I have never known you to be anything less than completely honest and upfront with the world. In light of this new evidence, I can only conclude that you truly were abducted. Heather, I am really sorry for ever doubting you at all."

"Frank, thank you for that. I believe you're sincere."

"I am, Heather. So, how am I doing?"

"Excuse me?"

"You told me to act like an adult, so I thought I would give it a try. So, how am I doing?"

"Not bad at all, Frank, my man." She laughed as she gave his arm another squeeze. "A bit more practice and who knows what could happen."

"Another course correction," announced Jim. Heather and Frank returned their gaze to the screen.

# On Our Way

"**R**eport," barked Freydis, as she strode onto the command centre of the ship. The creature who turned to face her was even taller than she, with more battle scars. His face was far more angular, and his scales were much more prominent. He was humanoid, but obviously of a different species. In fact, Drass was the last pure Nylass still alive, as far as they knew. As with the humans, the last of the Nylass had interbred with, a few had managed to keep the bloodlines pure, at least until now. In all the fleet, only Drass was left of the true Nylass, and a pure human no longer existed among them.

The union of the humans and the Nylass had created a superior warrior race. With the strength and warrior society of the Nylass joined with the natural tenacity and determination of the humans they had rescued, the results had been inevitable. The societies blended well together, as did the genetics. The Nylass had loved and adopted the mythology of their new kinfolk and that, too, was added to the mix. Now their descendants were on their way home.

"The fleet is ready to depart, my chieftain." He spoke in that slightly hissing speech of the Nylass. His inner eyelids flickered only once, but she caught it.

"Kett, move us out," commanded Freydis. "One half light speed." The great ship began to leave space dock and was swiftly joined by eight others.

Freydis stood like a statue as the fleet moved slowly away from the great docks and the five planets below. It was a long while later before the message came across the speaker system. "You are cleared for speed now, Nyman fleet. We wish you well, may you find that which you seek."

"Thank you, station master." Freydis' face was impassive as she faced the screen. "Pilot, your course is set?"

"It is. Chieftain."

"Ahead then, five times light speed."

"Five times, Freydis?"

"Five times, Kett, mark me now."

"Five times speed, Chieftain, marked and set."

"Well, we're on our way, folks. I'll be in my cabin. Join me for a game of Toffle, Drass?"

"It will be a pleasure, my chieftain," replied her second-in-command, as he followed her from the bridge.

"Alright Drass, talk to me." The tall, fierce-eyed woman sighed as she plopped into a chair and put her feet up on the table. "Just what kind of shape are we in?"

"The emperor was most generous." Drass chuckled as he closed the door behind him and sank into a chair facing her.

"Oh yes, indeed. Generous, my blistered buttocks. He gave us our old battered and far outdated ships, as well as a few ancient transports, and then sent us on our way to face the last of the Grey Raider fleet, which he probably stirred up himself. We're going to get our heads pounded, while he sits back building new and faster ships. If we defeat the Greys, he wins, and we're weakened. If the Greys defeat us then he is rid of us, and the Greys are weakened. Either way he wins, and we lose.

"After we broke the back of the Xtak invasion fleet, we became far too popular, my friend. We're a threat to the throne now, and he was more than happy to be rid of us. We'll make our journey at half speed to rest our people as much as possible. We should still arrive at the same time as the Greys."

"Perhaps things are not as bleak as you might think, my chieftain."

"Enough games, Drass, I can see the glee in your eyes. Tell me all of it now."

"It took a long time for you to get your audience with the emperor, Freydis."

"That inbred fool kept me waiting in the halls for weeks while he arranged the meeting between us."

"Yes, well, while you were awaiting the emperor's pleasure, we were still technically a part of the Imperial Fleet."

"Drass, you didn't..."

"Oh yes, we did, we completely refitted the ships. We also called in a few favours. Your beloved Mjolnir is now equipped with a prototype Tak engine capable of exceeding twenty times speed; she has the latest in oscillating force shields, ion and point singularity cannons, as well the latest energy recovery system available in the empire. There is one more little addition as well."

"My gods, Drass, all that and more? What more could there be?"

"We have equipped the Mjolnir, the Raven, and the Falcon the same. All the supply and transport ships have fifteen times engines, as well as new shields and cannon. Best of all, we managed to salvage a number of those special healing chambers from the defeated Xtakan ships. We also have an Xtak medic on every ship."

"Drass, my old friend, you never cease to amaze me. How in the name of Thor's beard did you manage to convince Xtak medics to join us?"

"Well, during interrogations it was discovered that there is a large Xtak rebellion. Many who served on their Imperial ships were unwilling to do so. We managed to find a few in the emperor's prisons, and they were eager to join us."

"Eager?"

"The prospect of a journey into the unknown with us was much preferred to the Imperial prison system and dissection chambers. Now, that brings me to another point."

"And that is?"

"Our medic wishes to be adopted into the clan. I said I'd speak for him."

"You trust this one?"

"I do."

"Alright, I'll consider it. Now, what is the bad news?"

"The Grey Raiders have at least twenty carrion ships as well as a dozen or more transports. The gods alone know how many stealth ships they already have at the planet."

"Where did you get this information?"

"The information came from the Imperial Intelligence Network."

"That means that they have deliberately discounted the numbers. Here we are with three war ships and six transports against ten times odds. Ah well, business as usual, I guess. What else?"

"As you know, Freydis, the Northwind was crippled at the start of the last battle. What you may not know, is that all our Untried were aboard that ship. When she was struck by the missile her captain withdrew, and as a result, none of the Untried were able to face an enemy."

"Oh dear gods, no. Are they in our fleet?"

"All nine hundred eighty of them, in fact, every Nyman left alive is with us, as far as I know. Freydis, Thordik was among them, as she is now."

"What? She was denied again?"

"Sadly, yes. She is with them now, still improving her skills and honing the skills of the others."

"Thor's balls, am I going to have a mutiny on my hands?"

"Unknown at this time, Freydis. Thordik holds them in check for now, but who knows how long..."

"Where are they?"

"They are on the Wanderer now."

"Dammit all. Bring them all aboard the Mjolnir, then crank up every bit of speed we can get out of this fleet."

"As you command, my chieftain." He grinned as he stood and slapped his huge fist against his chest in salute. Without another word he turned and headed out the door.

"Thordik denied again." Freydis sighed as she found herself alone in the room. "Is there no damned justice left in the universe? That girl embodies the hope for the survival of our entire race, and she is kept waiting like a child. Somehow I must do something to help her, to help us all."

Freydis sat brooding for quite some time, then her reverie was broken as she felt the pull of sudden acceleration. Grinning to herself, she rose from her chair and began a few stretching moves designed to limber her tall powerful frame. A moment later she emerged smiling.

"What's our speed?" she asked the helmsman.

"Sixteen, Captain, she's got a lot more in her, but the fleet wouldn't be able to keep up."

"Don't worry, Kett, you'll soon get your chance to see what she can do." He just chuckled as she strode away.

Freydis took close notice as she strode through the ship on her way to the armoury and training area. Drass had not lied; the Mjolnir was completely refitted. There was probably not a ship on the Imperial Line that could equal her. Once again, Freydis thanked Thor for the loyalty and ability of her second-in-command.

She entered the training area to find Drass grinning as an exceptionally beautiful young woman barked orders, and squads of young warriors in training leaped to obey her. "Tell me, Thordik, can you manage to survive here on my poor ship?"

The tall girl spun with the grace and speed of a hunting Kren. A smile lit up her face and the weight of the world was lifted from Freydis' shoulders. "We are honoured to be included in the crew of the, Mjolnir. As we are honoured to be serving Lord Freydis, Chieftain of Clan Pull-Karr, Earl of all Nyman folk."

"If you are so damned honoured, Thordik, will you now relent and allow me to adopt you into Pull-Karr clan?"

"I beg forgiveness of Pull-Karr. I am deeply honoured to be invited to join such a powerful clan."

"But you will not. A strong clan will have many seasoned warriors who could help you gain your status, Thordik. As it is now, you have none."

"I am the last of Freya's children, Lady." The girl sighed as she let her well muscled shoulders slump. "Thor's people are many and strong, as are the folk of Freyr, Ullr, and Skadi, but the clan of Erikr-Dak was destroyed at the battle of Kelonra Nebula when I was just a child.

"All Freya's children perished in that battle except me. She kept me safe that day. She has granted me Her strength and favours me with Her beauty as well as Her wisdom and Her magic. I cannot abandon Her. I must find a way to rebuild Her clan. Besides, how many other Untried can claim to be chieftain of their clan?"

"So, nothing has changed in your mind then?"

Everyone in the training area stopped to see how this encounter would play out. The two women stood gazing into each other's eyes for a long moment, then slowly Thordik sank to one knee while still holding Freydis' gaze. "I kneel before you now, Freydis Pull-Karr, as Chieftain of Erikr-Dak, to swear the loyalty of myself and my clan to the Chieftain of Pull-Karr, Earl of all Nyman folk."

Freydis felt a wave of relief wash over her, although she did not let it show. Thordik had rightly guessed her concern. Should Thordik lead the Untried in a revolt they would be hard to put down, and the entire social structure of the Nyman would be torn apart in the process.

By pledging herself and her clan to Freydis, in front of all the Untried, Thordik effectively put a stop to any and all rumblings and rumours. Thordik suffered no loss of face here either, for, as chieftain of a small clan, it was natural for her to seek the protection of a stronger folk. This girl was as smart as she was lethal.

"As Chieftain of Pull-Karr, I accept the hand of Erikr-Dak and welcome you to our hall." Freydis spoke formally as she took Thordik's hand and raised her up. "Pull-Karr will do all in its power to protect and assist their new allies.

"Hear me well, Thordik," she said more gently, "I will do everything I can to see you to your trial. That you have been denied so long is a heavy load you should not have to bear."

"Thank you, Lord Freydis. I promise you; when the time comes, I will be ready, as will my companions. All are eager to gain rightful status."

"That is good news, Thordik, for they will all be needed soon enough." Freydis turned on her heel and strode from the training area, Drass right at her side.

"Are they all aboard?" she asked as they neared the bridge once again.

"All are on the Mjolnir, my chieftain. Shall I call the captains now?"

"Actually, Drass, I think you're slipping a bit."

"Really?"

"Yes, I'm a bit surprised they are not already on board."

"They have been alerted and are standing by waiting for your orders."

"Then give that order, old friend. Let's get this show on the road, defend the home world, and prevent a mutiny."

"You still fear mutiny after she swore loyalty in front of the others."

"I'd feel a lot better if she'd stop being so damned stubborn and let me adopt her. As it is, the sooner I can get her into a battle, the better for all of us."

FREYDIS SAT AT HER table with the captains of the rest of the fleet gathered around her. "It is a damned dangerous manoeuvre, locking ships at this speed, Freydis. Why have you called us together now instead of conferring before we left?" The speaker was a shorter, thickset fellow with bristling red hair and glistening scales.

"I dared not, Brek, and I am sure you know why. I wanted you here now to help me lay my plans. This is where we stand. Drass has managed to see us refitted better than ever, but we are being sent against a much larger enemy."

"Sent? I was under the impression we wanted to go." This was the voice of a slim woman with saurian eyes and a liquid smile.

"Yes, Selian, but what do you think would have happened had we stayed?"

"Qullar would have had us all murdered in our sleep. Nyman folk are far too popular right now for their own good. A few generations in obscurity will be a lot safer for us than at the center of the empire."

"Exactly so," grinned Freydis. "We now know that we'll be vastly out numbered, and we have no idea at all what the home world is like, if it is still populated at all, or if the people there will welcome our return. They may very well see us as potential conquerors, and turn on us as well as the Grey Raiders."

"So you're thinking the war ships should go on ahead?"

"No, Brek, I'm taking the Mjolnir on ahead. You and Selian are needed to protect the rest of the fleet."

"She's right, Brek," sighed Selian, "as badly as we would like to go, we must remain while she has all the fun."

"I know, my beloved. How shall we ever pass the time?"

"Please don't leave us here with those two," groused another captain. "They'll just lock their ships together and spend the entire journey in Selian's sleeping quarters trying to over populate their clans." There was a great round of laughter at that, and Brek blushed as red as his hair.

"It seems we have been found out, my precious," purred Selian. "Whatever shall we do now?"

"I'm at a complete loss, my love. Perhaps we should retire to your ship to devise a plan."

"Splendid idea, Brek my darling."

"While those two are trying to repopulate the galaxy, Freydis," spoke up another of the captains, "you should take on as many extra fighters as you can."

"I agree with Tornan," said another. "My ship has over two thousand five hundred fighters aboard, and she's so automated ten people could fly her. Take a thousand of mine, Freydis."

"I can't, Corfort. We've just taken on all the Untried. We will, however, take as many weapons and provisions as you can spare."

"Freydis, I will gladly part with weapons and supplies, but it's madness to try to do this at high speed."

"Agreed, Corfort. Drass, signal the fleet. All stop. We shall take on provisions then see just what this new engine is made of."

"Kett will be thrilled to hear that." Drass chuckled as he rose easily to his feet.

Freydis turned back to the captains, her face going grim. "Selian..."

"Don't worry, Freydis," said Brek. "Sellie and I will see the fleet to Greenland, safe, sound, and battle ready."

"We will be swift, Freydis," agreed Selian, all seriousness now. "You will be alone no longer than necessary." As she spoke they felt the slowing of the great engines.

"Then as soon as we're stopped, my friends, make ready. Once again we go into the unknown against all odds."

"Just save a few Raiders for the Falcon," rumbled Brek as he rose and headed for the door, patting Selian affectionately on the butt as he went.

SEVERAL SLEEP PERIODS had passed before they got the fleet stopped and all was in readiness. Finally, Drass approached Freydis on the bridge and smiled. "It is done, my chieftain. The fleet has resumed formation and is ready to sail."

"Signal the fleet, ahead full. Alright, Kett, open her up. Let's see how fast you can get us to Greenland."

"As you command, my chieftain," he grinned as his fingers flew over the controls, "so shall it be." The rest of the fleet was amazed at how swiftly the Mjolnir left them behind.

# Confirmed

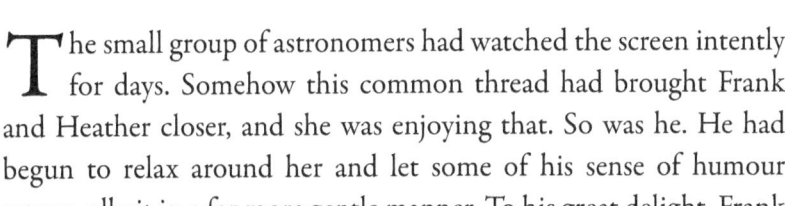

The small group of astronomers had watched the screen intently for days. Somehow this common thread had brought Frank and Heather closer, and she was enjoying that. So was he. He had begun to relax around her and let some of his sense of humour return, albeit in a far more gentle manner. To his great delight, Frank found he truly could make Heather laugh, and he thrilled to the sound of it.

For her part, Heather was torn. The screen held her focus almost entirely and yet, Frank's new gentle teasing was giving her a thrill. This tall, handsome, rich, young man truly was trying to woo her. Heather wasn't sure if it was the fact that he now claimed to believe her, or the fact that she was lonely and a bit needy for a man's attention, that was making her fall for him. Ah well, what did it matter, it felt good, and Heather decided to enjoy it while it lasted.

With a deep sigh Heather leaned back in her chair and began to massage her neck. "Thanks, sweetie," she murmured as a cup of coffee appeared on the desk at her hand.

"You're welcome, lover."

Heather spun around to shake her finger at Frank. She had thought it was Jim, and he knew it. "So, you're the kind of guy who takes advantage of distracted women are you?"

"Absolutely." He sighed with an exaggerated drop of his shoulders. "It's a curse I know, but what can you do? I was doing pretty good in therapy, but then I met a goddess and had a complete relapse."

"You're a shameless flatterer, Frank Hunter, but it won't do you one bit of good."

"Damn. Ah well, it was worth a try. Still nothing moving?"

"Not a darn thing." She took a sip of the coffee and returned her gaze to the screen. "Dammit, that thing, whatever it was, came right at us for several days then just vanished. Nothing has moved out there for a week now. Shit, we were so close. A bit more data and we could have gone public. Another week and there would be no way anyone could deny what we saw."

"Sure, and as soon as it looked like it might really be headed this way, the military would march in here and drop a cone of silence over the whole damn thing."

Heather turned to face Frank once again. "Are you serious?"

"Absolutely. My dad's companies have some government contracts, and I've seen this sort of thing before. So have you, Heather."

"Yes I have, Frank. So, what should we do, I mean, if we ever can truly prove what we know?"

"We play along with them while keeping full back-ups in a secure online site." He was acutely aware that she had just asked his advice and had said *we* unconsciously. That had given him a real thrill. "As soon as they get too pushy we let them take over and we get out of Dodge."

"Just let them take over?"

"We'll have all the data we need by then. When I was a boy, I was so intent on being an astronomer that my dad built me a small observatory in the mountains outside Denver. It is still there, and still functional."

"Frank?"

"Okay, so it's my special hide out. I go there when I need to hide or to lick my wounds."

"Is this where you take all your girlfriends?"

She was teasing, but he just shook his head. "There has been no one else there since I was fifteen, and the only girl I ever took there was my mother the year before she was killed in the car accident. The place is safe, Heather, even Dad has forgotten about it, I'll bet. So how about it, when the bullies chase us away, do you want to share my hideout with me?"

"Be careful what you wish for, Frank." She smiled as she returned her gaze to the screen.

"You know what I wish right now?" he asked with mischief in his voice. Her laughter was like music and it thrilled him.

"I don't want to hear it, Mr. Hunter. I really don't want to hear it."

"Actually, I do have a wish..."

"Frank Hunter, I swear..." she admonished, as she turned to shake that finger at him again.

"Easy woman, don't shoot. I just wish you'd tear yourself away from that screen for a minute and take a walk around the parking lot with me, you know, stretch out the kinks."

"Really?"

"Best behaviour, Heather, I swear it. That's the tenth time in the last hour you have rubbed your neck. You're all cramped up, and there is nothing moving out there right now. Come on, girl, stretch you legs a bit?"

"He's right, honey," Jim chimed in. "Go get some fresh air. I'll watch the monitors for you."

"Best behaviour, Frank?"

"How many black belts have you got, Heather?"

"Three."

"Best behaviour, count on it."

"Alright, Frank, let's go stretch our legs, but I swear, if there's a full moon out there I'll..."

"Gods, Heather, am I truly that transparent?" He grinned as they stepped through the door and into the cool night air.

They walked to the middle of the parking lot where she stopped, stretched as tall as possible then relaxed and started walking toward the hill beside the big domed building. Frank stayed a respectful distance from her as he followed her up the grassy knoll. To his surprise and delight, she moved right into his space and leaned against his shoulder once they reached the top. Tentatively he put his arm around her waist.

"Do you find this a bit ironic, Heather?" he asked softly, after they'd gazed at the sky in silence for a while.

"What's ironic, Frank?" Heather continued to gaze at the sky.

"We're both astronomers, but in the past year or more this is the first time I've actually looked at the sky. How about you?"

"You know, you're right. I've been glued to the damn screen. This is the first time in a long while I have actually looked at the sky." He realized she was staring in the direction they had detected the movement.

"They're not there, Heather."

"What???" She spun around look into his eyes.

"The grey bastards, they're not there. Whoever that is, they are too far away. The Greys are much closer. What can you tell me about them?"

"Excuse me?"

"Heather, you are looking at a fully converted, true believer. I can read all sorts of crap on the internet, but you've had personal experience. I need to know everything you can tell me about them."

"Why?"

"Because if they show up again I want to be able to defend you, and myself. So the more I know, the better I'll be able to do that." He was sincere and she could see that in his eyes.

"Frank, why?"

"Do you really have to ask me why, Heather?" She didn't speak, she just gazed deeply into his eyes. "Alright, here goes," he sighed at last. "I want to defend you because I'm madly in love with you, and from the moment I first saw you I have not looked at, or thought about, another woman. I know, I know; but these are my feelings, I can't stop them, nor do I want to."

"Frank, you're young, handsome, rich, smart, and charming as hell when you want to be. Why me?"

"Charming and handsome? You really think so?"

"Why me, Frank? No hiding behind the jokes now, tell me."

Frank Hunter sighed deeply, then gathered his courage and spoke softly as he gazed imploringly into her eyes. "You are, without doubt, the most fascinating woman I have ever met, Heather. You are so intelligent that it scares the hell out of me. You're a lethal weapon, you are completely fearless, yet there's a bit of the wounded bird about you, and you are so incredibly beautiful you take my breath away."

"Keep going, this is fascinating."

"Okay, so now who's doing jokes? Heather, I'm baring my soul here, and I am begging for a chance."

Heather gazed into his eyes for a long moment then stepped into his arms and laid her head on his shoulder. "Frank, since I was a young girl I have known what men want from me. You are the very first to pay me a compliment and mean it. I do believe you're sincere."

"But you wonder how sincere, or how long it would last, if we became close." He sighed as he tentatively put his arms around her. "You wonder if I would feel the same the morning after, or would I run away like all the rest."

"I'm sorry, Frank, I just can't help it. Every man I've ever known just wanted a roll in the hay then to get far away from the nut job as fast as he could."

"I'm different, Heather, and I can prove it."

"Oh yeah?" She leaned back to smile into his eyes, but not moving out of his arms. "Okay, prove it."

"I wanted you from the first. I can assure you, I would have stayed around just to be close to you, I have actually done so, and now we have proof that you are terribly sane, so now the story is reversed."

"Reversed?"

"Yes, Heather, I'm the crazy one now because you make me that way. Please just give me a chance to prove that it is you I love, issues and all. After all, I have a few of my own."

"Don't try so hard, Frank." She sighed as she laid her head back on his shoulder. "I like you, and would like to get to know the real Frank Hunter better, but you're always trying too hard, and he gets lost in the effort. If you truly want to get to know me, Frank, ease up a bit, I won't bite."

"Darn."

"Stop it, you fool." She laughed as she slapped his shoulder then gazed into his eyes. Slowly Heather allowed her eyes to flutter closed and melted into his arms. With pounding heart and trembling knees Frank gently pulled her closer. The kiss was not to be, however, as Jim's shout broke the mood.

"They're on the move," he bellowed from the doorway. Heather grabbed Frank's hand and raced back, towing him along behind. They ran straight to the monitor and bent over the screen, Frank's arm around Heather's waist. "Well, it's about bloody time," Jim muttered softly, as he nodded his head approvingly. He actually liked Frank Hunter, and he loved Heather MacKay like a daughter.

It was later that night when Heather suddenly sat back with a startled look on her face. "Heather?"

"Frank, my boy, I think we just might be overlooking the obvious."

"And that is...?"

"Well, if you were in San Diego and you could see a car leave Alaska for Frisco, what would think?"

"I'd think it was headed right at me," he mused after a moment's thought. "So you think there might be something else going on in our neighbourhood that we don't know about."

"We've been pretty focused on our friends out there..."

"Okay, you keep an eye on our distant cousins, and I'll poke around the backyard for a while." Frank went and sat to the other computer. It was hours later that she heard him cursing.

"What is it, Frank?" Heather abandoned her computer to peer over his shoulder.

"More company coming, Heather, at least I think it is. Look at this." The rest of the night was spent working on the numbers and plotting the direction of travel from both sides.

It was two days later that she sighed and rose from her chair. "I guess there is no use waiting any longer, we've got all the numbers. Okay Jim, you're on. Call your buddies in government. Let them know that company is coming."

"This is your show, Heather. You should be the one to make the call."

"She can't, Jim. Heather has a wedding to plan."

"Oh really?" Heather arched an eyebrow at him. "What makes you say that?"

"Remember what I said about the little grey bastards being a lot closer to home?"

"You think this new object might be..."

"They're a lot closer than the others, Heather. Yes, they're moving a lot slower, but they are in the neighbourhood. They could easily have been here before."

"But at the rate they are moving the other guys will get here first. It is all speculation right now, Frank, but I do have a few ideas in mind."

"Ideas?"

"About the wedding..." His rich laugh drowned out the rest of her joke.

They were still chuckling as Jim brought up the large screen. A man in a very expensive looking suit, flanked by two men in military uniforms frowned out at them. "This had better be good, Jim."

"Yes sir, Mr. President, it is. We have incoming extraterrestrials. Dr. MacKay and the rest of the team would like to officially..."

"You're a day late and a dollar short, Brady," snarled one of the uniforms. "We already know about sector 324. Something is out there and it is heading our way at close to the speed of light. We have two months to prepare and we are already preparing."

"Oh yeah?" Heather bristled as she stepped in beside Jim. "What about the two in sector 967 who will be here in about two weeks?"

"967? Christ Almighty. That will still take them years to get here..."

"Not if they're travelling over twenty times the speed of light."

"Dr. MacKay, are you certain about..."

"We've checked our figures several times, sir. They're moving fast and they've made a total of fourteen course corrections. Company's coming, sir, and they're almost here."

"Gather all your data, doctor. My people will be there within the hour," barked one of the uniforms.

"Listen carefully, you over paid medal holder. You, and those just like you, tried to convince the world that people like me are crazy. Well guess what, you can cover this up all you goddamn want for the next two weeks, and then you're screwed."

"Dr. MacKay, please relax. The military are not going to steal your findings, or cover up anything," said the president. "As you have so eloquently pointed out, that is pointless now. I will ask, however, that you keep a line to this office open and keep me fully updated on all developments as soon as they occur."

"Yes sir, we can establish a permanent feed of all our..."

"Just keep us informed," he replied curtly. Then the line went dead.

# Arrival

Freydis was once again pacing the bridge. "What's our speed?"

"Twenty-two plus, Captain," grinned Kett. "We've managed to get another 0.03 out of her but I doubt she can keep it up for long."

"What is the status of the enemy?"

"That remains unknown, Captain," replied another of the crew. "We're moving too fast to detect them. Once we arrive we'll be able to drop to sub-light speed and then our sensors can locate them easily. Any information we get at this speed is suspect at best."

"So we could drop out of speed and into the middle of an enemy armada?"

"Isn't it exciting," grinned Kett. "I just love surprises."

"I'm getting too damned old for surprises, Kett. What is our estimated time of arrival?"

"Three sleeps, Captain. Gods, it is just like Yule when I was a child."

Freydis laughed in spite of herself. Old Kett was still the best pilot and engineer in the empire, and his childlike enthusiasm always cheered her up. "So, you think the good folk of Greenland will welcome us home with a feast, do you, Kett?"

"Hope for the best, Freydis, but prepare for the worst."

"Wise words indeed, my friend. Hold your speed as long as you can, then drop her back. I'll be in the training area."

"I watched her train after last break," said Kett, as Freydis reached the door.

"Oh?"

"She scares the lights out of me, Freydis. If she smiles at you, you will give her anything she wants. To watch her move and strike is frightening, and to gaze into her eyes is to know her mind never stops. May the gods forgive me, but I hope there is somebody there for her to kill when we arrive."

"Our thoughts are one on that score, old friend," muttered Freydis, as she left the bridge to seek out Drass at the training area.

She found him there training with Thordik. Drass was one of the greatest masters of hand-to-hand combat Freydis had ever known, even better than she. It was difficult to watch him apply every bit of speed, strength, and experience he had, and to know that the girl was holding back, toying with him.

"Hold," commanded Freydis, and they instantly froze. "Thordik, I forbid you to humiliate my proven warriors any longer." Her grin belied the harshness of her words.

"Forgive me, Lord Freydis, but you misinterpret my purpose. Commander Drass is a master of the art, with much experience. He was teaching me new techniques."

"I was getting my head pounded." Drass grinned as he slapped the girl lightly on the shoulder. "Thordik, I have faced a hunting Kren and survived, and I swear you are faster." She beamed at his praise.

"Thordik," Freydis began gently, "I have heard there was a foreseeing called before last sleep."

"I confess that it was I who called, Lord Freydis. Kellass made the call, as I instructed, but the calling was for me. I admit I grow frustrated, as I am sure you are aware. My greatest fear is that I might be denied yet again. I asked for guidance."

"Did you receive it?"

"My Lady Freya will always answer a heartfelt prayer. She came to me through Kellass, but her words were a bit confusing, not at all what I had hoped for."

"Thus is ever the way of the gods. The young want definite answers for a single thread, but the gods see a much more elaborate cloth. Can you tell me what she said?"

"A warrior will come to us, wounded and weakened. She will lead us to alliance with our own people, and she will guide us to victory."

"She will lead?"

"Those are the words of the lady. All hangs in the balance. If I look into the eyes of my sister and do not know her, we will fall. If you do not recognize her worth, we will fail. I must find and embrace her, and she will lead us to glory." Thordik was shaking now, as the emotion of the reading gripped her once again. "Freydis, I am the last of my clan. I have no sister, and you are the earl, only you can lead."

"That was a powerful foreseeing, Thordik." Freydis gently gripped the younger woman by the shoulders. "As soon as we arrive you must keep your eyes open, for I believe your destiny will soon be upon you, upon us all. Do not fear child, an earl can take advice as well as the next. I will have no fear of your sister."

HEATHER EXITED THE building, reaching for Frank's hand as she did so. "Well, that's that, Frank. I guess we won't have to run off to your hideout in the mountains after all."

"Damn, I was hoping."

"Yeah, so was I," she said, as they reached the cars. Suddenly she turned and stepped into his arms. "The world as we know it is about to change, Frank, and I'm willing to admit I'm a bit frightened, as well as elated."

"I know what you mean," he replied, as he held her closer and kissed the top of her head. "It was one thing to look for evidence that they exist. It is something else to have the whole damned lot of them pounding on our door. Frankly, it scares the hell out of me, but it has brought one good thing into being."

"Oh? What might that be?"

"I'm standing here with you in my arms. As far as I'm concerned, it's all worth it just for this moment."

"God you're a nut, Frank." Suddenly she hugged herself tightly to him. "Frank, take me home today. I really don't want to be alone."

Frank didn't respond for a moment and she suddenly became uneasy. "Frank?"

"All right, Heather, I'll take you home with me," he finally replied gently, "but first we have to find a J.P.."

"A J.P.?"

"You promised to marry me and bear my children if I found extraterrestrial life for you. I've completed my task, Heather. Now it is time for you to live up to your end of the bargain. I got the job done, and now I want the girl, as I was promised."

"Frank, stop being such a joker and take me home."

"Heather, I'm not joking here. Make no mistake, I want you, but I want to keep you forever. As you said, the world is about to change, and I want this to happen before it does."

"Frank?" Heather gazed deeply into his eyes and saw the pleading there.

"Please, Heather, I'm begging you here..."

"Hush now," she whispered, as she stopped his words with a kiss. Bolts of lightning lanced through him and his knees began to shake. "I don't ever want to hear that phrase from the lips of my husband," she breathed as their lips finally parted. "I'm getting into your car now, Frank. I'm ready for whatever step you want to take."

She stepped out of his arms and walked from her own car to his. She got in the passenger's seat and closed the door.

"Okay, no begging, just decisive, manly, take charge behaviour. I can do it, just watch me," he said as he got behind the wheel. "Here we go. I swear to you, Heather MacKay, I will move heaven and earth to prove myself worthy of you." Frank reached for her hand and held it as he drove down the mountain and the ten miles to the small town where they all had rooms in the motel. He drove straight to the jewellery store.

"Frank?"

"Rings." Frank grinned as he went around and opened her door for her. He led her inside where he bought the most expensive wedding set they had, as well as a thick gold band for himself.

The middle aged woman smiled as she rang up the sale. "Will there be anything else?"

"Just point me to the nearest J.P., preacher, or judge."

"No problem." She smiled as she ran his credit card through the machine. She turned and called over her shoulder. "Charlie, put on the jacket and come out here."

"The jacket, this early in the morning?"

"Folks are waiting, judge."

A man came from the back room pulling on a suit jacket. "Hi folks, I'm Judge Charles Joyce, or Charlie as you wish. Now, how can I be of service?"

"Can you perform a legal wedding?"

"I can."

"Right now?"

"If that's what you want, then it's no problem at all."

"Okay, let's get started."

"You haven't said a word, miss. Are you sure this is what you want to do?"

"I have no choice, sir." Heather smiled as she hugged Frank's arm tightly. "I lost the bet."

"The bet?"

"I swore to marry him, and bear his children, if he could complete an impossible task."

"She thought she was safe, but I can be tenacious, and quite resourceful, when I have need. Heather is now honour bound to bear my children."

"Oh well then, if it is a matter of honour." Charlie smiled and nodded, seeing that she was all in favour as well. "Now then, let's get a bit of the paperwork out of the way."

In less time than it takes to tell it, they left the jewellery store with wedding rings on their hands. Heather sat in silence, gazing at the sparkling rings as Frank drove to the motel. "Okay, Mrs. Hunter, we're home."

"Frank." She spoke softly as she reached over to grip his arm tightly.

"Yes, my love?" Frank was suddenly afraid she would bolt and run away.

"Your place or mine?" She smiled mischievously.

"Yours." He grinned in relief. "Mine's a total mess."

THE INSISTENT BUZZING of her alarm brought Heather back to the land of the living. She'd been having the most delightful dream. She reached over to slap the offending machine into silence, but her arm struck an obstacle, bringing a grunt of protest from her new husband.

"Good god woman, you said you'd wake me with a kiss," grinned Frank, as he rose up on one elbow to gaze lovingly at her. "We're married less than twelve hours and already she starts the spousal abuse."

"Yeah, well, maybe I'd be easier to get along with if you'd let me have more than two hours sleep." She sat up and tousled her hair before beaming him a dazzling smile.

"I didn't hear any complaints."

"Oh my husband, I have no complaints at all." Heather rolled on top of him, kissed him deeply, then rolled out of the bed to make her way to the bathroom.

She was brushing her teeth as his arms enfolded her from behind. With a sigh and a smile, she relaxed back into those loving arms. "We've only got a few days before the world goes all to hell, Heather. Want to run away to the Far East for a week?"

She giggled and rinsed out her mouth before answering him. "I'd love to sweetheart, but..."

"Duty calls, Mrs. Hunter?"

"Sadly, that it does, Mr. Hunter."

"Okay," he yawned as he pulled on his jeans, "I'll just run next door and get ready to face the day. Maybe tomorrow morning we can move my stuff over here."

"Is that easier than cleaning up your place?"

"Immensely. Shall we see if we can get some breakfast at six o'clock at night?"

"Oh god yes, Frank. You have to feed me. You want me to keep up my strength, don't you?"

"Absolutely." He laughed as he kissed her cheek then headed for the door.

"Order me something, and I'll eat whatever it is."

Smiling to herself, Heather MacKay-Hunter gazed at her rings for a long moment, then finished dressing and went to join her husband at the small café next door. They spent the next eight days tracking the visitors, or lying in each others arms. The world as they knew it was about to come to an end, but Heather was happier than she had ever been before. She was in love with a man who knew what had happened to her, and he truly believed that it actually had. For the moment, her world was perfect.

FREYDIS' EYES SNAPPED open and she lay completely still, searching her surrounding with her senses. Glancing at the timepiece embedded in the wall she saw that it was several minutes yet until her sleep cycle was due to end. What had awakened her? Again she reached out with her senses. She could no longer feel the great engines. Suddenly a smile creased her face as she felt the delicate pull of the engines being reversed.

Drass was already on the bridge when she emerged from her cabin. "Are we there yet?" she asked as she leaned over Kett's shoulder.

"Not quite yet, Captain. I had to start slowing her down a bit early because of the speed we've been holding. After all, we don't want to overshoot the whole system, do we?"

"No indeed, that we do not want to do." She smiled as she patted his shoulder. "How long?"

"We'll be there before end of shift next."

"Did you sleep yet?"

"What, and let Elgess bring her in? Perish the thought."

"Drass, are we ready?"

"All is as it should be, and battle ready, my chieftain."

"Tessa, the very instant we drop sub-light I want to know the enemy position."

"Yes, my captain," replied a woman standing at another instrument panel. "I am calibrating the sensors as we speak. I'm seeking carrion ships, raiders, and stealth ships."

"That and anything else that might be out there, especially anything our cousins might have in the air. I don't want any nasty surprises."

"It shall be as you desire, Chieftain."

HEATHER AND FRANK WERE just arriving as the president came on line again. "There isn't a lot new to report," they heard Jim say as they entered the building. "Whatever it is, it sure appears to be coming here, alright. It is still changing course to come right at us. It's getting a lot closer, and it seems to be slowing down a bit."

"Keep me informed, Jim, anytime, day or night. I want to be appraised the instant anything new develops." With that he was gone, and Jim sighed as he relaxed back in his chair.

"Now I know why you two lovebirds insist on the night shift," grumbled Jim, as Heather brought him a coffee.

"Don't be a grumpy bear." She smiled as she lightly kissed his cheek. "Did you say they're slowing down?"

"Looks like it." He took a sip of the coffee. "What do you think, Frank?"

Frank was glued to a screen full of data. "Right on the money, Dr. Brady. At the speed they've been travelling, I'll bet it takes a while to get the brakes working. Check this out, honey, what do you think?"

"I think I'd be a fool to second guess the two smartest men in the whole world."

"Flatter me all you want, wife, but it is still your turn to do the laundry."

"Ah well, I tried." Heather smiled as she looked over his shoulder. "Good god, I'll say they're slowing down. Jim, go on home and grab a few hours sleep, but be back here before dawn. I don't want you to miss this."

"Sorry, but I am going to miss it, Heather." He sighed as he rose stiffly to his feet. "I called Laura earlier, and she's going to meet me at the lake house. I'll grab a few hours sleep, but by dawn my wife and I will be on our porch, having morning coffee."

"Jim?"

"Heather, I don't know what the hell will happen next, but if it is all over, I want to spend my last hours with Laura, in the house we worked so many years to build for our retirement. Why don't you two newlyweds run away to that hideout in the mountains Frank is always bragging about?"

"Do you really think this is the end, Jim?"

"I don't know, honey, I just don't know. What I do know is, this is all over the media. Half the planet is in the throes of a panic attack now, and Laura is scared to death, too. I'm not leaving her alone any longer."

"Drive carefully, dear friend," whispered Heather, as she hugged Jim tightly. "Give my love to Laura."

"I will, sweetie." He smiled as he pulled on his jacket. "Take care of her, Frank. I'm counting on you."

"I promise, Jim. Stay safe and keep your eye on the sky."

Jim slapped Frank's shoulder companionably on his way out the door, and then the Hunters were alone with their monitors. Suddenly Frank heard the motors cut in and the groan of protest as the big scope was refocused on the sky. "Heather?"

"Why not, Frank, it won't be long before we can get a good look at our visitors."

"You're right about that, lover, they're decreasing speed quickly now. I'd say they will be entering the solar system well before daybreak. Maybe we can get a look at them at that." They spent the next several hours intent on the monitors and the figures thereon.

By three a.m. they could delay no longer, Heather placed the call. "MacKay?" demanded a uniform as the line came instantly alive.

"That's Dr. MacKay-Hunter to you, and yes, it is I. They are definitely coming here, and they've just gone sub-light. They'll be in the solar system within the hour. Hell, they'll be at the White House for lunch at this rate. You've got incoming, General."

Heather broke the connection and sighed. She knew the rest of the world was as aware of this as she was by now. All eyes had been turned to the traveller for days, ever since she'd secretly leaked out the news.

"So, are you deliberately trying to piss him off, or what?"

"You could tell?"

"I'm your husband, I notice these things." He straightened up, then stepped over to take her in his arms. "What is it, Heather? Why do you have such a hate on for the military?"

"Because of their refusal to admit that what happened to me was real." She sighed into his shoulder. "All my life I've been marginalized and called crazy, because I refused to play dead for them. They cost me jobs, friends, lovers, time, money, and did everything in their power to discredit me. They raised hell when Jim pulled in a lot of favours to get me this job."

"Yeah, having the president for a brother-in-law gives you a lot of pull, alright."

"Yes, it does. That sweetheart even made sure I was listed as chief astronomer, when his experience made him a natural for the job."

"Jim Brady loves you like a daughter, Heather."

"He's the only father I've ever known, Frank. He really likes you, too. It was Jim that kept me from killing you the night you pulled the alien abduction gag. I was all for shooting you and tossing the body to the coyotes. Jim convinced me to give you another chance."

"Then I owe him a lot more than I thought."

"So do I, darling, so do I."

The gentle moment was shattered as the president appeared on the big screen before them. "Mrs. Hunter, are you there?"

"Right here, sir." Heather stepped in front of the camera and flipped the switch.

"Where are they now?"

"Frank, honey?"

"Okay, they just passed Pluto's orbit. That is one big mother of a ship, and it is coming in fast. Holy shit, I've just got it on monitors. Oh my god, look at the size of that thing. Okay, here's the feed."

"Alright, we've got it all on tap now people," declared a uniform as he stepped in front of the cameras. "Your help has been invaluable, but you are now off the case. You close up shop, we'll take it from here."

Heather started to protest, but the line went dead, and then so did the monitors. "The dirty rotten sons of bitches," swore Frank. "They've scrambled our link to the satellites."

"Bastards. Grab your coat, Frank. We'll make a run for Denver."

"No time, lover," he replied, as he began to readjust the huge scope, "we'll just have to make do with old Betsy here."

They watched with a growing sense of awe as the huge ship blew past Saturn's orbit, then suddenly opened up and a swarm of small ships spread out to comb the solar system. Moving at incredible speed, the smaller ships fanned out and made a swift pass through the entire system then returned to the mother ship which was still slowing down, just past Jupiter.

Having retrieved her scouts, the big ship moved towards Mars, still slowing. She came to rest at the edge of the asteroid belt. An hour later she moved into Earth's orbit and parked near the moon. A short time after that she made a single broadcast aimed at Earth.

# First Contact

"**S**ub-light," bellowed Kett, as his hand slammed down on a button, causing a loud Klaxon to sound throughout the ship.

"Battle stations," bawled Freydis, as she bolted from her cabin. "Tessa!"

"Got them, Captain. Thirty-eight carrion ships, twenty-eight raiders, and sixty-four mass transports. There are no stealth ships in the fleet, but there are over a dozen on the planet's surface, probably a lot more."

"Sixty-four transports, great Thor's beard," growled Drass. "What in the name of all the gods...?"

Freydis' eyes went hard as flint as she stared at the view screen before her. "I can guess. Our kinfolk must have been quite prolific, and the home world is probably crawling with humans. The Greys are in trouble, so they are coming to harvest the lot all at once."

"We could let them," said Drass quietly. The entire bridge crew fell silent at that.

"Drass?"

"Freydis, even as Thordik is the last of her clan, I am the last of my kind. The Nyman folk though, still number over tens of thousands strong, and all are in that fleet following behind us. Consider that you are no longer human folk, and that if the planet is truly crawling with humans, how welcome will we be? How willing to share with us, will they be?"

"So, are you suggesting that we allow the Greys to make their harvest, then we go in and take over what is left?"

"It is one option," he replied evenly. "We do not have to risk our entire species."

"I don't like it, Drass."

"Nor do I, but it has to be discussed."

"Fine, we have discussed that option. Now give me others."

"We can form an alliance with the humans against the Greys."

"I like that better."

"And I, as well. However, I suggest we keep an eye out for another likely planet to colonize, just in case."

"I have one now," grinned Tessa. "It is orbiting that gas giant up ahead."

"We'll take a look, later. Ready fighting scout ships. I want this system scanned as soon as possible. Tessa, have our cousins got anything up here?"

"They've put up a lot of junk around the planet, but no defences I can detect. Maybe the planetary defences are surface mounts. There is one orbital station, but it doesn't seem to carry weapons, or much of a crew."

"Or maybe they haven't got that far yet," muttered Kett.

"We'll know soon enough. Launch scouts."

"Scouts away, Captain," Kett announced a moment later.

"Tessa, anything new moving in?"

"No, Captain."

"What time do we have?"

"Plenty of time to breathe. The Greys seem to be coming in on sub light. They must be holding back to the pace of the transports. Our fleet will arrive with a span of time to spare."

"Good, now turn your attentions to the planet. I don't want them trying to blow us out of the system before we have a chance to introduce ourselves."

"There is an asteroid belt up ahead, Captain. That should mess up any real attempts to target us, and it is far enough away to give us manoeuvring time if we need it."

"Excellent. Snuggle us in, Kett. We'll hang around for a bit while Tessa sees what they've got for defences, then we'll introduce ourselves."

"As you desire, my chieftain. The scout ships are starting to return now."

Freydis stood waiting for the reports to come in. Two stealth ships were found on the far side of the planet's natural satellite, both were easily destroyed. "All scouts returned, Chieftain," reported Drass. "Two stealth ships destroyed, nothing else found."

"Very good. Kett, put us to bed now."

Kett easily manoeuvred the huge ship into the asteroid belt where she hung for a while. Tessa worked intently at her sensors for a long time before she sighed and straightened up. "This doesn't look too good." She sighed as she stretched the kinks out of her back.

"What is it, Tessa?"

"Well, as I can see it with sensors, and trying to interpret some of their communications, they are in a mess down there."

"Explain."

"They have no cohesive form of government, several factions have some weaponry, but it is all aimed at each other. It will take a while to get a clearer picture, but for now I believe it is safe to approach."

"All right, in we go. Kett, park us near that natural satellite. Morness, can you decipher their language yet?"

"No Freydis, there are far too many of them. This will take time, but there is one ray of hope."

"And that is?"

"There seems to be one place of legend left there, and the language is somewhat akin to the elder human speech. I believe I can talk to those folks."

"Greenland?"

"Iceland."

"Iceland? Very well, let our cousins know we've come home for a visit."

"WHAT THE HELL WAS THAT?" demanded the president. "That was a message, what did they say? Was that a human language? Is it in our database? Somebody decipher that message. Where the hell is Jack...?

"Here sir, we're searching for the deciphering key right..."

"Somebody's answered them," shouted a voice. A switch was flipped and the bunker room was filled with the sounds of a voice speaking in a halting manner, as though the speaker was unfamiliar with the language. As suddenly as it began, it stopped.

"Bring that back up. What the hell are they saying? Who is talking to them and what are they saying? Somebody get me some answers. Where...?"

"I can't bring it back up, Sir. The visitor has put some sort of dampening field on the transmissions. We have the visitor's original message on tape, as well as a bit of the reply, but..."

"It's Iceland, sir," shouted another voice. "The Icelanders are talking to the visitor."

"The Icelanders? What the hell are they saying?"

"We've got an interpreter on the way, Mr. President."

"I have the Icelandic ambassador on the line for you, sir," declared another voice as a young woman passed him a video phone. The room went silent as he spoke.

"Helga, this is Thomas Mooreland, how are you this morning?"

"Actually I am quite busy this morning, Mr. President." The middle aged woman who appeared on the screen smiled politely, but it did not reach her eyes. "As I am sure you are aware, we have a visitor from afar. My people are in contact as we speak, and my government will be contacting you later today, or so I am told. Please forgive me, sir, but I am packing to return home, as I have been recalled."

"Recalled?"

"All Icelanders are being called home, Mr. President. Forgive me, but I truly must return to my task. Good day to you, sir." With that, she was gone.

"The interpreter is here, Mr. President," said a young man as he hustled a woman into the room. "This is Anna Mayweather."

"You know what is going on?"

"Yes, sir, I do."

"Can you tell me what has been said? What did that message from the ship say, and what did the Icelanders say?"

"Mr. President, the language seems to be a form of an Old Norse dialect," the woman said carefully.

"Can you translate it?"

"Yes. I had a chance to study the message on my way here."

"Well, what did it say, woman?"

"It says, 'Rejoice for the children of Erik Rhode have returned to the Green Land. We will stand at your side in the coming battle."

"What? What battle are they talking about? What does that mean and who the hell is Erik Rhode?"

"Eric the Red, he's the Viking who founded the Greenland colony. There is an old legend of an entire village disappearing from Greenland, early in the colony's history. Apparently, they must have been abducted by aliens."

"Correct me if I misread this," mused a man in uniform, "but..."

"That's right, General, up there beside our moon, and darned near as big, lies the twenty-first century version of a Viking warship.

I was shown the photo. That symbol on her side is a Thor's Hammer. I can't read the runes beneath it."

"ARE YOU SURE THAT'S what it said, Heather?"

"My Icelandic is a bit rusty, Frank, but I'm sure that's what they said. Those folk consider themselves Greenlanders."

"Man, I'll bet they're pissed at the state of Greenland now. It was a thriving Norse colony at one time, and I'll bet that's what they expected to find."

"Yeah, well, Iceland is still here, and they've opened up a dialogue. I guess there's hope for the future yet."

"I hope you're right, sweetheart. Can you make out that symbol on her side?"

"It's a Thor's Hammer," replied Heather as she continued to peer through the lens of the scope. "As near as I can interpret the runes painted below the symbol, her name is Mjolnir. That was the name of Thor's magic hammer."

"Well I'll be damned."

"Yup, a real futuristic Viking warship."

"How come you know all this stuff, Heather?"

"Mom's an Icelander. She wanted me to know my roots. 'How can you know where you're going if you don't know where you've been?' she used to say."

"I didn't know that about you, Heather." He sighed as he took her in his arms. "In fact, there is a lot about you that I don't know. We've done what we can here. I say we abandon ship and head for Denver. We can see her well enough from there, and maybe I can get our satellite feeds back so we can check up on the other guys."

"All right, my husband, let's go. You're absolutely right, there is nothing more we can do here. It is now time to get the hell out of Dodge."

# Calm Before the Storm

Frank drove on for hours, quizzing Heather constantly about her likes, dislikes, and everything else in between. He said he wanted to learn everything there was to know about her. Smiling, Heather answered the questions and fired a battery of her own back at him. There was much she wanted to learn about her husband as well.

Several times they had to detour around traffic snarls, destruction, and panic stricken mobs. Frank's big four wheel drive turned out to be a blessing more than once. Terror had suddenly gripped the nation by the throat, and it was starting to get to them as well. What should have taken less than a day actually took three, but they finally arrived. The place was well provisioned, and there was a note on the table as they entered. Frank picked it up and read bemusedly.

"Son, I had a hunch you might retreat here with your new bride. The world has gone completely mad, and we must be prepared. The larder has been stocked for a long siege, and the locker has everything you might need. Call me if you can, I'll be on the island. You know which one.

"Love, Dad."

"Frank?"

"It seems that dear old Dad was one step ahead of the game, as usual. He's like a clam, so I told him about what we'd found. Actually, I told him we'd gotten married, and I was so full of excitement, I blabbed on and on about the exquisite Mrs. Hunter. I even told him about the quest and how I succeeded. I guess he must have talked to the press."

"No, dear, I did that."

"Heather?"

"They covered everything up so many times before, Frank. I just couldn't allow that to happen again. I sent everything we had to some folks I know. I'm the one who spilled the beans."

"I can understand why you did that, Heather, and in truth, I do agree with your reasoning."

"What did he mean that what we need will be in the locker?"

"Here," replied Frank, as he moved a book near the top of the bookcase. The case slid aside and a small room appeared behind it. It looked like a weapons locker. The walls were bristling with guns of various sizes and shapes, and there were boxes of ammunition stacked neatly on the floor.

"May you never have to use these against our fellow human beings," read Heather, as she picked up the note on a box of grenades. "God willing, you will not have to use them at all. If, however, you do have need, please son, be careful, and may we see each other again soon. I am anxious to meet my new daughter.

"Dad."

"My god, Frank, there's an arsenal in here. What is going on?"

"You saw the riots we had to evade, sweetheart. Dad knew this would happen, so he fortified the place for us. He trusted that I would take you to the safest place I knew, and so he prepared it for us."

"Wow, I don't know what to say, Frank. Do you know how to use any of this?"

"Every damned bit of it, Heather, Dad saw to that at an early age. How about you?"

"Sorry, I concentrated on the martial arts. Guns aren't my thing."

"Mine either really, but these are unusual times. Come on, let's close this up and get this place going. You check the kitchen, while I get the defences turned on and line up the scope."

"All right, but if I hear one barefoot and pregnant joke..."

"I'll be on KP for months, I know."

"How I do love a man who understands me," she laughed, as she began to inspect the kitchen.

The smell of food brought Frank back from the upper floor, where she'd heard him busying about. In truth, Heather was enjoying her new role as wife, but she wasn't yet ready to tell Frank just how much she loved cooking. Her bright smile at his approach faded as she saw the gun protruding from his belt.

"Oh god, that smells good," he sighed, as he hugged her gently. "Sorry about the gun, Honey. Maybe I'm just getting paranoid. I've got all the remote cameras going, and I've got our new neighbours on the scope. I'll wash up after we eat, and then show you the set up. You can keep an eye on the visitors while I try to hack into some satellite feeds. Heather? Are you okay, lover?"

"I'm sorry, Frank. I knew the bubble would burst once they arrived. I guess I just wanted the illusion to last a bit longer."

"Illusion?"

"That everything was rosy with my world."

"Isn't it, Heather?"

"Whoa there big fella, don't get panicky on me. Frank, you are the one bright spot in a swiftly destabilizing world. You, and this mad marriage, are all that anchor me right now. I love you madly, and will never part with you as long as you help with the dishes."

"Now there was a hint if I ever heard one." He grinned as he headed for the table, the relief clear on his face.

"ANY PROGRESS, MORNESS?" asked Freydis, as she appeared from her cabin to find a young woman at the helm. "So, Kett finally fell asleep did he?"

"Yes, ma'am. That he did. I am allowed to sit in his chair, but I am to keep my hands off the controls. The mad desire to spin her about, just once, is torturing me."

"Restraint is a powerful weapon, Elgess," said Freydis.

"It makes a fine defence as well," added Morness. "We've been getting quite a history lesson, Freydis, but not much else yet. I have, however, progressed to their language as they now use it, that's making things easier."

"So, what have you learned?"

"Greenland, as our ancestors knew it, is long gone. The folk of Erik Rhode thrived there for many generations, but the climate turned cold, and eventually they had to leave. Most returned to Iceland or the other nearby islands, but that was also long ago. There is little trace of our people left in that cold land."

"Pity that. What else?"

"Well, the first Freydis is our greatest hero of legend, the victor of the Battle of Vinland. However, to these people she is known as a murderess and a traitor."

"Really?" A snarl fleetingly crossed Freydis' face.

"Apparently she lived at a time of great upheaval. There was a new religion sweeping the lands in her time, a religion that basically enslaved women and granted all the lands and power to the men. Freydis fought for the old ways, ways that we still hold to. Her brother Leif brought the new religion to the lands, and they fell into conflict. Freydis lost the political battle."

"And the winners write the histories. Ah well, I will not mourn battles lost so long ago. Have you learned anything we might find useful now?"

"Nothing yet, really," replied Morness. "Perhaps Drass and the scouts have had better luck." She turned back to her monitor as Freydis left the bridge.

Freydis found Drass at the healing deck, the Xtakan healer busy working on his arm. "Practicing with Thordik again, eh Drass?"

"It's good for us both, Freydis. I'm one of the best and she needs to test herself against that. She's too fast and strong to be real, and that will sharpen my skills as well."

"If it doesn't get you killed first."

"Yes, well, there is that to consider."

"Mmm, mmm, mmm," came the musical voice of the Xtakan healer. It was a strange creature with four arms that seemed to work completely independent of the creature's two very large dark and gentle eyes. The head was large, and the smallish body was covered in blue fur. It wore a loose fitting jumpsuit of a strange glittering material that almost seemed alive.

"Yes, of course," said Drass, as he nodded at the creature. "Lord Freydis, Earl of Nyman kind, and chieftain of Pull-Karr, this one has a name we cannot pronounce, but he is content to be called Skeezix. Skeezix has asked to be adopted into Pull-Karr and I have agreed to speak for him. I believe he will bring loyalty and strength to the clan. Will you consider his request?"

"I will consider your request very carefully, Skeezix. However, I do ask your patience until the current situation has been dealt with. Is this acceptable to you?"

"Thank you, Lord Freydis," purred the soft voice. "This one is grateful for your consideration. May I now show you that which I have brought to the Nyman folk?"

"Of course."

"Here it is, Great Lady." He showed her a long coffin-like chamber with a soft interior. There was some sort of control panel at the other end. Freydis eyes opened wide as she saw the soft interior suddenly move and ripple gently.

"Yes, my captain, inside is a living creature. Skeezix puts the wounded person inside, then I go here, lock minds with the wounded person, and then work the controls to show the creature how to heal the wounds."

"You lock minds with the wounded?"

"Not at the surface, Lady. Skeezix can gain no knowledge from this link. We lock minds at a much deeper level. The mind knows what is needed to heal, and Skeezix can tell the creature. The creature can then do what is needed to enhance the healing. Now, this object is a knowledge crystal I have made."

"Knowledge crystal?"

"Yes. Place it here and all the history and language of the Nyman folk is learned while the wounds are healed."

"Are you saying I could bring you a person from the planet, and they can learn all our history and language?"

"Yes, that is true, Great Lady. Skeezix is now making a skills crystal."

"Skills crystal? You mean one can learn the skills of a warrior in that thing?"

Freydis was surprised to see the small creature back off and get defensive, folding its arms around its chest. "No, Lady, Skeezix will make art skills, weaving and craft skills, skills of a bard, but I will not make a crystal for fighting skills. This I will not do.

"I refused to make war crystals for my own people, and so was sent to serve on a small old ship. They hoped I would die in a battle with the Nyman folk, but I survived and was taken prisoner."

"So, how did you end up with us?" she asked kindly. It worked, he relaxed completely once again, and excitedly told his story.

"I was taken prisoner, stripped of my cloth, tortured, terrorized, examined, and not very gently. Great Drass found me and took me from that small cold box. He brought me food, water, cloth, and tools for grooming. Great Drass said the Nyman folk are going on a long journey, far away, and they're not coming back. Skeezix could come as a free man, or stay as he chose. It was an easy choice to make. Drass promised that I would be treated well by the Nyman folk, and so I have been. All is good here, Lady Freydis, but I will not make war crystals, not for anyone. Harm none, is the oath I took as a healer, and I live or die by this oath."

"I will not ask you to break that oath, Skeezix. You are the healer, and your task is to heal. We have plenty of warriors, and that is a skill best learned slowly over time. Now, if Drass is all patched up and ready to return to duty..."

"Command me, my chieftain." Drass smiled as he rose to his feet and followed her out of the infirmary.

"I grow weary of just sitting here, Drass," she said as he fell into step beside her.

"So, what is our next step?"

"I want you to take some of the Untried and hunt down those stealth ships, but first we must make sure our brothers on the surface won't shoot us for going down without permission. Let's go see if Morness is making any further progress."

"ANY NEWS?" ASKED FREYDIS, as they reached the bridge.

"Not really. I'm now starting to get a sense of the political situation down there. It's not encouraging."

"That figures. Tessa, where is our fleet?"

"Still ten sleeps out at best guess, Captain," replied the slender woman peering at a monitor.

"The enemy?"

"Twenty sleeps or more I'd say."

"Alright, we still have time to prepare. Morness, I grow weary of this waiting. I want you to send a new message for the Icelanders to pass along to the rest of that world."

"FRANK, THIS IS SOME set up," Heather said admiringly.

"I told you so. Check out the scope now, while I see if I can eavesdrop on the Icelanders."

Heather laughed then peered through the scope. She had a good view of the ship. On a whim she tried to focus on sector 967. There was nothing to see so she dialed back to the big ship hovering near the moon. She was still gazing at the ship when she heard him start to swear.

"Dammit, now what the hell?" There was an insistent beeping alarm. Frank moved to another monitor and Heather looked over his shoulder. There was a coyote snuffling up at the security camera back by the gate to the long driveway. Frank hit a button and the speaker mounted beneath the camera started to bark wildly at the coyote, which fled for its life. "That'll learn ya, sucker," muttered Frank, as he reset the alarm.

"My god, Frank, this place is like a fortress."

"Yeah, well, Dad is a bit of a survivalist. When he built it for me, he had it made pretty tight. He wanted his only son and heir to be safe."

"Only son and heir? So I married money, did I?"

"Yes, you did. Is that a bad thing?"

"Actually, I married Frank Hunter, the only man who ever wanted more of me than a roll in the hay. I have come to love this man very much."

"And he is so very pleased to hear that, Mrs. Hunter. So, shall we call it a day, or do you want to go back on the night shift?"

"No, let's call it a day, lover. Maybe tomorrow you can hack back into the satellite feeds so we can check up on the rest of the folk who haven't arrived yet. The first batch doesn't seem to be offering any harm, at least according to the Icelanders."

"So far, so good." He smiled as he swept her into his arms and carried her off to bed. Heather shrieked and clung tightly to his neck until he deposited her on the covers, then she kissed him deeply. The future was so uncertain, and she was determined to draw every ounce of delight from whatever time of peace they had left. There wasn't going to be a lot of it.

# Shattered

"Report," said Freydis, as she exited from her cabin.

"Same, same," replied Kett. "There's nothing new to report, unless you count Thordik pacing a deep path through the bulkheads."

"Morness?"

"The Icelanders are all returning home, so it will be easier to defend them, Captain. The rest are posturing, and making demands of the Icelanders. They want to know what is going on, who is in charge, and how they can take advantage. We have to do something soon, Freydis. They're starting to come unglued."

"Have you figured out which is the most common language yet?"

"Yes, and Drass has Skeezix working on a language crystal. He thinks he can get it to work ship wide during a sleep cycle."

"That would be useful. Alright, tell the Icelanders what's coming, and ask them to pass it along to the rest."

"Yes, my captain, it shall be as you desire."

"Call Drass to the bridge. I have an errand for him."

"Yes, ma'am."

A short while later Drass appeared on the bridge, exhausted and a bit battered. "Practising with Thordik again were you?"

"Getting my head pounded again. Keeping her distracted is going to be the death of me yet." There was a round of laughter at that. "So you all think it's funny do you? Alright, who is going to be the next volunteer?" There were a few snickers, but no volunteers.

"Actually, I have a better idea," said Freydis. "Kett, you need a bit of exercise. Take Thordik, and a half dozen more, down to the surface and see if you can find a stealth ship for her to tear apart."

"Now that sounds like fun," replied Kett. "I'll send Elgess up here, but don't let her touch anything." Freydis was still chuckling as he disappeared through the door.

"FRANK, HONEY, SOMETHING big is going on," declared Heather, as she listened intently to the radio. "Oh shit, Frank, this is bad, really bad."

"Heather, what is it?" He came flying down from the observation room above.

"Iceland has just relayed a warning from the visitors to the whole earth. You were right."

"About what, honey?" Frank was holding her close now and Heather stood trembling in his arms.

"They're coming, Frank."

"Who is coming, sweetheart?"

Heather gave a shuddering sigh, then regained control of her emotions. "You were right about the second group headed this way. The Greenlanders have warned us that a large fleet of Greys, the Grey Bastards of my past experiences, is headed this way. They're coming to harvest a full crop of humans. Frank, they've been here for a long time, capturing a few here and there to experiment with, but staying hidden in what the Greenlanders call stealth ships."

"Okay, so why are the Greenlanders here?"

"They say they are here to help. They say there aren't enough Greenland ships to stop them all in space, so some of the Greys will make it to the surface. We've been warned to prepare for war."

"And you were right, Heather, they've been here all along abducting folks and experimenting on them. Did they say what the Greys want us for?"

"Breeders, war slaves, but mostly as food for their fighters. I tell you this, the bastards will never take me alive again. Show me how to work some of those guns, husband. I mean to defend us to the death."

"As do I, Heather, as do I," he breathed softly. "We have a couple of weeks grace here, we'll start first thing in the morning. Now what the hell???"

All the perimeter alarms sounded at once then the electricity failed. Everything was deathly silent. "Oh Christ," gasped Heather, "they're here."

"Who is here, Heather?"

"The Greys, Frank. Quick, get your guns."

He hurried to the bookcase and grunted with the effort of moving the case aside manually. He grabbed an automatic and jammed a full magazine into place then handed it to Heather. "Move this tiny lever to remove the safety," he whispered as he cocked the weapon. "Just point and pull the trigger. Don't worry about trying to aim, just spray the bastards with lead." He took down another auto for himself and loaded it then shoved several extra full magazines into his pockets. "Alright, let's get into position. What are we up against?"

Before she could answer the yard was filled with a bright light. "Don't look at the light. Do not look into the light. They'll be coming soon. They're grey with big bug eyes. Shoot to kill, Frank, no prisoners... Frank? Frank!!!"

Frank Hunter was having trouble concentrating. The light hurt his eyes and he couldn't focus his thoughts. The wall seemed to be gone somehow, and he really wanted to see what was in that light.

By now Heather, too, was feeling the pull to enter the light. Fighting to stay focused, she closed her eyes tightly then reached for

Frank. As soon as she felt him at her side, she opened fire, hoping she would not hit her husband. She continued to fire blindly into the light until the gun was empty. She had no idea if she had hit anything, but it had an effect. Frank came back to his senses.

As soon as his mind cleared, Frank opened fire. Mag after mag poured from his gun into the light until the gun was too hot and he cast it aside. The mind numbing started again and they both fought it. Heather suddenly felt herself alone. Frank was gone into the light. Opening her eyes she saw a group of greys lead him away, three more were reaching for her and she fought the urge to go to them.

Suddenly, all hell broke loose. The light vanished and the ship exploded away leaving Heather alone with the three grey creatures. Her mind clear now, she struck with all her martial arts training. She swiftly felled two and was choking the life from a third, when the most beautiful woman she could have imagined suddenly appeared before her.

Heather was bleeding heavily from several wounds inflicted by the weapons of the Greys, but she didn't seem to notice. She wasn't even aware as the creature in her hands ceased to struggle and went limp. The beautiful woman reached out to her and smiled with the radiant smile of a goddess. "Greetings, my sister." She spoke in Icelandic, and her voice was like music. Heather fainted from loss of blood, with that wonderful voice ringing in her ears.

"THEY'RE ESCAPING," shouted Thordik, as she hurled herself from the small ship. Alas, even her great speed was not enough. The stealth ship vanished with its lone captive. She arrived to see a tall human woman, bleeding from a dozen wounds, finish off the last of the Greys that had been left behind. They had been too late to save both humans. She was impressed with the fight they had put up though, even without protection, these two had managed to fight off the effects of the mind control weapon of the Greys. Sadly, Thordik had been denied once again.

Torn with the mad desire to kill something in her frustration, she faced the human. Finally the rage began to subside, and she looked closely at the woman standing there with a dead Grey in her hands. The woman's face could easily be mistaken for Freydis at first glance. Gazing deeply into those wary eyes Thordik knew, this was the one. She spoke a greeting, but the stranger fainted from blood loss before she could reply.

Scooping the wounded Heather into her strong arms, Thordik carried her back to the small scout ship. She laid her tenderly on a bench, then began to bandage her wounds. "We should take her back to her own people so she can get attention," Kett said.

"We must take her to the Mjolnir," Thordik replied firmly as she continued to tend the woman's wounds.

"Thordik, we cannot..."

"Kett, you saw what she did."

"Yes."

"She is proven then. She has killed in battle and deserves to be honoured."

"Thordik..."

"Go back without me then, for I will not abandon this woman," replied a hard-eyed Thordik, as she turned to face him. "Better yet, I can leave you here and take her back myself."

"You would defy me, Thordik?"

"Yes, but I do hope that will not be required. I ask you now to take her back to the ship while life still clings to her. Do it now, or I will do it for you."

"All right, Thordik, but it's on your head. All are aboard?"

"All are here," replied one of the others.

"Here we go." Like a Valkyrie, the small ship leaped into the air and sped right toward the Mjolnir above. "Have the healer meet us," Kett barked into the transmitter as the small ship cleared the atmosphere.

"You have wounded, Kett?" came Freydis' voice. "Who?"

"A human woman, she's badly hurt."

"What are you thinking, Kett? You should have dropped her with her own kind."

"Freydis, it is I, Thordik," said Thordik, as she leaned over Kett's shoulder. "I threatened his life if he would not bring her. Mine is the fault here."

"She is the one, Thordik?"

"You should have seen her, Freydis. With her bare hands, and no defence against the mind fogger, she still killed three. With just her bare hands, Freydis, she tore them asunder, but she is badly wounded. Freydis, she wears your face; I thought you might want to meet her."

"The stealth ship?"

"Escaped even as we arrived," replied Kett. Thordik had returned to the human woman's side.

"And Thordik?"

"Denied. Three Greys were killed, Freydis, but it was the human woman who fought that battle. She is a proven warrior. Perhaps Thordik is right about this."

"How did Thordik convince you to bring her, Kett?"

"She threatened to leave me behind." Kett chuckled as the small ship disappeared into the belly of the Mjolnir.

Freydis arrived at the healing bay just as Skeezix lowered the lid and Heather screamed.

"Thordik..."

"Forgive me, Lord Freydis, but I had no choice. If, when she is healed, you insist, I shall return to the surface with her and remain there."

"You believe this is the one?"

"I do, as will you when you see her. We arrived almost together, Kett and I, but the stealth ship was already gone with its captives, and she had killed the three who were left behind. She fainted from blood loss. I had to bring her here, as I have no idea if her own people could help her or not. She is the one foretold, Freydis, and I will not leave her side until this affair has been concluded."

"All right, Thordik, don't get all worked up on me. I'm not going to shove the two of you out the air lock. Skeezix, can you use the learning crystal on her?" The small blue creature did not look up, he just patted the crystal with one hand to show her that it was already in place.

"All right," said Freydis. "Come on, Chieftain of Erikr-Dak, let's get some food. Your new sister isn't going anywhere for a while. Since you obviously are not destined to be a warrior, perhaps we can make a nurse of you."

"Lord Freydis, it is cruel to beat the defenceless about the head," sighed Thordik, as she fell into step beside Freydis.

"After we eat you can go out again. There are other stealth ships down there, and we have to clear them out before the armada arrives."

"Forgive me, Lady," said Thordik, as she took a tray of food then sank onto a bench at the long table, "but it will do no good at all. Send others. They will have better luck. For good or ill, my destiny is tied to that woman in the healing chamber. I just hope she lives."

"She will live, Thordik, don't worry." She did worry though, and for the next three days she rarely left the infirmary. On the third day, Heather awakened just as Thordik left for her sleeping space.

HEATHER WANDERED IN and out of consciousness as the small craft hurtled toward the mother ship. Groaning under the slight gravitational force, she nonetheless withstood it. She had been taken again, but this was different. The beautiful young woman stayed ever at her side, soothing her hurts, and crooning to her in that magical sweet voice. She was taken into the mother ship, then carried to what she thought was a soft bed. She screamed as a blue creature began to lower the lid, and she felt the creature inside fold itself around her.

Heather tried to struggle, but it was no use. She was enfolded as though in a mother's womb. She stopped her struggles, as a voice calling to her caught her attention. It was a soft sweet purring voice, and she liked the sound of it. "Let me out please," she thought and then she tried in Icelandic. This time it answered.

"First you must sleep, healing comes in sleep."

"Frank, I have to help Frank. They took him and..."

"Sleep and heal first. You cannot help Frank until you are healed."

"But..."

"Sleep now and heal," purred the voice again. "Many things you will see and learn as you sleep."

"Learn?"

"Yes, learn in sleep. You will learn the language and the ways of the Nyman folk, of their customs, and of how they came to be. Sleep now, sleep and heal."

Heather drifted off then. The voice continued in her mind, or so she thought. She wondered how she was able to breathe, but the question faded as well. All sense of time was lost as images drifted in and out of her awareness. So much information, so much confusion, and yet somehow, it all seemed to make an odd sort of sense.

Finally the flow of information slowed to a crawl, and eventually stopped. With no further information coming, she started to get restless. Heather began to stir, and the warmth of the enfolding creature withdrew from her. The lid was then raised from the chamber. The light hurt her eyes for a moment as she tried to sit up.

Hands reached out to help her, and she struggled from the healing chamber.

# Cousins

"Frank, where is Frank?" asked Heather, as she was helped to stand.

"He is not here, Great Warrior of Greenland," purred that familiar voice. It came from the blue creature she had seen before. Involuntarily she shrank from him and took a defensive stance. When the creature did not move she slowly relaxed.

"You locked me in there."

"Yes, I did. That will not harm you; it is a healing chamber. It healed your wounds, Greenland Warrior."

"It's alive."

"Yes, it is. The creature feeds on pain and sorrow. It takes them away from you. The creature finds the ways your body uses to heal itself, and it enhances them. The creature saved your life, Greenland Warrior."

"Why do you keep calling me that?"

"I know how you came to be here. Allow your mind to embrace the knowledge. You know now how the Nyman folk came into being."

"So, what does that have to do with me?"

"Turn around and find out," chuckled a rich feminine voice.

Heather spun around to see a tall woman with fierce blue eyes like her own. The woman was older and had a few battle scars, but her face was so very familiar. Heather had seen it a million times in the mirror. "Oh my god," she breathed as she reached her hand toward the woman's face. Suddenly she snatched her hand back. "Sorry," she muttered as she withdrew her hand.

"Let's both do it." The woman smiled as she reached out to gently stroke Heather's cheek. "Thor's beard, your skin is so smooth."

"You have scales." Heather smiled in wonder as she touched the woman's face lightly. "They're beautiful. You look so very much like me. Can we truly be related?"

"I think I have a few cycles on you. Therefore the face was mine first. I should be charging you rent. Skeezix, introduce us if you please."

"Of course, Captain," purred the blue creature as he tentatively approached Heather. "This one is the Greenland Warrior that Thordik brought to me for healing. Warrior, this person is Lord Freydis, Chieftain of Pull-Karr clan, and Earl of all Nyman folk."

"The earl," said Heather. "It is a great pleasure to meet you, Lord Freydis. I am deeply honoured. I thank you for saving my life."

"And I you, Greenlander, but I am not responsible for your rescue. It was Thordik who brought you to us, and it was Skeezix who healed you. It is he you should be thanking."

"Yes indeed, forgive me for a moment." Heather smiled as she turned to the blue creature. "Skeezix, I beg your forgiveness. You are the first of your kind I have seen, and after being attacked by the Greys, I was fearful. I ask your forgiveness for my fear and bad manners, and I ask you to accept my gratitude for the healing. I surely would have died had you not helped me. I am in your debt."

"I am honoured to have been of service, Great Warrior. There is no debt between us."

"So, warrior, have you got a name?" asked Freydis.

"Oops, sorry. I'm Heather MacKay-Hunter. Heather will do just fine."

"Freydis works for me. Do you know the history of your family, Heather? I truly believe there must be a connection between us."

"For some reason, I appear to know the entire history of your people, Freydis. I seem to have learned your language as well. I know you folk are descended from Greenlanders, and so am I, I believe. My mother claims that if you follow back through the line of women, I am descended from Erik Rhode through his daughter, Freydis."

"As am I, Heather. It seems there is truth to our combined belief. Now cousin, tell me, who is Frank?"

"My husband," Heather replied softly, a tear forming at the corner of her eye. "The Greys took him. God help me, he's probably dead by now."

"I doubt that, Heather. They got away with him, but they're still on the planet somewhere. Not one single stealth ship has left the surface since our arrival."

"Then I have to find him," exclaimed Heather, as she tried to surge to the door. She didn't get far before she ran out of gas.

"We will find him, Heather, but you're not quite ready for battle again yet."

"Why am I so weak?"

"It's the gravity."

"You're heavy worlders?"

"The ship is kept at Nyman normal one. That's about one point four times Iceland norm. You need a few more days to adjust. You rest and recover. We'll keep an eye out for the stealth ships."

"They said there are a hundred ships coming," said Heather, as Freydis helped her to a seat and threw a blanket around her bare shoulders. "Can we truly survive?"

"We shall do more than survive," Freydis replied with a wolfish grin. "We'll pound their heads for them, but there are so damned many. It isn't going to be over quickly, and a lot of them will reach the surface. Your people must be ready."

"Freydis, can you tell me something?"

"Yes?"

"Was I delirious, or was I truly saved by a goddess of your people?"

"Close. That was Thordik. She is the last of her clan, and enjoys being a clan chieftain, even though she is still an untried warrior. Heather, she is like no other we have ever known. She is beautiful beyond compare, stronger than she should be, faster than any warrior in the fleet, so intelligent she is frightening, and her mind never sleeps. She is the greatest hope our people have."

"Oh?"

"Thordik is young yet, but one day she will be the greatest Earl the Nyman folk have ever known. If anyone can lead our people back from the brink, it is she. However, she is still an Untried, and each time we get her close to a battle, something intervenes. She has become so frustrated that we are afraid for her, for us all."

"For all?"

"Should Thordik lose control, it would take half the fleet to get her stopped. She could as easily be our destroyer as our saviour. I have tried to adopt her into my clan, where several of the older warriors might help her to her trial, and to the status that eludes her, but she is determined to rebuild her own clan.

"Ah well, enough of this, you're tired. You rest for a few days, Heather, and then we will discuss your future."

"My future?"

"I have a mighty task for you, Heather Mak-Kay Hunter. One that might make a big difference to your people as well as our own. I won't compel you, however. If you wish it, I will have you returned to the surface where Thordik found you. Rest now, there's no need to make decisions yet."

With that, Freydis left Heather alone with Skeezix. "It seems that my cousin carries a heavy burden," said Heather as Freydis disappeared through the door.

"That is true, Great Warrior. Lord Freydis carries the fate of both your people and her own. It is a heavy load. You must help her if you can."

"You are of a different people aren't you, Skeezix?"

"Yes, warrior. My own people warred against the great empire for many generations, but eventually, with the leadership of Lord Freydis against us, Skeezix's folk were defeated. Freydis' folk became too popular then, and so have come to the far edge of the empire to find a safe haven.

"The Nyman folk asked Skeezix to come along as their healer, and so I came. I have asked to be adopted into Clan Pull-Karr, but I doubt it will ever happen. Lord Freydis would not mind, I am certain, but too many folk remember the bad things my own people did to theirs during the long wars."

"Then why are they helping us?"

"You are same folk almost, how can she not help you? What would you do, Heather the Warrior?"

"I honestly don't know what I'd do, Skeezix."

"You are tired now, Heather. Go back into the healing chamber where I can help you grow strong again, stronger than you have ever been before. I swear you will be safe. Heather, why do your eyes drip water?"

"Frank," she sniffed. "My poor Frank. I swear to any god who will listen, I will avenge you, my beloved husband. I swear I'll kill every damned slimy Grey son of a bitch in the universe. I will hunt them to the end of my days, on this or any other planet they try to hide on. I will find you, Frank, or I will die in the attempt."

"Rest now, Heather," soothed Skeezix, as he eased her back into the healing chamber. Heather sobbed out her sorrow at the loss of her beloved husband as the symbiote enfolded her. This time Heather gave herself to the sweet sleep, and her pain was swept away.

When she awakened again her rescuer was waiting with a bright smile of welcome. "Greetings, you selfish robber, you," laughed that wonderful voice.

"What do you mean, robber?"

"You had three Greys, and you didn't save me a single one to play with, you kept them all for yourself."

"I've heard a rumour that more are on the way." Heather smiled as she stood up and tested her weight. She was no longer weak, but felt strong again. "You're my rescuer, it's to you that I owe my life. My name is Heather MacKay-Hunter, but Heather will do nicely."

"I am honoured, Heather," replied Thordik, as she passed Heather a garment and helped her into it. "I'm Thordik, Chieftain and only member of Clan Erikr-Dak, the Children of Freya. Thordik will do fine, my sister."

"You called me sister back at the cabin, why?"

"I call you sister because that's what we are, sisters. Only distant cousins by blood, Heather, but we are sisters, at least I would like us to be."

"I'd like that too, Thordik. When you found me, did you see a tall man?"

"I glimpsed him only, Heather, as the Greys took him. Who was he?"

"He is my love and my life, Thordik," Heather replied in a cold deadly voice. "He is the world to me. Those things took him from me, so I killed them. They have him now, and I want him back." Her voice was so cold and deadly that Thordik actually shivered and Skeezix backed away from her.

"I will get him back for you, my sister," vowed Thordik. "Get me to my trial, then I will personally tear apart every Grey ship in existence until you are reunited. I'm enslaved, Heather MacKay-Hunter. Freya herself has sent you to help me. Set me free to find him for you. Release my bondage and we will hunt them together."

They were gazing into each other's eyes fiercely, and neither saw Freydis enter. Freydis froze in place and made no sound. She heard the whole exchange.

"There is something that must happen first if we are to be sisters," Heather said at last. She didn't know why this was suddenly so important, but it was. With Frank gone she needed someone, and here was a volunteer, a volunteer like no other in the world, any world.

"Name it, my sister."

"Adopt me into your clan, Thordik, then we will be sisters."

"Are you certain this is what you want?"

"It is, Thordik. We are both alone now. Let us truly be sisters, and face whatever comes, together."

"Then so be it. As chieftain of Clan Erikr-Dak, I adopt you, Heather MacKay-Hunter. Now you must take on your new role as chieftain of the clan."

"What???"

"You're the elder sister, and you're the only proven warrior in the clan. You must accept the role. You know our ways now, so you know what you must do. Get me to my trial, Heather, and I swear I will find him if he yet lives."

"Alright, Thordik my sister, I accept the adoption and the role. I may do some very strange things in the near future, but I beg you to trust me."

"It shall be as you say, my chieftain. Now you have a decision to make."

"I do?"

"Yes. As chieftain, I pledged the clan to the service of Pull-Karr. They are powerful allies, and I felt it to be a good alliance. It is now up to you to keep that pledge or to cut us free."

"We will keep it, Thordik, it was a wise decision."

"I am happy to hear that," chuckled Freydis.

"You knew she was there," admonished Heather, as she rounded on Thordik. She spun back to Freydis and dropped to one knee while meeting the gaze of the earl. "As chieftain of Erikr-Dak Clan,

I pledge the loyalty of myself and my clan to the Earl and to the Chieftain of Pull-Karr."

"Well said, Heather." Freydis grinned as she offered her hand. "I accept you and your clan. Now then, Chieftain of Erikr-Dak, I need you to be my ambassador to the planet."

"Excuse me?"

"Heather, I need someone who understands the background of both peoples. You also have first hand knowledge of the Greys. You're intelligent, fast with your thoughts and tongue, and you have courage, as you have proven. Will you take on this task?"

"I will, but first there is something I must ask of you, Freydis."

"Ask."

"I ask for your trust, as I have asked Thordik for hers. The things I say or do might not make sense to you, but I swear I will do my best for you, for us all."

"Alright, Heather," agreed Freydis after searching Heather's eyes for a long moment. "I'll trust you to keep the faith. Thor's beard, you might look like me, but there is a lot of Thordik in you too. Truly you are sisters. Rest now, Heather, another sleep cycle, then we have to get busy. The fleet is nearly here and we must be prepared."

"Okay. Are you ready to put me back to sleep, Skeezix?"

"First I would ask a favour of you, Heather MacKay-Hunter, Chieftain of Erikr-Dak clan."

"Of course, Skeezix."

"Forgive me, Lord Freydis, but Skeezix knows that many of Clan Pull-Karr are still angry with Xtak folk. I am sorry to put you in a place where you must make such a decision. Heather MacKay-Hunter, will you accept me into your clan?"

Thordik's eyes hardened slightly and Skeezix flinched. Heather didn't speak for a moment then she winked at Thordik and grinned. "What do you think, Sister Thordik? A skilled healer might be a welcome addition to the clan if we're going hunting for Greys, don't you think?"

"I do believe you might be right," Thordik replied with a sudden bright smile. "It's your decision, my sister, but I have no objection at all. I think Skeezix will be a welcome addition to the clan, and I will speak for him." His eyes opened wide in surprise at that.

"Agreed then. Welcome to the family, Skeezix my brother. Now put me back to sleep. I'm tiring fast." She dropped the garment to the floor then winked at Freydis, as the excited Skeezix tucked her back into the healing chamber.

"Join me for a morsel, Thordik?" said Freydis, as she exited the healing bay and headed for the great hall.

"I'd be delighted, Freydis." Thordik grinned as she fell into step beside the earl.

"That was a bold thing to do, Thordik, handing over the leadership of your clan like that," said Freydis as they sat at a table in the corner of the huge room. "You, of all people, will not be at ease as second."

"She was sent by Freya to save us, Lord Freydis. She cannot do that if she is constantly asking my permission, or making suggestions, hoping I might agree."

"So you trust her already?"

"I trust my goddess. She sent Heather to me, and I trust that. The future will hold the proof of the metal."

"It will that, girl, and sooner than we think. You'd better get some rest, because ready or not, she will have to get busy the next time she awakens."

"I hear and obey, my Captain." Thordik rose from the table and headed for her sleeping space.

"Please, Lady, let this be, for I'm going mad with impatience," sighed Thordik, as she curled up in her small space. She was actually too tall to fit it properly.

"Patience is a powerful weapon, child," whispered a voice at the edges of her reality. "Be at peace, she will set you free and lead you to greatness." Thordik was unsure if it was real or if she was dreaming, but she was comforted nonetheless.

# Freed From the Chains

Frank Hunter fought the fuzziness in his mind, but it was useless. He had no idea where he was or how much time had passed since their capture. He knew that he'd been taken, but he wasn't sure how. Frank had been unable to resist the light or the small, friendly people who had come to guide him home.

No, that was wrong; they didn't take him home, they'd brought him here, wherever here was, and they damned well weren't friendly. Tired of the struggle he let his thoughts drift away again.

Frank awakened with a deep pain in his abdomen, but he was unable to move. A moment later he realized that he was restrained. There were a lot of chittering sounds and a scurrying of feet, but he was having trouble focusing on anything but the pain. Finally he got his eyes cleared a bit and looked down his chest. There was a small, bug eyed, grey creature, cutting at his abdomen. He could feel the passage of the blade and the pain it caused, but they ignored his screams, or did he just imagine that he'd screamed. Frank fainted from the pain.

Awareness returned again, sort of. The pain was much duller now, but his thoughts were still cloudy. Slowly Frank became aware of the tubes sticking into his body, and the restraining material that held him suspended above the floor. Suddenly his thoughts turned to Heather. Heather! She must be here as well. Frank had to escape and find her. He struggled for only a moment, then the light came, and his thoughts scattered once more.

Pain brought him around again, and as it burned through the fog in his mind, he realized that they were cutting into him again. Frank tried to fight them, but he failed. He was fully aware of what they were doing, but he was unable to make a sound or to move a muscle on his own power. Again the pain became too great, and he passed out.

A long time passed before he regained his senses, or had it, he couldn't tell. Frank had lost all sense of time and had no idea where he was. This time his mind cleared slightly and he realized he was naked; naked and in a glass cage. With a deep sigh Frank began to explore the wounds on his body. There were many, and had been only crudely repaired. He staggered to his feet, but the floor lurched under him and he fell. He lay there cursing and trying to get the rest of the fog from his mind. Somehow he had to escape and find Heather.

Heather! Frank was suddenly filled with a mad desire for Heather, and his body responded. The cage opened and a naked woman was thrust in with him. Frank nearly went mad with lust. "Heather, my beloved," he croaked as he gathered the limp body of the woman into his arms. Ever so weakly, she tried to resist him.

The human sense of smell may not be very strong, but it can wield power. Something was wrong, and Frank sensed it. "Heather," he breathed, but the limp woman did not respond to him. Suddenly it penetrated his befogged mind, she smelled wrong. Somehow that cleared his mind a bit, and he sat back up. Her hair was dark, not gold, and her eyes were brown. This wasn't Heather, and Frank pushed her away.

"God damn those little grey bastards." He ranted and railed, and the rage cleared his mind. Frank could now see the half unconscious woman in the cage with him. She definitely was not his Heather.

"You little bastards." He shouted as he gave in to the rage, and the clarity of thought that accompanied it. "I'll kill you all." He shouted more threats as he pounded on the glass wall. "I'll kill every fucking one of you little grey bastards..." Frank Hunter got no further as the light returned and his mind fled once again.

THIS TIME, WHEN HEATHER awakened, she was alone with Skeezix. "Greetings, my chieftain." He fairly purred as she emerged from the healing chamber and dressed herself in the garment that waited for her.

"Greetings, kinsman." She smiled with delight as she tested her strength and flexibility. "I feel like my old self again."

"You are that and more, my chieftain."

"What do you mean by that, Skeezix?"

"You are far stronger than ever before, Heather MacKay-Hunter. The Nyman gravity will no longer hamper you. Skeezix did not tell all of his healing secrets, my chieftain. You now have more skills than before as well."

"Skeezix, what did you do to me?"

"I did nothing harmful, my chieftain. That is the code I live by as a healer. What I did was enhance your natural abilities and skills. The creature can magnify a person's natural gifts many times over."

"Is that how Thordik came to be as she is?"

"That is true, my chieftain. It was not Skeezix, but she has been in a chamber before. She was found on the wreckage of a Xtak ship as a small child. It is said that she slept in the chamber each night until her rescue. I believe she was helped by the ship's healer during the great battle that killed all her clan.

"Who knows what plans my people had for her, but she was recovered by her own folk, and no one will ever know what was done. I believe, because of his grief at the pain our soldiers inflicted on her folk, that the healer must have tried to give the child full access to all her potential. She herself has done the rest. I beg you, my chieftain, keep this secret. If it becomes known..."

"They will want you to enhance all the warriors, and that is against the Healer's Code that you live by. I understand, Skeezix. The knowledge will remain between us."

"Thank you, my chieftain. I believe I have chosen my clan well."

"Family is important to you isn't it, my friend?"

"Yes. Among my people, to be without family would soon result in death from loneliness or starvation."

"Well, you have clan now, Skeezix, and we are glad to have you."

"I was afraid Thordik would object, but her mind works so very fast. In a mere moment she evaluated the situation and chose another path."

"Her hesitation was a natural reluctance to embrace one of those who took her entire clan from her. She bypassed the instinct, understood that you were not one of them, and that you are indeed a good friend, and so she embraced you as a brother. Thordik will cherish you as I do, Skeezix, do not fear."

"Is this truly so, my chieftain?"

"It is, my kinsman. You have saved my life and become a trusted friend. Now, Brother Skeezix, where is everybody, and where can I get something to eat around here?"

"Come with me and I will show you," he purred, as he led her from the healing bay. Skeezix led her to the great hall, where many people were seated at some of the amazingly long tables, enjoying a variety of foods. Freydis was there, and her companion looked up, saw them, and spoke. Smiling, Freydis motioned for them to join her. Heather's status among the Nyman had just been established.

Prattling on the whole time, Skeezix helped Heather choose a platter of food, then he left her to return to his healing room. Heather approached Freydis and sat facing her and her companion. She smiled with delight as she was introduced to Drass.

"It is an honour to meet a true Nylass," said Heather. "It is also an honour to meet Thordik's combat instructor."

"Her favourite punching post is a better description," replied Drass. "It is a pleasure for me to meet the Chieftain of Erikr-Dak and the Ambassador to Greenland."

"I prefer Heather, and it will be a lot easier to say."

"Drass is best for me."

"So tell me, Drass, what is all this Skeezix has piled on this platter?"

"Not a word, Drass," chuckled Freydis. "Try it all, Heather. See what you like. Start with that one."

Heather daintily tried a few things then gave in to her appetite. "Dear gods, that was wonderful." She sighed as she finally came up for air. "I had no idea I was so hungry. How long has it been since I have eaten anything?"

"It has been a while," replied Drass. "That chamber will nourish you, but it isn't the same, and you always come out ravenous."

"Now that you're finished, Heather, I want to put you to work," said Freydis.

"I am here to serve, cousin. How can I help?"

"I need you to speak to your people. In the past while, they have begun to launch missiles at us, and they are hampering our efforts to find the stealth ships. They can't hurt us of course, but they're depleting their weapons, weapons they will need in plenty very soon. Something must be done, and it must be done now."

Heather nodded her head slowly for a moment, deep in thought. "All right," she said at last, "I'll need you to trust me, Freydis. I swear I will always act in the best interest of both peoples, even though it may not seem like it at the time. I will also need you to make some of this ship's resources available to me."

"Come with me," said Freydis, as she rose from the table. Heather followed her swiftly disappearing back and Drass stayed at Heather's side. They strode onto the bridge and straight into Freydis' command cabin, where she indicated that they should sit.

"Thank you for the escort, Drass."

"It was not in fear of sabotage, Heather. The Mjolnir is a big ship, and it would be easy to lose sight of a guide that runs away."

Freydis shook her finger at Drass then laughed. "What do you have in mind, Heather?"

"Freydis, I believe that, with a few demonstrations, we can accomplish many of our immediate aims. What I have in mind depends upon the capabilities of this magnificent ship of yours."

"What do you need?"

"Can we see what is going on down on the surface? Can we see it as it happens?"

"We can."

"Is it possible to broadcast it to every communications system down there?"

"Yes. What are you up to, Heather of Erikr-Dak?"

"With your permission and assistance, Lord Freydis, I intend to unleash Thordik, stop any interference from the surface, and give those people an idea of what they might be up against. That should bring them onside easily enough."

"Tell me more," encouraged Freydis, as she leaned across the table. Drass was still chuckling with delight as they returned to the bridge.

"People, hear me now," said Freydis. Everyone stopped what they were doing and turned to hear her words. "This person is a distant cousin of mine. She is Heather Mak-Kay-Hunter and chieftain of Erikr-Dak clan. In the next few short spans, she may forget herself, and start barking orders on my bridge. Obey those orders as though they were my own." There were several surprised faces staring at Heather.

"This one is Morness, our communicator, and this one is Kett. Kett is the best pilot and engineer in five galaxies," said Freydis as she introduced her bridge crew. "Kalla will..."

"Forgive me, Captain," interrupted Drass, "but I request permission to man weapons myself."

"Don't you want to play pilot?"

"Oh, Thor's beard, yes, that's a delightful idea, my Captain. Kalla, the guns are yours."

"All right, Heather," Freydis said as Drass left the bridge, "the ship is yours."

"Is it permissible to have an Untried on the bridge?"

"Morness," grinned Freydis. "Get Thordik up here."

"Thordik, to the bridge, now," barked Morness's voice throughout the ship. "Battle stations."

"THEY'RE MOVING," SHOUTED a voice, bringing tension and life to the bunker where the President of the United States of America was still in residence.

"What? Where?"

"Unknown, sir. They seem to be circling the globe slowly."

"Where, dammit?"

"Away from us, that's all we know at the moment sir."

"Looks like those damned fools might have pissed them off. I hope we all don't have to pay the price for this," said Thomas Mooreland.

"Amen to that, Mr. President, amen to that," agreed a voice behind him.

"The Icelanders just called with a warning, sir," shouted a voice. "The ship is going to broadcast in English at any moment."

All eyes immediately sought the huge wall screen. A scene of horror played out before them as a band of desert raiders attacked and brutally destroyed a village somewhere in sub Saharan Africa.

"WHAT ARE WE LOOKING for?" asked Kett as he easily manoeuvred the ship around to the bright side of the planet.

"I'll know it when I see it, Kett," replied Heather, her eyes glued to the viewing screen. "Easy now, there's Africa down there, can you get a better look at this area right here?" Heather was pointing at the screen. Slowly the ship moved directly over Africa and the landscape below came into view.

"I need a closer view." She had it instantly. It was just like adjusting the zoom on the world's biggest scope. "Slowly now, easy does it, the bastards have to be around here somewhere... There!"

The scene from below that leaped to life on the huge screen was horrific. Heather heard a soft snarl from Thordik, who was peering intently over her shoulder. On the screen they could see a large number of ragged men, heavily armed, terrorizing a village. They were shooting and killing at random, and the unfortunate villagers who were unable to escape were either cut down by gunfire or chopped to death with machetes.

Thordik nearly broke Heather's arm, she gripped it so tightly, as they watched a woman being mutilated with machetes. "Why have you brought me here to witness this?"

"Look at those men," commanded Heather, as she thrust the girl toward the screen, "mark them well. Hear the words of your chieftain, Thordik of Erikr-Dak. Those men are my enemies. Destroy them."

With a cry of delight Thordik leaped away and bolted from the bridge.

"Morness, I need to speak to the planet now," said Heather, as she turned to the woman bent over her station.

"Stand here and speak, all will hear you," replied Morness.

"People of Earth, hear my words," began Heather. Her voice was cold and remorseless. "I am Heather MacKay-Hunter, and I have been chosen by Lord Freydis as ambassador to Earth for the Nyman people. The atrocity you have just witnessed against these villagers is what you can expect from the enemy once their armada arrives, and you have little time left to prepare for their arrival. Watch your screens carefully, for we are about to give you a small demonstration."

The screens split and they saw both the village in Africa and the small fighter streak from the belly of the Mjolnir. Straight towards Africa it sped. Several missiles were fired at it, and dozens of war planes rose to the air, but it was all useless. The small ship was much too fast and agile. Easily avoiding the attempts to interfere, it zeroed in on the African landscape.

Suddenly it appeared over the village, and the near-naked body of a woman fell out from a great height. She tumbled over and over in the air and then, at the last moment, she turned upright. Two small flashes of light or flame sprouted from the objects strapped to her wrists, and she dropped easily to the ground. She was naked except for her boots.

# Thordik Unleashed

"Thordik, what in the name of the gods are you doing?" demanded Drass, as he saw her strip off all her weapons then her clothing.

"Just pay attention, Drass, there's another missile coming at us. I'm going to face those men alone and naked, Drass. I want there to be no mistake in Heather's mind about my worth." She strapped on a couple of grav packs, then opened the door.

"We're too high," bawled Drass, but his words fell on empty air. She was already in free fall.

Thordik tucked and fell at terrible speed, but it was necessary to avoid the gunfire. At the last second she turned and cut in the grav packs strapped to her arms. It nearly tore her shoulders from their sockets, but she managed to land lightly on her feet. In the midst of the carnage, she slowly turned around in a full circle, a wolfish grin on her face.

The men on the ground just stared in wonder as the tall woman fell from the sky to land easily in their midst. She was naked, except for her boots, and she was like no other woman they had ever seen. Taller than a man, with a flowing mane of auburn hair tied back with a silvery band, she turned about, her sea-green skin glittering in the sun and her fierce eyes taking in everything in the village.

As they stared, she dropped the things from her arms to her hands, then locked eyes with a man in a turban and sneered in derision. With a sudden scream of rage he attacked as she spat in his direction.

He came at Thordik with a bladed weapon, casting aside his rifle and not even seeing as she hurled the objects in her hands. Two of his men were already dead before he reached her and met his fate. As he swung the machete she ducked, grabbed his wrist, and broke it. She then easily broke his neck and cast aside the body.

Thordik was now armed with a machete. They came at her then, and she fought them with a fury born of a savage madness. Her speed was incredible, her strength astounding, her skills unequalled, and there was no mercy at all in her.

Thordik was ready when they charged. She leaped to meet them, and they met their fate on her blade, at her fists and feet, and at the hands of their comrades as they missed their target and struck their own. Like an enraged leopard, only much faster and more deadly, she tore into them.

The entire world held its breath as, in desperation, some of the men opened fire with automatic weapons. Several of their own were killed, but she had taken only a few scratches. She was so very fast, and she was never still, not even for a heartbeat.

Horrified, the men saw as she turned and charged right at the gunmen, easily avoiding their fire as she fought her way towards them, killing as she ran. Now all was very different, as the men fought to escape this demon from a hell they could not imagine. It did them no good at all, for she pursued and slew them as they fled.

A few managed to escape her for a short while, but she swiftly hunted them down. Horrified at what they had just seen, the world watched as Thordik ran down the last of the men and literally tore his head from his shoulders. Her head came up and she sniffed the air, her eyes searching everywhere, but she was now alone. The remains of the villagers cowered in their huts in fear.

Suddenly the small ship reappeared, and she fled from it. With laughter on her lips, she fled from the pursuing ship, and the world watched in wonder as it banked above her. Suddenly she leaped impossibly high into the air and disappeared into the small craft, which then sped straight toward the huge spaceship above.

Several missiles were sent after it but they fell behind, then back to earth, as the craft broke from the atmosphere and into space. Only one missile followed, and a lancet of light from the Mjolnir destroyed it.

Suddenly, Heather was back on the screen. "Hear me well, people of Earth. The one you saw was only an Untried, a cadet, if you will. She has had training, yes, but before this day, she has not ever been tried in actual combat. What you have seen was the work of a naked female trainee.

Now, imagine if you will, what it might be like to have ten thousand battle hardened and fully armed Nyman warriors landed on the surface of the planet. Think long and hard on this before you send another missile our way. Oh yes, about that last missile that you fired at us, watch and learn.

"Kalla, have you located the source of that last missile?"

"I have, Heather."

"Destroy it." A beam of light flickered, then the screen shifted to a gigantic gaping crater somewhere in Siberia. The crater had to be the size of a small city, and its bottom glittered in the light like polished glass.

"Now then," Heather went on mercilessly as her face returned to the screen, "now that we have your attention, hear me well. We are not your enemies, we are your allies. In the near future you will face a terrible enemy, and we are here to fight beside you. There are far too many of them for us to destroy in space. Some will surely reach the surface of the planet. There you must fight them. Prepare yourselves.

"There are several enemy ships already hidden on your planet. We are going to seek them out and destroy them. Do not attempt to interfere, for we have run out of patience with you. I will contact you through the President of Iceland once we have accomplished this task." She made a jerking motion and the screens went blank.

"Heather!" She spun around at that cry to catch Thordik in her arms. Thordik was laughing and swinging Heather around in the air as she hugged her so hard the poor woman couldn't breathe.

"Put her down, Thordik, you're killing her."

"Are you pleased, my sister?" asked Heather, as Thordik set her back on her feet.

"My pleasure holds no bounds, my chieftain. You have kept your promise to me, and now I must keep mine." She spun to face Freydis and saluted.

"I can see it in your eyes, Thordik," said Freydis, as she took the red sash from her own waist and tied it around Thordik. "Drass has born witness, warrior. You have proven yourself worthy. What would you have of me as gift this day?"

"Lord Freydis, I made a vow to my sister, and I must now keep that vow. I ask permission to hunt the stealth ships on the surface."

"The task is yours, Thordik. Take what you need and get it done."

"I need a dozen proven warriors as witness," barked Thordik, as she spun toward Morness, "and I need the Untried at the launch bays." She was already gone from the bridge as the klaxon sounded and the voice of Morness gave the instructions.

"Come, Heather, Drass, let's see them off," said Freydis, as she led the way towards the belly of the great ship. Even as they went, Heather could feel the deck move gently beneath her. "Relax, Heather, Kett is just putting us back into our berth by your moon."

"Sorry cousin, I'll get my sea legs soon." Heather staggered slightly as she followed Freydis into the elevator.

They reached the launch bay to find it full of people, and Thordik herself just arriving from another direction. She was now armed to the teeth and wearing body armour. Thordik had asked for a dozen proven warriors, but hundreds had shown up to volunteer.

She grinned as she saw them all. "I need about a dozen proven warriors for pilots and to act as observers." They all stepped forward.

"Thank you, one and all." She pointed directly at one of the women. "You and the twelve to your right, ready fighter scouts." The thirteen leaped towards the rows and rows of fighter ships. The rest grumbled a bit and moved back out of the way.

"Gordrall," bellowed Thordik, and a young man appeared as if by magic. "Ten to a ship, go." The young fellow began swiftly bawling orders and the Untried sorted themselves out as if by magic.

"Thor's beard," muttered Freydis, "she's got them more disciplined than seasoned troops."

"That she has," agreed Drass.

"Hear me people," shouted Thordik, and the entire bay fell completely silent. "We go to find the stealth ships, we go to see as many of you as possible to your trial, but we also have a more important mission. We seek a human held captive by the Greys. The man's name is Frank Hunter. Repeat that to me."

"Frank Hunter," shouted a hundred voices.

"Again."

"Frank Hunter!"

"Find those accursed stealth ships and bring them down, but do not destroy them. Tear them apart and release every captive you can find, kill every Grey you can find, but above all, find me Frank Hunter. When you have him, abandon all else. Abandon the battle, abandon your comrades, abandon the planet as swiftly as you can, and put Frank Hunter in the healing bay. That is the most important task of all now. As soon as we have him, then we seek and destroy every stealth ship on the planet. Understood?"

"Understood! Find Frank Hunter!"

"Ready then," she shouted, as she leaped aboard one of the small ships. The rest followed her lead and Freydis gently pulled Heather back a step. A moment later there was a snapping sound as a force shield came up and the big launch bay doors opened to spill over a dozen scouts out into space. They fell towards the planet's surface at terrifying speed.

Heather watched as the great doors closed behind them, then she heard Thordik's voice at her shoulder. Freydis reached over and touched a small pin on Heather's tunic then nodded.

"Yes, my sister?"

"I will find him, my chieftain," came that gentle voice. "I will find him if I have to tear this whole damned planet asunder. I will return that which you have lost." With that she was gone.

"My dear god, what have I done this day?" Heather sighed as her shoulders slumped.

"You have unleashed the storm, Heather, and neither of us knows how strong that storm will be. At this point, I personally am quite happy she is an ally and not an enemy."

"I heard that," agreed Drass.

"You were concerned?"

"She had been denied so often, Heather. It was becoming frustrating for us all. Thor only knows what would have happened if she had cracked. See how disciplined those Untried were? Had Thordik come apart, with them to obey her, we could have been nothing but a floating derelict by the time the fleet got here. You've saved us all a lot of grief this day, cousin, and now I have a reward for you."

"Oh?"

"Yes, Drass and I are taking you to the hall where we can feed you. You're starting to look a bit pale, and there is nothing to do now but wait; wait for Thordik, wait for the fleet, and wait for the enemy. When all you can do is wait, it is best to spend your time eating. Come." Smiling, Heather fell into step with Freydis and Drass.

"MR. PRESIDENT, WHAT do we do now?" Everyone in the bunker was still staring at the blank screen. There had been absolute silence while Heather's demonstration was in play, and they still had the image of Thordik's utter mayhem in their minds.

"What?" he asked absentmindedly.

"What do we do now, sir?"

"We stop pissing them off, for a start. Dear god in heaven, she could as easily have wiped Washington off the map as she did that missile silo in Russia. We have just been given a demonstration of the power of our new allies. If that truly is an invasion fleet coming, I'm quite content to have those people on our side."

"We only have their word for that, sir, that the other fleet is an enemy, I mean."

"True, but I believe them, son. If they wanted, they could have taken this planet for themselves by now, but they've left us alone."

"Until we started shooting at them..."

"Exactly. Get every damned head of state in the world on the phone, and make sure they keep their fingers off the triggers. Somebody get me Jim Brady on the phone too. Heather MacKay. How the hell did she get up there, and how did she gain command of that ship?"

"Dr. Brady, sir," said a woman as she passed him a phone.

"Jim."

"Tom."

"Did you see that transmission?"

"I did. Pretty impressive, wasn't it?"

"Yes it was. Listen, how well do you know Heather MacKay?"

"That's Heather MacKay-Hunter now Tom, and I can say I know her pretty well."

"What do I need to know?"

"She's a pitbull when she locks onto something, and she hates the military as well as most branches of government. After all, they went to great lengths to discredit her, and I doubt she'll be all that merciful. Heather is honest and up front, Tom, if she says it's crap, you can bet that it's crap. You play fair with her, and she'll play fair with you, but if she says she'll blow your ass to Mars, start packing."

"Can we trust her?"

"I would."

"Have you any influence with her?"

"Maybe, but how am I supposed to contact her, and what do you want me to do?"

"I want you to bring her on side, Jim. If we can get a handle on this thing we can..."

"I'll try, Tom, but no promises."

"Fair enough, I'll send someone to bring you and Laura to the bunker. You'll be a lot safer here than where you are."

"Incoming!" bawled a voice. "More ships just went sub-light."

"From where?"

"Sector 967, sir."

"Looks like the gang's all here," sighed the president, "and our only chance seems to be in the hands of a madwoman."

# Reunited

Frank Hunter slowly returned to consciousness. He was hanging in the slimy stuff again, tubes sticking out of his body. How much time had elapsed now, he wondered. Ah well, what did it matter? Heather, where was his beloved Heather? Tears came to his eyes and the power of the emotion began to clear his mind once again. They'd been taken, so she must be here somewhere.

Slowly Frank managed to focus his eyes and look around. There were a lot of other people hanging like he was. He searched as best he could in the dim light, looking for the one thing he hoped he would not find. Suddenly he saw a mass of golden hair. There was a naked woman on the floor in the corner and she wasn't moving.

A mad and terrible rage gripped his heart then, and his mind cleared. The cold rage fuelled his desire for revenge, and he sought for the means to extract that. Frank began to struggle wildly, and he managed to get one arm free. Okay, the hard part was done, the rest should be easy.

Ignoring the pain, he tore the tubes from his body then wrenched hard at the substance that held him. It gave easily, but would not tear. Further struggle worked him loose, and he fell heavily to the floor just as the floor leaped upwards. Frank lay on the cold metal, gasping for air. The sudden force of acceleration sent him sliding across the floor, grasping wildly for something to hang on to. A few more twists and turns then he felt a bump, and the floor was still once more.

Struggling to his feet, Frank made his way towards the woman in the corner. She still had not moved, and he feared she might be dead.

He was right. Frank reached for her shoulder and gently turned her around. She was definitely dead, but she wasn't Heather. Frank wept with relief then, and his thoughts began to slip away.

"No!" He began to swear as he fought the desire for sleep. "No goddamned way, you little bastards, not this time. This time I'm going to wring your filthy little necks. Help, I need help. I've got to wake some of these folks somehow. He peered at several people until he found what he was looking for, a very muscular young man with a Marines tattoo.

The young Marine came to with someone slapping his face and cursing at him. "Sorry, Sarge," he muttered.

"Come on, dammit, wake the hell up." The command was followed by another hard slap to his face.

"Knock it off, goddammit," snarled the Marine as he began to struggle. "What the hell is going on here? Where am I? Who are you? Cut it out, you son of a bitch, or I'll rip your lungs out through your asshole."

"Atta boy, now you're awake," grinned Frank, as he jerked a tube from the man's belly.

"Ow, what the hell is the matter with you?"

"Listen soldier, we've been taken prisoner. I'm sorry about the abuse, but they've got some sort of mind numbing weapon. Rage is the only way to clear your mind, so get pissed, really pissed, and stay that way."

"Screw you, asshole."

"Good man, now take a long look around and tell me what you see."

"Good God Almighty, where the hell are we?"

"Spaceship would be my first guess."

"I knew those bastards were..."

"Not the newcomers," said Frank. "I think they might be allies. These guys have been here for a while."

"Yeah, little grey guys with buggy eyes. E.T. phone home."

"That's right brother, that's exactly who took us. Come on, get pissed. Think, how did you get here? What's the last thing you remember?"

"Light, plenty of light..."

"Yeah, and then what?"

The Marine thought hard for a moment then suddenly ground his teeth as he spat out the answer. "There was a little guy who said something about home... The little bastards, I'll kill the lot of them. Get me out of this slop."

"You can't tear it," growled Frank, as he began to jerk at the man's restraints, "but you can squirm out if you work at it." A moment later the Marine was free.

"Alright, that's a lot better," declared the Marine. "I'm Leroy."

"Frank. Listen Leroy, we need to wake up as many people as we can. Look for potential fighters first. Remember, stay mad. Strong emotion clears the mind."

"Got it, Frank, let's get busy."

FREYDIS, DRASS, AND Heather had barely reached the table when the klaxon sounded. "Incoming fleet," Morness announced with delight. "They've just gone sub light."

Freydis tapped the pin on her shoulder. "Morness, Freydis here. Send our greetings and ask the captains to assemble in my cabin as soon as they arrive. Are they reporting any problems?"

"None, Captain."

"Excellent." She smiled as she tapped the pin again. "Well, the Nyman folk are all together again."

"They made good time," grunted Drass. "I would have thought we had another two sleeps to wait yet."

"Brek would be beating the drum all the way. Heather, you will soon meet the rest of our ragged warrior fleet, better eat hearty."

"If you get the time." Drass grinned as he glanced past Heather's shoulder. Both she and Freydis turned to see a tall young woman, wearing the blue sash of an Untried, standing a respectful distance away.

"Yes?" asked Freydis.

"Forgive me, Earl Freydis, but I wonder if I might have a word with the Chieftain of Erikr-Dak?"

"Me? What do you want with me?" Both Drass and Freydis were chuckling now, and the girl was blushing with embarrassment.

"Well, Lady, you see..."

"What's your name?"

"Clerisa."

"Well Clerisa, I'm Heather. Come sit beside me." Shyly the girl sat. "Now, how can I be of service? What is it you need from me?"

"I want to be adopted into your clan, we all do."

"I saw that coming," grinned Drass.

"All of you?"

"Yes, all of the Untried. We have been denied for so long. Thordik helped us train, and she made us far more than we ever expected to be. We asked her many times to adopt us, but she wouldn't."

"Did she say why she wouldn't?"

"She said she wanted to pass her trial first. She said no one should have to follow an Untried chieftain. She promised that once she was proven she would adopt us."

"But then I happened along and messed up all the plans."

"Lady..."

"Heather, Clerisa, call me Heather."

"Heather, I know I'm an Untried, but I swear I'll do everything in my power to bring strength and honour to your clan. We all will.

Please, will you consider us? I know an Untried is not the first choice, but will you consider me if I can pass my trial?"

"Well, Heather, I think Drass and I have things to do on the bridge. You're on your own with this one."

"Do I get no guidance from my earl?"

"Not a drop, cousin," laughed Freydis, as she and Drass walked away.

"Clerisa, did you say there are more of you wanting to join Erikr-Dak clan?"

"All of the Untried, Heather, we all want it."

"You are completely certain?"

"Yes."

"Why?"

"We believed that Thordik would be the greatest chieftain ever," replied the girl. "When she made you chieftain, we knew that you were the one to lead us. If Thordik trusts you to guide her, then there can be no one greater."

"I think you're expecting a bit much from this poor little Earthling. Ah well, I guess my job is to rebuild the clan. All right girl, welcome to the clan, but I warn you, I'm a hard taskmaster."

"Oh thank you, Heather. You won't be sorry, I swear it."

"All right kinswoman, go to the others and gather together everyone who wants to be adopted into the clan. Once they're assembled, come for me and we will get it done."

"Right now?"

"Yes, right now. Get going, girl." Heather chuckled as the girl fled the eating hall. "Dear gods, now what have I done? Ah well, what the hell, Frank said he wanted a big family. Oh my dear Frank, I dare not hope, but if anyone can get you back for me it's Thordik." She sighed and returned her attention to her food.

Heather had barely finished her meal when Clerisa returned. "All are ready, my chieftain. Right this way."

Heather followed the girl through a few corridors and two elevator rides, until they reached the training area. "My god, how many of you are there?"

"Over eight hundred, Chieftain," grinned Clerisa. "The rest are on the surface with Thordik."

"Do you all truly want to be adopted into Clan Erikr-Dak?"

"We do," was the resounding response.

"I believe it is customary to have a clan member speak for you, is that not so?" Only silence answered her this time. "Clerisa, my kinswoman, will you speak for these people?"

Clerisa grinned her delight as she answered. "Yes, my chieftain, I know them well and all are strong and true. All will bring honour to the clan."

"Very well then, I accept you, Children of Freya. You are now Erikr-Dak. It may take me some time, but I swear to you I will learn the name of every one of you. I also swear to do my best to be a good chieftain to you. Know that my name is Heather MacKay-Hunter, but I prefer to be called Heather. Come to me now by ones, so we may clasp hands together to seal the bargain." Each one came forwards, giving her their name, expressing their thanks, and vowing to bring honour to the clan. By the time it was over, Heather was exhausted, and the fleet had arrived.

FRANK AND LEROY HAD awakened several more people. With more people awake it seemed to be easier to stay clear. The ship suddenly accelerated again and everyone was sent sprawling, just as several Greys opened the door. They had no time to wonder before Leroy was on them like a whirlwind, his combat training serving him in good stead.

Frank was busy laying about with something he'd snatched from a Grey. He'd managed to hit a few, but he wasn't sure if he'd actually killed any or not. Suddenly there was weapon's fire, and Frank felt a burning pain in his leg, then another in his side. Leroy was down, and it looked bad, when the floor bucked and sent everyone, including the armed Greys, flying.

Frank could hear sounds like hissing metal as the ship writhed in her death throes. There was the feeling of a sudden plunge, and then a hard landing. A Grey ran past and Frank grabbed it by the leg, swinging it hard against the wall and killing it instantly. The wall hissed then and began to melt. All hell broke loose as the Greys tried to flee and the attackers burst through a hole they had cut in the wall. It was complete mayhem for a time, then it went quiet.

Frank sank to the floor, the pain in his body more than he could bear. He was hurt badly and he knew it. Ah well, what did it matter? He'd gotten a measure of revenge after all. The sound of his name slowly brought him around a bit, and he listened. A young male voice was calling his name, asking for him. "Here," he managed to croak.

The heavily armed warrior was at his side in a heartbeat. "Frank Hunter?"

"Yes, I'm Frank Hunter." Excitedly the warrior slapped his shoulder then began to babble in a strange language. It almost sounded like the Icelandic he'd heard Heather speak. The youngster stopped speaking, then with a grin of pure delight, he helped Frank to his feet and led him from the wreckage of the alien ship.

Trying to help himself, Frank was, nonetheless, practically carried out by the young warrior. As they reached the sunshine, a small craft landed and a goddess leaped out to run to them. She was beautiful beyond compare, and her smile of delight lifted his spirits completely. "Frank Hunter?" she asked, in a rich voice that sounded like sweet music.

"Yes," he managed, as he began to sink to the ground. She swept him into her arms and carried him as easily as a child. She was barking orders over her shoulder, and he could hear the hiss and crackle of metal being super heated. He knew the alien ship was being destroyed, and he rejoiced as his consciousness fled from the pain in his body.

HEATHER WAS ON HER way to her small cabin when her shoulder spoke in Thordik's voice. "Heather, can you hear me?"

It took the exhausted woman a few tries, but she managed the pin on her shoulder. "I'm here, my sister."

"Meet me in the healing bay, Heather. I'm coming home with a friend who says he knows you."

"Frank? Thordik, you really found him?"

"He's badly wounded, but he's alive. Quickly now."

She was gone and Heather was lost. Which way was the healing bay? In desperation Heather tried the shoulder pin, but had no success. She ran in what she thought might be the right direction, it wasn't. Completely lost, Heather stopped and slammed her fist against the wall in frustration. "Chieftain?" asked a young male voice.

Heather spun around to see a young Untried standing a respectful distance away. "Hassless?"

"Close," he laughed. "It's Hassness, my chieftain. Can I be of service?"

"I'm completely lost, and I need to get to the healing bay right now. Thordik has found Frank and he's hurt."

"This way." Hassness sped away. As tired as she was, Heather struggled to keep up with him. They arrived just as Thordik carried Frank in. "Frank, oh my god, Frank," gasped Heather, as she saw him.

He was naked and bleeding. He had severe burns on his side and leg as well as several crudely stitched up cuts on several parts of his body. Some of them were bleeding freely and he was barely conscious. "Heather?" he asked weakly. "Is that really you, or are those bastards playing with my head again?"

"No, my love, it really is me," she replied, as she gently pushed the matted hair back from his brow.

"I'm sorry about the kids, Heather. I know I'm not going to make it. I did get a few of those little grey bastards though..." His voice trailed off as he faded from consciousness.

"You are so going to make it." Heather sighed, as Skeezix gently tucked Frank into the healing chamber and lowered the lid. "You owe me a half dozen children, Frank Hunter." She laid her forehead against the lid of the machine. "You get your ass back here and keep that promise."

"Come, my sister," soothed Thordik, as she gently pulled Heather away from the chamber. "This is in the hands of Freya now. With her help, our kinsman will bring him back to you in short order. Come, you're exhausted, and you need to sleep; I will take you back to your cabin."

"I can find it, Thordik. You still have work to do on the surface." Heather shook off the emotion that threatened to consume her. "Take Hassness with you and throw him at the first Grey you find."

"With great pleasure, but you must promise to sleep. I hear that we have a very large clan to govern now, and you have to be at your best."

Just then Heather's shoulder pin spoke. "Heather, this is Freydis, come to my cabin and meet the kinfolks."

"Thordik here, Lord Freydis; my sister is exhausted from adopting half the fleet. Might she be allowed rest before you put her back to work?"

"She has had a busy day at that. All right Thordik, take her to her booth. We'll take this up again after the next sleep cycle."

Heather tried to object, but Thordik and Hassness escorted her to her cabin. The next time Heather saw Hassness he was wearing a red sash, a bandage, and a huge grin.

# Short Respite

Heather gratefully prepared for sleep and climbed in. She was alone as Thordik and Hassness had abandoned her at the door. As she crawled into the bed, she broke down and wept. She had recovered Frank, but he was so injured. In desperation she prayed to the goddess whose people she was now supposed to lead. As she slept she had a sweet dream of happy laughing people, and Frank playing with a passel of children. There was a hawk flying overhead and she was at peace as she watched it.

Awareness came slowly to Heather, and she savoured the delight of waking up gently. Suddenly she remembered that Frank had been brought to the ship and was now in the healing chamber. Leaping to her feet, Heather swiftly dressed herself. She smiled at how natural the loose-fitting uniforms of the Nyman folk felt to her already. A swift brush of her hair, a splash of water on her face, and then she bolted through the door.

Skeezix was still in his seat at the head of the chamber, purring softly to the machine. One of his many arms rose to salute her, then point in the general direction of the great hall. Heather took the hint and went for some breakfast. She found Thordik there with Hassness. Heather swiftly filled a platter and joined them.

"What news, my sister?"

"It's done, my chieftain. We have found all their stealth ships on the surface, freed their captives, returned your husband to you, saw a number of our clan through their trial, and all that is left to do is for you to finish what you started."

"What I started?"

"There are more folk who wish to be adopted into Erikr-Dak."

"Forgive me, Thordik. I should have consulted with you about that..."

"It was well done, my chieftain. These are my brothers and sisters. I will gladly call any one of them kinfolk. You're our chieftain, Heather. You need to consult no one at all about clan business."

"A chieftain who doesn't consult with her most trusted advisors, is a poor chieftain and a complete fool," replied Heather.

"I agree with that bit of wisdom," chuckled the voice of Freydis, as she sat down beside Heather. They were soon joined by Drass and the other captains. Hassness seemed a bit overwhelmed to be in such company, but Thordik was completely at ease.

"So, Thordik, I hear that you've been proven," grunted a short, thickset, red haired fellow, as he plopped down beside her. "Now that you're free to marry, shall we abandon these folk to their fate and run off together?"

"As much as the idea appeals to me, Brek, I'm afraid that Selian would skin me alive for thinking it. Sister Heather, this is Brek of Torvaless-Pem clan. He is their chieftain and Captain of the Falcon. Brek, this woman is my sister, cousin of Earl Freydis, and chieftain of Erikr-Dak. Her name is Heather Mak-Kay-Hunter."

"A pleasure to meet you, Heather Mak-Kay Hunter." Heather smiled shyly and nodded.

"I want that ship of yours, Brek," grinned Thordik. "Why don't you retire and give her to me. That will give you a lot more time to address the needs of your beloved Selian."

"Why you young upstart, I'm not giving up my ship to anyone. With that attitude, it's easy to see why you were supplanted as chieftain."

"Brek and I are old friends, Heather." Thordik, gently squeezed his shoulder as she spoke to Heather. "It was the Falcon that rescued me from that barren planet. I spent several turns on her, and Master

Brek tried so very hard to teach me the ways of hand-to-hand combat."

"You mean I tried to keep you from constantly pounding my head, girl. I've heard a bit about your exploits, Heather Mak-Kay-Hunter. They are most impressive. This one is Selian, chieftain of Mulla-Tess clan, and she is the captain of the Raven."

"Your skin is so smooth." Selian tentatively reached toward Heather.

"And your scales are so very beautiful, Selian," replied Heather, as she reached for Selian. They gently stroked each others faces for a moment then let their arms fall away in embarrassment. "Selian, Drass claims to be the last true Nylass, but surely you..."

"Almost, but not quite, Heather. When the Sessassas crashed on that planet so very long ago, there were only three women aboard. Stuck on that planet, the men had to wed the human women that the raider had held captive. When our people returned to the skies, they found that the Greys had completely destroyed the home world. There were no more Nylass to be found anywhere at all. I am told that once, and only once, in the history of my line, was a Nyman woman chosen as a mate."

"You are exquisitely beautiful, Selian," smiled Heather, "and I am honoured to meet you."

"Freydis said she had found a distant cousin, but I did not truly believe the resemblance until now. You two could easily be sisters."

"Especially the way you handled the planetary situation," agreed another of the captains. "We saw the vid of Thordik's trial, and your demonstration. That was just what one would expect of Freydis herself. My name is Corfort. It is a pleasure to meet you."

"The pleasure is mine, Corfort, and I will take your words as high praise indeed."

"And so you should," said Freydis. "So, Heather, are you ready to get on with the show? We don't have a lot of time left before the Grey fleet gets here. We need to lay our plans and to set them in motion."

"This is a war to be fought in space, Freydis," said Heather. "I have no idea at all how this is done. Thordik will be far better able to advise you than I."

"Sorry cousin, but the council consists of clan chieftains, and ship's captains."

"Then I happily retire as chieftain and name Thordik as my successor."

"Declined with gratitude, my sister. You are a far wiser woman than I, and will be a much better chieftain for the clan."

Heather made a face at Thordik, then laughed. "All right, but am I permitted to check in on Frank before you put me to work?"

"He's sleeping, Heather, and he will be for some time, but he did say to give you his love, and he hopes to see you the next time he awakens."

"He was awake? You spoke with him, Freydis? What did he say? Will he be all right? Will he recover?"

"Easy cousin, easy. Yes, I was there and spoke with him. I have already told you what he said, and yes, he will be just fine, but he needs a few more sleep cycles in the chamber, just as you did. He was injured pretty badly, but Skeezix is working his magic as we speak. Come now, we must prepare for war. Go claim the rest of your adoptees, then repair to my cabin."

FRANK HUNTER SLOWLY awakened from a deep sleep. Light flooded into his eyes as the lid of the healing chamber was raised. The first thing he saw as he sat up was Heather. With a smile of delight he reached for her but she took his hands gently and held them. "Look closer."

Her voice was rich and full, and definitely not Heather's. As his vision cleared he saw that this woman was not Heather, although she looked very much like her. This woman was taller, a bit older, she had a few scars, and she was covered in small, delicate, sea-green scales. "Oops, sorry." He grinned sheepishly as he tried to cover himself.

She tossed him a cloth and laughed. "I'm the one who should apologize, Frank Hunter. Heather is resting from a most difficult day, and she has another to face, so we didn't wake her. Skeezix said you were about to awaken, so I came to see you. I thought you might like to see a familiar face."

Frank chuckled at that and blushed. "That is my very favourite face, ma'am. I just expected to see it on someone else. Is Heather all right?"

"Heather is well and has had many adventures. She will want to tell you about it herself, I am sure. I just wanted to see how you are making out, and to welcome you to my ship."

"Your ship? Then you are..."

"I am Lord Freydis, Chieftain of Pull-Karr clan and Earl of all Nyman folk. But I prefer to be called Freydis. Heather and I believe we are distant cousins. I must tell you, Frank Hunter, she has performed miracles and moved worlds to find you. I do hope you are worthy of the price she has paid."

"What did she do? What does she owe you, Freydis? I can pay whatever..."

"Hush now, Frank Hunter, all will be revealed. Forgive my little bit of drama, I implore you. Heather is well, she has granted the fondest wish of every warrior in our fleet, she has gained a new sister of terrible power, and she has gained so much more. I do hope you want a large family, Frank Hunter, for that is what you now have.

"Now, I have tormented you enough for one day. You need to rest again. I will seek out Heather as soon as she rises, to tell her you are recovering nicely. She will come to you at her first opportunity.

This one is called Skeezix. He is our healer, and he is your kinsman. Heather holds him in high regard. You can trust him."

With that she smiled and withdrew, leaving Frank alone with the blue furry creature which had not made a single sound up to this point. "Give Heather my love," he called after her retreating back. Frank turned and eyed the four-armed wonder for a long moment; neither spoke nor moved. "So, you patched me up, did you? Thank you for that. Can you speak?"

"Oh yes, I have been talking to you for many divisions now," purred that soft voice.

"I remember that voice. Tell me, what is this language I'm speaking, and how in the name of time did I learn it?"

"It is the learning crystal. In the healing chamber you sleep very deeply, so your body can be healed. Your mind will absorb much information very quickly at this time. Explore your thoughts. You now have the language of the Nyman folk, as well as an understanding of their history, and an idea of how their society works. I have done this to make it easier for you to interact with them once you are fully healed."

"She said you healed Heather, too. Did you do this for her as well?"

"I did, and she would not be pleased if I did not do the same for you."

"Why is her displeasure so frightening to you, and what did Freydis mean, you're my kinsman?"

"Heather will explain, Frank Hunter," purred Skeezix. "You must rest now."

"Okay, I can be patient." Frank groaned as he eased himself back into the healing chamber. He sighed deeply as Skeezix lowered the lid. The next time he awakened he felt a lot better. Heather wasn't there to greet him, but the goddess who'd saved him was.

"WELL, HOW DID WE COME out of it so far?" asked Thomas Mooreland.

"Three hundred and eighty-three of our people recovered, Mr. President, and no casualties. There were actually five of those damned ships on our soil."

"The rest of the world?"

"Sir, a few folks got a bit uppity, and tried to assert their territorial authority. The result wasn't pretty. She wasn't kidding about losing patience with us. All attempts to interfere were met with instant and deadly force. In fact, sir, they almost seemed to be taunting some of those people. Our people were very respectful, as you directed, and we didn't take a scratch. In fact, after the first two, we just followed them around with paramedics."

"What's the story on Jim Brady?"

"He tried, sir, I'll give him that, but the Icelanders won't pass on the message."

"Goddammit anyway, who the hell do they think they are? Get the President of Iceland on the phone. Sweet Jesus Christ, we're the most powerful nation on the frigging planet. They should be keeping us in the loop."

"Iceland, sir," said a tech, as they brought up the screen.

"Ragnar, what the hell is going on there anyway? I'm told you refuse to pass along our request to the ship."

"It is good to see you too, Thomas," replied the hard-eyed face on the screen. "In response to your question, there is far too much going on to explain. We are preparing for war, my friend. The Nyman fleet has agreed to help arm us in exchange for our protecting some of their people. The young, elderly, sick, and/or infirm, are all being brought down with some of their warriors and weapons for the defence of Iceland.

"We have not passed along your messages because their earl has asked us not to clog the communications with unnecessary chatter. Having said all that, and in view of our past friendly association, I will see what I can do about contacting their ambassador for you."

Before the president could say another word the screen went blank. "Son of a bitch," growled Thomas Mooreland, "I think I've just been snubbed." He paused for a moment then sighed deeply and allowed his shoulders to sag. "People, I think it is about time we faced a hard and unpleasant reality here."

"Mr. President?"

"The Nymen are arming the Icelanders, and they are landing forces. We have already seen what their weapons are capable of, people. They are bringing down warriors, and we have seen those, too. We are no longer the main power on this planet. It is time to start kissing Icelandic ass if we hope to survive. See if you can get him back on the line for me."

"I am somewhat busy this day, Thomas," said the Icelandic President, as his face came back on screen.

"Forgive me, Ragnar, I will take only a moment of your time. I called to apologize for my manner a moment ago. I plead stress, bad coffee, and lack of sleep."

"I can easily sympathize with you there, Thomas. We are a small nation, as you know, and our population is about to double in less than thirty-six hours, for we have called all Icelanders home from across the globe, and we are expecting a large contingent of Nyman folk as well. We are not ready by half."

"Ragnar, I understand, I do. I am just a bit frustrated that I have no idea what is going on. We are about to be invaded, and we have no idea at all what we are up against, or how best to defend ourselves. Any and all information you can share with us will be greatly appreciated."

"I can sympathize with your position, Thomas. Gretta Gudrirsdottir is our liaison with the Greenlanders. I will have her contact you at the first opportunity. She will give you all the information we have. Forgive me, but I now must return to my tasks."

"Thank you, Ragnar, we will be grateful for any and..." It was too late, he was talking to a blank screen again.

# Calm Before the Storm

Heather arrived at the training area, guided by Hassness. Thordik was there with close to a hundred newly promoted warriors and a few Untried. "So, why have I been summoned here?" Heather had a small grin playing at her lips.

"We, the assembled people here beg to be considered for adoption into Erikr-Dak clan, Great Chieftain," declared a tall girl with red hair, and what appeared to be freckles under her scales.

"Do you now?" Heather approached the girl. "Who are you who seeks to join my clan?"

"I am Helgess, Great Chieftain," she replied, mischief in her eyes as well.

"Well Helgess, is there anyone whom I can trust who will speak for you?"

"I will vouch for her, my sister," laughed Thordik, "and the rest as well."

"Thordik, don't we have enough already?"

"The more warriors we have in the clan, my sister, the more there are to defend you in your old age."

"That's going to cost you, Thordik." Heather laughed as she shook a threatening finger at her sister. The others laughed with her. "Alright people, hear me well. All joking aside, we are very pleased indeed to welcome you to Erikr-Dak clan. We accept you. I'm Heather MacKay-Hunter, but I prefer to be called Heather. Come to me now, one at a time, so we may grasp hands and exchange names to seal the bargain. Helgess, you first."

It took a while before it was finished, and once it was done, Heather retraced her steps to the great hall, grabbed a snack, and then headed for the bridge. She found everyone waiting for her around the long table in Freydis' cabin. "Well cousin, have you finished adopting the cream of our next generation?"

"Laugh if you will, Freydis," groused one captain, "but in twenty full turns she will have the most powerful clan of all, and the rest of us will be begging for her protection as we try to fend off old age and wait for the grandchildren to be proven."

Heather was grinning as she took her seat. "It's all in the timing, folks. So, what have I missed while I was out playing with the youngsters?"

"Well, we've got about three more turns before they hit us," said Drass. "They'll reach the outer planets just after second sleep period."

"Do we have a plan?"

"Heather's right people," said Freydis. "We've spent enough time catching up and trading tales. It is time to get down to planning the task. Drass, your assessment?"

"We are all fully armed, we have readied the provisions for the Icelanders, and right after next sleep cycle we will take the elders, sick, infirm, young mothers, and children down to the surface. Five hundred heavily armed warriors will accompany them."

"So few?" asked Selian. "Are you certain that will be enough?"

"We can only hope," replied Drass. "They will be fully armed. The Icelanders will be given weapons, and will be ready to defend them as well, so it isn't as bad as it sounds."

"Brek, did you leave long range scouts out?"

"I did Freydis, but we didn't see yours out there. You have hidden them well."

"There are none, Brek, we know what is coming. Bring your folk in and rest them as best you can. Alright, let's have a look at the terrain and the odds."

She moved a dial on the panel that was right at her hand. A holographic image of the entire solar system appeared above the middle of the table.

"Now, we know from experience that our ships are bigger, faster, more manoeuvrable, more heavily armed, and we have better shields. The downside is that we have only three battle ships and six transports. Our transports are well armed and shielded, but they aren't battleships. Any suggestions, Brek?"

"Well, as we see here, they have started to split up. The carrion fighters and raiders are picking up speed now that they're getting close. If they're true to form, and since they have no imagination at all and haven't changed battle tactics in three generations, I believe they will be; the carrion fighters will swarm us at speed, trying to knock us out with one blow, shoot past us, turn and come back in for the killing stroke.

"The raiders will try to duck past and make for the surface of the planet. The problem is, it just might work this time, as there are so few of us."

"You're smiling, Heather, you have seen it haven't you?"

"I know nothing of space battles, Freydis. I was just thinking about the way our ancestors would have dealt with a superior force."

"Lock shields and strike where they least expect it," chuckled Selian. "So, we leave the transports out where they can see them, and hide the warships."

"Exactly," said Freydis. "We leave the transports out here by the red planet where the enemy can see them blocking the path to Greenland. We hide three thousand small striker ships here in this asteroid belt. We take the Mjolnir, the Raven, and the Falcon, and hide them out here behind the moons of this giant. When the carrion fighter ships come past, we lock shields and strike from the side, splitting them asunder. Before they can regroup, the small fighters will be among them. We then race past and put ourselves here, blocking the path to Greenland."

"What of our poor old transports?" asked Corfort.

"Once you see us attack, the transports rise up from the plane of the system and the battle. As soon as you're clear, shoot past the battle and lock shields. See if you can split their transport fleet and keep them busy until we can get loose to help you."

"And if you can't?"

"If you see us failing, Corfort, take the fleet of transports out of this system while you can. Find a place of safety and try to rebuild the clans as best you are able. We will leave some from each clan on every ship, just as a precaution."

"It doesn't look good, does it, Freydis?" said Heather.

"No, their numbers are so many. That in-bred maggot of an emperor sent us off with far too few ships. With the number of folk we have with us, we could easily have brought a dozen battle cruisers. Ah well, it solves little to mourn what is not. Do not despair, Heather, we're not finished yet. They may have the greater numbers, but we will meet them in combat nonetheless."

"We have two great advantages, Heather," said Selian, "and they offset the numbers somewhat. We have far superior ships, and they are all stocked and armed with free-born fighters."

"Free-born fighters?"

"Let me explain, cousin. Their fighting ships are all manned with slave fighters. We call them carrion fighters, because that is what they look like, and that is what they are fed on. The Greys send out their stealth ships to explore new species. They seek strong folk for fighters and breeders, they use the rest for food. By the look of Frank Hunter's scars, I'd say they were trying to make a slave fighter out of him.

"Heather, the Greys did not evolve great strong bodies, but they evolved powerful minds. They control their captives, and their slaves, with their minds. A mind-numbed slave is no match for a free fighter, but if the Greys can cloud the minds of their enemies, it's a different matter. We all are wearing a protective device, this one here." She touched another pin on Heather's red sash.

"It emits a scattering energy that counters the effects of the Grey's mind numbing abilities. "That is why Thordik chose to make you chieftain. You fought the numbing and killed three with your bare hands, and you didn't have the advantage of the blocker. That's also why Thordik stripped off her clothes and faced her trial naked. She wanted to be worthy of so strong a chieftain."

"Heather, do not fear the enemy." Brek smiled as he gave her shoulder a friendly squeeze. "We are far stronger, and we will prevail. Remember, most of their number are slaves. Slaves make you weak, they make you dependant."

"So, the key is to kill the masters and set the slaves into confusion."

"Exactly so, cousin. You see, we're not finished yet, not by half. Now, we must all begin to prepare. Heather, what would you like to do for the people on the surface? We can spare no more weapons or technology and they have been warned; what more would you like to do?"

"I would like to give them another demonstration, if we have the time."

"Time is short, so you should be about it. Take what you need, do what you must."

"Thank you, Freydis. I will be as swift as I can. May I borrow a small ship for a while, and may I access Morness and Kett?"

"You may. Heather, what are you going to do now?"

"I will take a few folk down to the surface with me, just for show. I will go to where most of the world leaders gather, and there I would like to show them what they face. Can the ship direct holographic images to the surface?"

"Of course, but it won't fool anyone."

"I don't want to fool them, I just want to show them what they're up against, and I want them to see it. I also want to give them as much information as I can."

"Do it, Heather, but before the end of next sleep cycle we must abandon this orbit and slip away to lay our ambush."

"It will be done before this waking cycle is complete, Freydis." Heather rose and left the cabin. As the others filed out they saw her deep in conversation with Morness.

"No problem, Heather. It shall be as you require."

"Okay, I'm on my way. You bring Freydis up to speed on this, and I'll get a move on."

FRANK HUNTER AWAKENED slowly once again, savouring the experience and trying to recall the recent events as clearly as he could. Surprisingly, his mind was extremely clear. He remembered everything about speaking with Freydis and he remembered fully his rescue by the young warrior who summoned a goddess to bring him here. Frank assumed that he was indeed aboard the visiting craft from Sector 967.

He grinned with delight as the lid began to rise, as he was expecting to see Heather. She was not there, but the young goddess was, and her radiant smile nearly took away his senses. "It is a great pleasure to find you well, Frank Hunter." She smiled, and her voice was like the song of angels. "I'm Thordik, and I'm Heather's adopted sister. I believe the customary greeting is to clasp hands, is it not?"

"Huh? What? Oh, yes, of course." Frank grinned sheepishly, as he pulled the cloth Freydis had given him over his lap. "I'm Frank Hunter, Heather's husband, but you already knew that."

"Yes, I did." She shook his hand then released it. He was startled at the strength of her grip. "I have come to see how you are recovering and to beg your forgiveness, Frank Hunter."

"Frank, Thordik, call me Frank. I swear, smile at me like that and I'll forgive you anything at all. What do I need to forgive you for?"

"Beware, Frank," she laughed with delight, "for I will remember that and take full advantage. Frank, it took me longer to find you than I had hoped. Those damned Greys kept moving their stealth ships about from place to place, and it took some time to find you. I am sorry you had to endure that for so long."

"You were looking for me?"

"Yes. I swore to Heather that I would find you or die in the attempt. I keep my oaths."

"I believe you, Thordik. Can you tell me why you would swear such an oath? I'm quite thrilled that you did, but I wonder what could make you do it. We haven't met before, and you owe me nothing."

"I owe Heather Mak-Kay-Hunter everything. When we first met she swore to grant my lifelong desire before another day had passed. She kept that promise. Since she had given me the one thing I truly wanted in the entire universe, I swore to do the same for her. She said the Greys had taken you, and she wanted you back above all else. We tore apart nearly a dozen ships before we found you."

"Thordik, I owe you my life, and one day I hope to be able to repay the debt. Is there any chance I can see Heather now?"

"She is in a council of war now, Frank. I knew you might awaken so I wanted a friend to be here for you when you did. Stand up now and see how you feel."

Frank stood, tying the cloth around his waist as he did so. "I feel good as new."

"Skeezix my brother, what do you say to that?"

"Frank Hunter must sleep again and very soon. When he awakens next he will be whole and sound and ready for battle."

"Battle?"

"The enemy is nearly upon us, Frank," Thordik replied with a wolfish grin. "Back into the chamber with you now, my brother. Heather will need you at full strength when we engage the enemy."

"Heather? I thought that other one, Freydis, was the leader..."

"Heather is our clan chieftain, Frank. Freydis will give her instruction and Heather will decide how it gets done."

"The old chain of command trick, eh?"

"Enough now, you're just stalling. In you go." With a soft chuckle, Frank allowed Thordik to tuck him back in the healing chamber. She laughed as she whipped away the cloth, and he silently vowed revenge as Skeezix lowered the lid. He drifted off to sleep in the loving embrace of the living chamber. "The one thing in the universe that she truly wanted," he mused as he drifted off to sleep again. "God, how I love you, Heather MacKay-Hunter."

"THE PRESIDENT OF ICELAND for you, sir," said a young man, as he passed Thomas Mooreland a telephone.

"Ragnar, it is good to hear from you."

"Thomas, I have little time. The Nyman ambassador is coming to speak at the United Nations in a few hours. You should be there. She is going to give us a look at the enemy, and as much helpful information as she can. I can tell you this, make sure all your computers are shut down and unhooked before the enemy arrives. It is their custom to knock out all communications with a large electromagnetic pulse before they attack. I must fly now, for Heather MacKay-Hunter will be arriving in Reykjavik at any moment." With that he was gone.

"Dear sweet Jesus," breather the president. "Did you get all that, General?"

"Got it, sir. We'll be shut down before they get here, with fully shielded back-ups ready to go the moment they hit the ground."

"Get on it man, get on it. Dear god, we're a nation that is completely dependant on electronics. If we'd been caught with our pants down on that one..."

"I told you that you could trust Heather," said Jim Brady. "She's made you sweat a bit, as retribution for the past, but when the chips were down she was there for us, and I'll bet she'll bring us more. We won't have a lot of time to prepare, but we won't be going in totally blind either."

"I guess you're right, Jim. Get your coat, you're coming to New York with me. I want her to see the face of a friend at my side."

# Warning

"Thordik, man a small ship with ten well-armed Untried, if we have any left. We're going down for a visit," barked Heather, as she bolted from the bridge. She was beginning to know her way around the ship by now, and managed to make her way to the launch bay without difficulty. She found Thordik and ten Untried waiting for her. Swiftly they prepared and the small ship dropped towards the surface of planet Earth.

"Are we going into battle, Chieftain?" asked a soft voice behind Heather.

"No, this is a diplomatic mission."

"But you said to come well-armed..."

"Thordik is always getting into trouble. You may be required to bail her out." There was a round of snickers behind her.

"Where shall I land, oh wise sister?" asked Thordik.

"Reykjavik, Iceland."

"Which way do I go?"

"Damned if I know, Thordik. Ask Kett."

Thordik chuckled and called the ship. Kett set the coordinates and they landed easily a few meters from the President and his people, who were waiting for them. He stepped forward and extended his hand, as Heather emerged from the small fighter ship. "It is an honour to meet you, Ambassador MacKay-Hunter."

"The honour is mine, President Thorvaldsson," replied Heather as she took his hand. "Please call me Heather."

"Thank you, Heather, and I am Ragnar."

"Are you all set to go, Ragnar?"

"I'm as ready as I can be. I'm not as young as I once was, Heather; are the G forces going to crush my poor old body?"

"The ship has G force dampeners, Ragnar. You'll hardly notice a thing."

"Would you like to have a look around at our preparations before we leave, Heather?"

"We have not the time to spare, Ragnar. We trust you to do your best for our people, and we will do all we can to keep Iceland safe. Come now, we must be about the business."

They boarded the ship and Heather made him comfortable before taking a seat beside him. "Gently now, Thordik, off we go."

"Where shall I go now, my sister?"

"Kett has the coordinates, dear." Heather grinned as she winked at one of the Untried. "You just enjoy the view and let Kett guide the ship."

"Older sisters can be so cruel," Thordik chuckled as she smoothly accelerated into the air and turned towards North America. She had already received directions from Kett while Ragnar was greeting Heather, but Heather had known she would. Suddenly she banked gently and swooped low over a long fjord below. "There, my brothers and sisters, lies all that remains of our ancestor's home, the place where we all began."

"You are all descended from Erick Rhode and his people?"

"Yes, Ragnar, the ancestors of these folks were captured by the Greys near this place, but they broke free with the help of a race called the Nylass. Trapped on a rocky planet together with no way off, the two peoples joined together and became one, the forebearers of the Nyman folk. All are descended from the Greenlanders, as am I."

"I did notice the resemblance you bear to Lord Freydis."

"We believe that Freydis Eriksdottir was our common ancestor."

"There should be a monument or something down there," muttered Thordik, as she hovered the craft over the empty landscape.

"The people who now claim this land would rather not acknowledge that our folk were ever here. They prefer to focus on their own heritage," Ragnar said gently.

"One battle at a time, my sister," Heather soothed, as she gently gripped Thordik's shoulder from behind. "On to New York now, time grows short, and the enemy will soon be upon us."

"As you desire, my chieftain, so shall it be," replied Thordik, as the craft suddenly leaped back into the sky and hurtled out over the ocean. "One day I will return to this place." Ragnar clung to his seat with the delighted grin of a child.

"Erikr-Dak will all return, Thordik, and we will mark this place well."

"WE'RE JUST IN TIME, Mr. President. The Nyman craft has left Iceland and will be here within moments."

"Okay, how do I look?"

"Impressive, sir."

"Good, it's always best to look impressive when you're sucking up." Thomas Mooreland sighed.

"Absolutely," chuckled Jim Brady, as he came forward to stand beside his brother-in-law. A few short moments later the small craft came to rest on the rooftop, mere feet away from where they stood. There were over a hundred troops in the honour guard standing behind the President.

"Jim," shouted Heather, as she leaped from the ship and swept her friend into her arms. "Oh gods, it is good to see you, Jim. I was so very worried about you."

"I hear that you've managed to get yourself a new job," he said, as he returned her embrace.

"Yes I did. Jim, are you and Laura staying at the president's bunker?"

"Yes."

"Good. Stay there until it is over, okay?"

"I will, sweetie. Now, let me introduce you. Thomas, this is Heather MacKay-Hunter, Ambassador to Earth from the Nyman ships. Heather, this is Thomas Mooreland, President of the United States of America."

"It is a pleasure to meet you in person at last, Mrs. MacKay-Hunter." He smiled easily as he offered his hand.

"Heather, please call me Heather. Sir, we don't have a lot of time here. We need to get down to business."

"Please call me, Thomas. Right this way, Heather, Ragnar."

As he began to lead the way, several security men stepped in between Thordik and Heather. In a move too fast to follow Thordik grabbed one and threw him into the ten Untried. He was instantly unconscious. The rest of the security men went for their guns, but they were easily brought down by the ten Untried. By now the honour guard was into the brawl and losing badly. Thordik just stood by smiling.

"Stand down," shouted Heather. "Tell them to stand down, Thomas, before they all get killed."

"Stand down, stand down," he bellowed, and his men slowly stopped fighting. There were not a lot of them still on their feet.

"Hold," shouted Heather, and her people instantly froze in place. "All of you people back away. My fighters will provide whatever security we may need. Thomas, lead on before something else goes amok."

"My god," he breathed.

"These are trainees only," said Heather. "I didn't dare bring warriors, gods only know what might have happened. They'd probably have killed the lot of them. Lead on, sir, let's get to it." He didn't see the sly wink she gave Thordik.

They were led to the elevators, then down to the main floor, through some more security, then onto the floor of the United Nations. The weapons of her fighters set off all the alarms, but no one dared to challenge them. Thomas gave Ragnar a glowing, if long winded introduction, then Ragnar introduced Heather.

Heather took the podium, looked all around at the gathered world leaders, then took a deep breath and spoke. "People of Earth, I am Heather MacKay-Hunter, Chieftain of Erikr-Dak clan, and Ambassador to Earth for the Nyman people. I have come to you this day with a warning. There is an invasion fleet of ships about to enter this solar system. They are coming here, and they are over a hundred strong. They are coming to harvest a crop of humans."

She paused for a moment, then went on. "Hear me well, your fate at the hands of the invader will not be pleasant. They want you for slaves, they want you for breeders to make more slaves, and they want you for food to feed their slave warriors."

There was a buzz of voices at that, but she held up her hand for silence. "Hear me, I am not playing around here. Kett!" A holographic image of a grotesque creature appeared in the air. "This is what you will face very soon now. This is a slave warrior. These things will capture humans and herd them into huge transport ships. They will kill those who do not comply. This is what you will become, what you will be mated with, and this is what your bodies will be used to feed."

Again Heather paused until the noise level subsided a bit. "Kett!" A new hologram appeared beside the first. It was a more familiar sight, the image of a small grey humanoid creature with huge eyes. "This is the true enemy," Heather went on. "These things present less physical danger, but they are the slave masters. If taken, this is what you will serve, in whatever way they choose, and believe me, they are neither gentle, nor compassionate.

"I have come to warn you this day, of the danger that will soon fall upon you. The Nymen have come to stand beside you in the coming battle. We will fight and destroy as many of them as we can before they reach Earth, but their numbers are so much greater than our own. Some will get through and reach the surface of this planet. Here you will have to fight them yourselves.

"This is the danger you will face. The slaves will be heavily armed, but make no mistake, the Greys are the ones in control. They will be far fewer and harder to reach, but they are your first target. Kill the masters and the slaves fall into confusion.

"Hear me well, the masters are not helpless. They are by far the worst danger. The Greys have abilities far greater than their slaves. They have strong mental and psycho-hypnotic abilities. They project a bright light then they dull your mind to make you compliant.

"Believe me people, this is truly hard to resist, but resist you must. Strong emotion is your best defence, it keeps the mind clear. In the face of the enemy, a powerful killing rage is your strongest weapon."

Suddenly a man in Arab dress leaped to his feet. "We have only your word of this, woman. What proof of this foolish deception can you offer?" He was trembling in rage, and Thordik was sneering at him. She had been for some time.

"Proof? You want proof? Wait three days, you will have all the proof you need."

With that Heather stormed away and left the huge room, Ragnar at her side, and her Nyman guards right at her heel. Mooreland and his people hurried along behind. "Mrs. MacKay-Hunter, wait please..."

Back on the roof, Heather stopped and turned to face him. "I beg you, sir, for the love of God and this nation that I cherish, please heed the warning. Tell your people, rage is the only thing to block the mind control."

"Is there nothing else you can tell us?"

"They may be wearing personal defence fields. Those can stop a bullet, but a slow moving blade or club can penetrate them. Warn your people, this will be a hand-to-hand struggle. Please, Mr. President, keep Jim and Laura safe." With that, she returned to her craft and the door closed behind her. The craft rose easily then shot straight toward Iceland.

Ragnar grinned as they left the roof of the United Nations building. "That went rather well."

"You really think so?" Heather sighed deeply. "Ragnar, do you think they will listen?"

"I hope so, for many reasons. We will have a much easier time of it if they put up a good fight. If they don't, our task will be more difficult."

"The Americans will fight."

"I agree, Heather, and the Europeans as well. As soon as the first ship touches down they will become believers and they will fight. So will the Chinese."

"I do hope so, Ragnar, for I've done all I can for them. They're all on their own now."

"Here we are," Thordik said, as she lightly touched the craft down in Reykjavik.

"Farewell, Ragnar, may you be victorious, and may we meet again in happier times."

"Farewell, Heather, fight hard, and hold to the courage of your ancestor. We will meet again in brighter days." With that, he stepped back to join his own people as the small fighter craft leaped skyward.

"Chieftain?"

"Yes?"

"Did we succeed?"

"Yes, you did." Heather smiled as she turned to face the young man who'd spoken. "I must thank you as well, for not killing any of them. They will be needed very soon."

"We suspected something like that." He smiled in return. "We assumed you would not want your own folk killed, but you still deliberately gave us a chance to see our trial. Truly we have chosen our clan well."

"You have proven yourselves worthy, my kinsmen. Stay ready, for a greater trial awaits you in the near future."

"Erikr-Dak will be ready, Heather," Thordik said "We will not disappoint you."

Heather reached over to grip Thordik's shoulder. "My sister, I could never be disappointed in you, any of you. I am the one who will strive to be worthy of such a mighty clan." She sighed deeply then fell into silence. No one disturbed her until they were back on board the Mjolnir.

# Setting the Trap

Heather stopped off to speak to Skeezix. Frank was still sleeping. "Frank will be fully recovered and ready when he awakens this time, my chieftain. I have fully prepared him for you."

"What do you mean, fully prepared him?"

"Like you, my chieftain, Frank will no longer be able to survive on the planet for extended periods of time. His body is now fully adjusted to the heavier gravity of Nyman folk. To remain at lighter gravity for long periods will cause bone and body to deteriorate. Heather and Frank are now Nyman folk."

"We can't go home?"

"Not to stay, Heather. Three months of Greenland time at most, and only one is best. I am sorry, Heather, but when I healed you, I was unaware of the difference. When Thordik brought Frank Hunter to me, I knew how important he is to you, so I prepared him for you. Had I not, you would have had to leave him behind, and I did not think you wanted to do that. Forgive me, my chieftain, did I do wrong?"

Heather's shoulders sagged as she absorbed this new information. "So I guess we really are Nyman now. Relax, Skeezix, you did what you thought was best. I imagine I would have done the same in your place. You have done nothing wrong, my friend. I'm just a bit shocked. I had not thought that I would never be able to go home again. Ah well, Frank and I will just have to make a new home here among our new people."

"You have already done so," said a soft voice behind her. It was Drass and he was holding a uniform with Erikr-Dak insignia on it. "Freydis wants you on the bridge, Heather. I will await the awakening of Frank Hunter."

"I see you brought him clothes, Drass, but the weapons?"

"He will need to learn their use. Forgive us, Heather, but we can carry no passengers now. Every pair of able hands must be put to work. I will find where Frank Hunter can best serve, and then I will inform you of his position and where to find him."

"Thank you, Drass, I know you're right. Please, just make sure he's ready for whatever you assign him to."

"I will place him in no more danger than necessary, Heather. A sudden grin lit up his face as he went on. "After all, he is the chosen mate of a very powerful clan chieftain."

He was still chuckling as she slapped his arm and fled towards the bridge.

"Are you ready, Heather?" demanded Freydis, as Heather bolted through the door.

"Ready."

"Drass found you? You know what must be done?"

"Yes."

"Excellent. Morness, Kett, do it."

The klaxon sounded throughout the ship as Morness sent a signal to the fleet. Suddenly the big ship began to move slowly. "Watch there, Heather," said Freydis, as she pointed to a three dimensional display near the front of the bridge. Heather could see the whole solar system laid out before her, including the massive number of ships approaching. She saw their own ships begin to move slowly closer together. As she watched the Nyman ships began to shift position and back again. She staggered a bit as the ship shifted suddenly. Laughing, Freydis caught her arm to steady her.

The ships were moving closer together and changing position much faster as they began moving away from Earth and toward the invading fleet. "Can you guess what we are doing, Heather?"

"What? No. Wait, give me a minute. We need to hide behind Jupiter's moons, but the enemy has sensors too, and they would easily see us do it, right?"

"Yes, Heather."

"We should have been in position long ago. You held back on my account."

"You needed time to complete your task, Heather. Don't worry, all is well, but can you guess what we are doing?"

"It's the old shell game."

"The old shell game?"

"A pea is placed under one of three shells. You then distract the observer with idle chatter, while swiftly moving all three shells as quickly as you can. The pea is removed during this process so no matter which shell is guessed, the pea will not be there. We are moving the ships close together and moving them about to confuse the enemy sensors. During this dance the war ships will slip away and take up their positions."

"Brilliant reasoning, cousin," laughed Freydis, as she steadied Heather once again, "and right on the mark. Our path will place the gas giant between us and the enemy for a brief moment, and in that moment we slip away. The transport ships will continue the dance until we spring the trap, then they will abandon their position and attack the enemy transports."

Heather was clinging to a rail now and avidly watching the 3-D display. She wondered how these massive ships could move so swiftly and so close together without crashing into each other.

———✦———

"THEY'RE ON THE MOVE," shouted a voice, bringing Thomas Mooreland to his feet.

"What? Where?"

"The whole Nyman fleet is moving away from Earth, sir," replied the voice of a young woman; she never once took her eyes off the screen before her. "I have no idea at all what they are doing."

"What do you mean?"

"They're all bunched up and moving around so fast we can't really tell which is which any more."

"Where are they going?"

"Right at the other fleet, sir."

"So they will help us." He sighed as he turned to the rest of his people. "General Drake, are our forces ready?"

"All our people are now back on American soil, Mr. President," replied the uniform with the chest full of medals. "All are being armed with knives, throwing stars, nun chucks, billy clubs, and any other form of weapon we can find. They are also carrying conventional weapons just in case. The general population is being advised to do the same."

"Good. Are we certain our computers are safe down here?"

"The systems in the bunker are completely shielded, Mr. President. We also have people topside with standard electronics. They will warn us the very instant the EMP hits."

"Alright then, I guess it is time to speak to the nation. Get me a video feed."

FRANK SLOWLY AWAKENED and became restless. The warmth of the cocoon-like environment he was in began to withdraw and then light flooded into his eyes as the lid was lifted. He swung his legs over the side then stood and stretched. Suddenly the floor bucked and he fell sideways. A helping hand came from nowhere to steady him.

Turning swiftly, Frank saw who had helped him. It was a tall humanoid with strong looking scales all over his body. The women he had met so far had much finer, more delicate looking scales. With a smile, the creature offered Frank the clothing he held. "I am Drass, Frank Hunter. I'm Second on this ship. Put these on now, we have much work to do."

Frank struggled into the clothes, with a bit of help and some direction. Finally dressed, he faced Drass who chuckled softly. "Not bad at that. Now, Frank Hunter, we must find where best to place you."

"Place me?"

"We're about to go into battle. Everyone must fight, and we must find a place where you can serve."

"Is Heather aboard, or is she safely back on Earth?"

"Heather is with Freydis on the bridge. That is her place as clan chieftain, and that is where she will remain during the battle. Trust me, Frank Hunter, Heather is as safe on the bridge of the Mjolnir as she would be anywhere on the planet. Come with me now. I promise you will soon see your chieftain."

He led Frank from the healing bay and down to the training area. The ship was moving around quite a bit now, but Frank was able to stay upright. By the time they arrived he seemed to have gotten his sea legs. All those trips on the boat with his father weren't wasted.

They arrived to find Thordik overseeing the training of several dozen young people. Drass called out and she turned with a bright smile of greeting. Once again Frank was struck by the beauty of this tall young woman.

"Thordik, Second of Erikr-Dak, I Drass, Second of Pull Karr, bring you a new kinsman. Put him to work." With a chuckle and a friendly slap on the shoulder for Frank, Drass turned and walked away.

"You seem ready for action, Frank Hunter," said Thordik, as she approached. "Get that look off your face, or I'll tell my sister, and then you will be in a battle that you are surely not ready for."

"Man, you're tough." Frank laughed, then he turned serious. "Thordik, is Heather all right? I really do want to see her."

"Our chieftain is well, Frank, have no fears. Under normal circumstances she would have been waiting there when you awakened, but these are not normal times. We are going into battle. We must find where you can best serve and where we can best protect you. Tell me now, what are your skills."

Frank started to grin but the look on her face said that was a bad idea. Play time was over. He'd been shanghaied and she was the new bo'sun. If Frank had learned anything from Heather, it was to recognize when it was time to play and when it wasn't. "I'm good with most guns."

"Useful on the planet's surface or in hand-to-hand, but not here, Frank. What else?"

"I'm pretty quick with technology, but I'm sure yours is different. I am pretty fast with video games."

"Explain."

"Video games, let's see. You have a control devise and a screen that gives you multiple targets to hit. The degree of difficulty increases as you go along."

"Sounds like a gunner's turret to me, Thordik," grinned a young fellow who had just approached.

"And to me as well, Gordrall. Put him in the simulator and see how he does."

"Thordik, can I ask a question?"

"Of course, Frank Hunter, what would you know?"

"What does this sash mean? Drass explained that this symbol here means I am of Heather's clan, but I don't understand the sash."

"What is it about the sash you would like to know?"

"Is there a certain significance to the colour? Mine is red and so are yours as are many others, but I see a lot of blue ones as well."

"Red means that you have proven yourself in battle, Frank Hunter. Blue denotes one who has yet to face such a trial."

"But I haven't..."

"When I found you there were dead enemies all around you," said the young man. "One of the others said it was you who first threw off the yoke of the mind numbing and woke the rest. It was you who led them in the fight to bring down the ship."

"Yes, it was you who found me. Thank you for that. So, you can speak English?"

"No, Frank Hunter, the woman who spoke to me was Icelandic. Come with me, we'll see just what kind of a gunner you will make." He led Frank away, and Frank noticed the affection with which the young goddess slapped Gordrall on the shoulder as he passed by her. He smiled to realize that even in the face of impending battle, young love would still show its face.

Gordrall led Frank to a small booth and indicated that he should take the centre seat of three. Once ready, he carefully explained how the machine worked. "Grip this and this, Frank Hunter. Now, squeeze this." There was a popping sound as he did. "Good, now move this around and watch that screen." Frank saw several red blips and an equal armed cross. As he moved the control the cross moved. The controls were amazingly delicate.

"Okay, so this is the joy stick, and this is the trigger. So, I move the cross hairs onto a red marker and squeeze the trigger like this?" As he did so the red dot exploded. Another red dot fired a yellow glowing ball that exploded onto the screen blanking it out.

Gordrall laughed as he reset the screen. "All right, Frank Hunter, you've got the idea. Now, this is how the system works. You have to hit both the reds and their missiles, the blues are your allies, don't shoot them. Usually there are three gunners to a turret. When a gunner begins to tire, or cannot keep track, he moves aside and another takes his place. It is always best to change often, so a fresh pair of eyes is always on the screen. I have set the system to level one. Let's see how far you can get before they shoot you down."

"Let 'er rip." Frank leaned forward as the screen began to move. He didn't last long. Frank squirmed in his seat for a moment then grinned. "Okay, I've got a feel for it now, Gordrall. Crank it up." Gordrall reset the machine again.

It was much later that Thordik stuck her head in to see how things were going. "Well, Gordie, how is he doing?"

"I think you may have a challenger here, Thordik. Frank is already up to level nine and still going."

"Wonderful," she said with a smile. "We have a new rail gunner. Get him ready and put him as near Heather's cabin as you can."

"I'll take him with me," replied Gordrall. "I've been assigned to the ship as gunner, and I have no seconds as yet."

"Is he truly that good, Gordie?"

"He's just hit level ten."

"Alright, I guess you've got your second gunner. Take care of each other, my men, for if you fail, Heather and I will be alone, and who knows what trouble we would get into."

"I don't even want to imagine. Where are you being stationed?"

"Ten Erikr-Dak are assigned to each ship; the rest are in the fighters. I'm to lead a fighter wing."

"Carefully, Thordik," Gordrall said softly, as he gently squeezed her arm. "Lay them low, but carefully."

"I will return," she grinned, as she gripped his arm tightly, "and you'd better be here when I do." With that, she was gone.

Gordrall turned his attention back to the screen to see that Frank had reached eleventh level. A moment later it was over.

"Dammit," exploded Frank, as his screen went blank.

"You're amazing, Frank Hunter. Are you certain this is your first time in the simulator?"

"It is, but we have had similar things on Earth for a while now, and I got a lot of practice when I was growing up. Tell me, who holds the record for this thing?"

"Thordik. She has reached level twenty-one. It will not go higher. No one else has ever passed fifteen and few ever get there."

"Alright, I can see how hard that could be. Tell me what the real thing will be like. What level are we facing out there?"

"Level ten or more," grinned Gordrall. "You're being stationed with me in the starboard turrets near the bridge. It's not so far from the sleeping booths. Now, it's time to work on the next phase."

"Okay, so what's next?"

"The enemy will not wait for us to change places, Frank Hunter. We must do it smoothly without a break in the defences."

"Frank, please just call me Frank, Gordrall. Okay, so how do we do this?"

"The right hand always works the controller, so when we shift we move to the left. If you're in the left seat, then you stand, and once the others have moved you take the right chair and you're next at the controls. All right, let's try it. I'll go here, and set it at level eight for a start. Wait for a break in the action, then when I slap your shoulder get ready to move. I bring my hand down to the controller and on a count of three we change, then you abandon the chair, moving to the left."

They tried it a few times and it was getting better. "That's enough for now, Frank. I'm hungry, let's go to the great hall and get some food, then we can practice more."

"How fast do we have to get at this, Gord?"

"We must be a lot faster than we are, and we have little time to practice. Come, we must eat."

Frank was trying to take it all in as he followed Gordrall along the corridors to the great hall. He was gazing all around the hall in wonder, when he heard a squeal of delight, and Heather was in his arms. "Frank, oh my darling Frank, thank the gods you're all right."

"Heather, my beautiful Heather," Frank whispered over and over, as he hugged her tightly to him.

"Oh, Frank, I thought I'd lost you." She laid her head onto his shoulder.

"Not a chance, woman, you said I get to keep the girl, and that's what I plan to do. Heather, I was so worried about you, but it seems that you've been busy without me."

"Far more than you know, Frank my love. Come join us and I'll fill you in as best I can."

# The Trap is Set

F rank sat trying to take it all in as Heather brought him up to speed on her adventures. "I met Thordik, she brought me to the healer, Skeezix. She said you two are sisters, but you and Freydis look like sisters to me."

"Cousins only, Frank Hunter," said Freydis.

"Heather, what did you do for Thordik that would make her tear apart every ship in the galaxy to find me?"

"She set her free," said Freydis. "Thordik is unique among us, Frank, greater than all who came before her. The gods seemed to be putting obstacles in her path, for we were all unsuccessful in getting her to her trial. Heather climbed out of the healing chamber, took over my ship, and cut Thordik loose within a matter of hours."

"Here," grunted a man who was sitting near. Heather had introduced him as Kett. "Watch this."

"What is it?" asked Frank, as he looked at the small handheld screen the man passed to him.

"Thordik's trial," replied Kett.

Frank was horrified at what played out before him. As it ended he passed back the screen. "I'm glad she's on our side," he said at last.

"So say we all," agreed Freydis. "Now good people, we have much to do. Their ships are near, but as soon as we settle into position I believe we will have time for one short sleep cycle. Give her back, Frank Hunter, she is needed on the bridge."

"And poor old Frank needs more practice in the turrets."

"The turrets? You've made gunner then. Is he any good?"

"Level twelve first time in the simulator," said Gordrall.

141

"I am well pleased," said Freydis. "The Mjolnir needs good gunners. Come, Heather, Kett. To the bridge."

Heather grabbed Frank by the collar and kissed him soundly. "Later. We'll have time together soon." With that, she was gone. Frank sat bemused as he watched them leave the hall.

"Frank?"

"When first I met Heather, I was struck by her beauty, her intelligence, and her inner strength, but there was another part of her, too. A small, wounded child that needed protecting."

"And now?"

"Now I think that small child has grown up, and she is pissed off. She is so much stronger now and reaching for her potential. I just hope..."

"Seek no troubles, Frank Hunter," Gordrall said, as he gripped Frank's shoulder. "Enough will find you all on their own. I believe you are growing stronger as well, Frank, and always remember what she has done to get you away from the Greys. The gods have done much to keep you together, embrace that. Come, we have to practice until sleep cycle arrives."

AS THEY REACHED THE bridge, Kett relieved Elgess at the controls. "Where are we, Ellie?"

"Almost ready, Kett. We'll be behind the gas giant in just a few moments."

"Got it. Get some food and then come back. I will need to sleep before the fun starts."

"Perhaps I should sleep first, then you can take a long rest while I get the show started." She grinned as she danced towards the door.

"The gods will get you for that, Ellie," grunted Kett, "and so will I." She was laughing as she left the bridge. A few moments later the ship made a sudden leap then, just as swiftly, came to a stop. "We're here, Freydis. There's nothing to do now but wait."

"Ship wide, Morness."

"Ready, Captain."

"This is Freydis. We will soon be in the fight of our lives. I want all crew to rest as much as possible. The ship will go on automatic with minimal crew awake until the sound of the klaxon. At that sound everybody to full battle stations, and you will not have a lot of time to get there. Rest now my sisters and brothers, and may the gods favour us in the battle to come."

Freydis sighed deeply, then smiled and shooed Heather off the bridge. "Go on, Heather, get some rest. Call that young fellow and have him bring your mate to you." Heather blushed deeply and Freydis laughed as she pulled Heather into a gentle hug. "You have faced much, Heather, and soon you will face more. You've earned these few moments of reward. Take them, enjoy them, cherish them in the days to come, for I fear it will be a while before they return."

"Freydis, I can't thank you enough for all you have done for me," said Heather, as she returned the embrace.

"Go now, cousin, time is wasting."

Drass watched as Heather fled the bridge. "Will she be ready?" he asked.

"You've seen as much as I, Drass. She will not wilt under the fire of battle. However, I don't want that to ever become the issue. You are to remain whole and sound, do you hear me? That's an order."

"Yes, my chieftain," he grinned as he saluted Freydis' retreating back. "I hear and obey."

HEATHER RACED TOWARDS her cabin, but it was empty. "What is his name, what is that boy's name? Gordon, no, Gordall?

Worth a try," she muttered, as she touched the pin at her shoulder. "Gordall?"

"Gordrall here, is it me you seek?"

"This is Heather MacKay-Hunter, are you the young man who..."

"Yes, my chieftain. Frank Hunter is right here." He reached over to touch the pin on Frank's shoulder then nodded.

"Heather?"

"Frank, my beloved, tell that young man to stop laughing. Gordrall."

"Yes, chieftain."

"Stop teasing and bring Frank to my cabin."

"On our way, my chieftain."

"So, Gordrall old buddy, how much time do we have, do you think?" asked Frank, as they left the training area.

"Not a lot, Frank. You should try to get a few moments sleep at least."

"Yeah, yeah. Listen Gord, are we ready?"

"As ready as time will allow, Frank," Gordrall replied seriously. "Here we are, this is the chieftain's cabin. Frank, when the klaxon sounds, get to the turret as fast as you can. Come through that door, turn to your right, go to the end of that passageway then turn right again. The turrets will be on your left. Ours is number thirty-seven. Don't wait for me, just get inside. If no one is there, get in the chair and fire up the weapons."

"Don't worry, Gord, I won't let you down."

"Good man." Gordrall slapped Frank's shoulder then jogged away down the long corridor.

Frank turned and knocked on the cabin door softly. It was swept open instantly and Heather was dragging him inside. He hugged her close and kissed her deeply. "Heather, my darling Heather. I was so afraid I had lost you."

"That will never happen, Frank my love, not ever. Now then, we have to get some sleep, but first I want to discuss something with you."

"Now, Heather? Okay, what's on your mind?"

"Those six children you owe me, buddy."

"So, no rest for the weary?"

"None." She smiled wickedly.

"All right then, I'll see what I can do to keep up my end of the bargain."

"See that you do," she breathed, as she melted into his arms.

Their lovemaking was swift and urgent. They had been parted too long and under too much stress. Their passion swiftly satisfied, they lay in each others arms, drifting on the aftermath of the orgasms. "Frank?"

"Yes, love?"

"Tell me this madness will all be over soon."

"It will, my darling, it will. One way or the other, it will all be over soon. Sleep now, my chieftain, my beloved." She closed her eyes and snuggled closer into his arms. Frank kissed the top of her head and he too, drifted off to sleep. The klaxon sounded all too soon.

"ANYTHING NEW HAPPENING?" demanded Thomas Mooreland, as he emerged from his rooms.

"They're still dancing about, sir," replied the young woman, glued to her screen. "Three of them dropped away and are hiding behind the moons of Jupiter, or so we believe. It is hard to tell with them moving so fast and all. The rest have taken up a position between the asteroid belt and Jupiter. Oh my god, it looks like they're disintegrating."

"What??? Disintegrating? How???"

"No, wait, they're still there. That was so weird. For a minute it looked like they had come apart and scattered into the asteroid belt, but they are still there. Now they're falling back."

"Falling back?"

"Yes sir, falling back towards Mars."

"What the hell is going on?"

"I think I might have an idea," said General Drake who was standing right behind him. "I'd say that, because of their small numbers, they're going to use guerrilla tactics. They've hidden the big guns behind the moons of Jupiter and all their small fighters in the asteroid belt. The ones falling back are the bait to lure them into the trap."

"They're coming here anyway, why not hide them all?"

"Because the enemy can see them as well as we can, except from a different view point. By using this tactic, they convince the enemy that they are all still blocking the way. Our allies may be few in numbers, but they seem to be experienced warriors. I'm actually heartened with this news. The more they stop in space, the fewer we have to deal with down here."

"Incoming call from Iceland, sir."

"Ragnar, good to hear from you," Thomas smiled, as the Icelandic president came on the screen.

"Thomas, I have little time, but I have some information for you. I am sending the assembly specifications for the mind control blocker. I do not know if you have time to make any, but I hope you do. I would have sent the information sooner, but we only just got it ourselves from one of the Greenlanders. Good luck, Thomas, and may your gods be with you." With that, he was gone.

"Have we got those specs?"

"Yes, sir, we've got them right here," replied a young woman. "It actually doesn't look too hard to make. We should be able to whip up quite a few before the enemy arrives, but we have to hurry."

"Get on it, and send those specs to everyone you can, including the internet media. Somebody get me a video feed. I'll tell the nation that we have the specs, then we can post them."

"Camera ready, Mr. President. The specs have already been posted to the official website."

"My fellow Americans," began Thomas Mooreland, as he faced the camera and got the prompt. "A dark day is nearly upon us..."

# Battle Joined

Heather sat up with a start as the klaxon sounded. She slapped Frank's bare bottom hard as she leaped for the facilities. He was already dressed when she returned to pull on her clothes. She kissed him deeply at the door then they both sprinted away in different directions.

Frank reached turret thirty-seven just as Gordrall came pounding along the corridor. They entered together to find a grey-haired warrior sitting at the controls. "Just my luck," he groused. "I get harnessed with a Fresh Proven and a Greenlander. You're both late. The ship could have been overrun in the time it took you to get to your post." He still hadn't faced them and Gordrall was about to jerk the old timer out of the seat when Frank winked at him.

"So, let me guess," chuckled Frank. "You're the one who was posted here all through last sleep cycle."

The old fellow turned with a great bellowing laugh and clasped Frank's forearm just above the wrist in the warrior's greeting. "I'm Larthaness. I heard that I was about to get some of Thordik's young blood up here, and glad am I for it."

"Frank Hunter," replied Frank, as he returned the man's grip. "Shift over now and get some rest."

"There'll be no rest now." He grinned as he turned to Gordrall. "Larthaness."

"Gordrall," he replied, as he accepted the warrior's greeting from the old fellow.

"Got to you, didn't I, young warrior?"

"You did." Gordrall sighed as he let his shoulders slump.

"Let the rage come too easily and trouble will follow it in, Gordrall. Rage can be a powerful weapon, but you must use it wisely."

"As Thordik has told me many times before."

"This one has too much energy, Frank. He gets the chair first, then you." He moved easily to the left seat and Gordrall slid into place. Frank had barely enough time to grab the rail before the ship nearly leaped out from under him.

HEATHER BURST ONTO the bridge to find Freydis waiting for her. "Sorry I'm late."

"Not bad, all things considered." Freydis grinned as she turned to Morness. "Report."

"Message from the North Wind, twelve Grey raiders have dropped back to escort the transports in."

"Blast them all to Hell," muttered Freydis.

"The Raven and the Falcon are standing by, Captain."

"Selian, Brek, are you ready?"

"Ready," came the reply.

"Move together, lock shields."

At that command Heather, who was watching the 3-D display, saw the three ships leap towards each other even as the deck leaped away from her feet. This time she didn't fall. Freydis nodded her approval as the air suddenly tingled for a moment.

"Shields locked, Captain. I have the board," declared Kett.

"Steady, steady," said Freydis, as Heather saw dozens of enemy ships gliding past Jupiter. "Now!" All three war ships leaped away at terrifying speed, and Heather clung to the rail for dear life.

As an axe splits the block, the locked ships shot towards the enemy, the Mjolnir leading and the other two flanking her tightly. Suddenly they were in the midst of the enemy ships, weapons fire everywhere, but they didn't slow down. Kalla's hands were a blur as she worked the big forward ion cannons.

Heather's eyes were wide as she clung to the rail. There were so many ships, and she wondered just how the hell Kett was managing to work his way through them, for it was he who now controlled all three ships.

As suddenly as they had struck and been engulfed in the midst of the enemy, they emerged out the other side. Kett continued on for a moment then the ships curved upwards and banked hard. The pursuing enemy ships could not match the manoeuvre and were left behind. Heather could see that the entire enemy fleet had been thrown into disarray.

Kett pulled hard and the banking turn was tight and swift. As soon as they faced the enemy once more, the ships leaped ahead and attacked again. Again they fought their way through and Kett drove right around the back side of Jupiter. Using the gas giant's gravity as a slingshot they came back around for another run. Once again they shot towards the enemy ships.

"Brek, Selian, get ready." Freydis waited until they were once again in the midst of the enemy before she gave the order. "Break!" Suddenly the Raven and the Falcon peeled off in different directions, taking the fight to the enemy as they went.

Like killer whales feeding on seals, the three Nyman warships used their greater speed and mobility to keep the enemy scattered. There were over a dozen enemy ships floating awkwardly in space now, drifting freely toward Earth so far away.

Heather had her legs under her now and was able to keep a much better eye on the battle. As it raged she felt the explosions of the missiles against the shields. "Dammit, we can't keep taking this pounding. Even these shields can't withstand this forever," grunted Drass.

"They'll hold," said Kett. "I modified them myself."

"Shields weakening," announced Tessa.

"Skeeter. Elgess, take the chair and don't crash my ship."

"Can I ram a few of theirs?"

"Not until I get the shields back up to maximum."

"Brek, Selian," bawled Freydis.

"Shields weakening," they replied in unison.

"Reform shield wall." At her command the other two ships pulled alongside the Mjolnir and Heather felt the tingle as the shields were locked once again. "Kett?"

"We're at max as long as we stay locked. It'll take me a while to recharge them to full."

"Get on it. Kalla, point singularity cannon, start picking off some of those damned raiders who went back to defend their transports. Elgess, keep as many off our backs as you can."

"Yes, ma'am. I'm on it."

Heather thought she heard a strange whine coming from the ship as Kalla charged her weapon. Suddenly the whole ship shuddered as Kalla fired. Heather saw two of the distant enemy ships vanish instantly. "Good shot, Kalla," grunted Drass. "How long before it can recharge?"

"It'll be quite a while before I can fire another shot, a sleep cycle at least." Just then the Falcon lanced out with her own cannon and another distant ship vanished. A heartbeat later the Raven took out three transports. "Dammit, Elan got three. I hate it when he does that."

"Well now, it has had the desired effect," said Freydis, as she watched the enemy transports scatter in all directions.

"Shields are back at max," bawled Kett as he leaped towards the controls. Elgess easily slid out of his way and relinquished the helm.

"Brek? Selian?"

"Shields at max," they reported.

"Break," commanded Freydis. The three war ships split apart and went on the attack once again. Like wolves attacking a flock of sheep they took a terrible toll, but the enemy numbers were too great. Heather could see that it would be impossible to stop them all. At least half were likely to reach Earth. She schooled her thoughts to concentrate on the battle at hand.

"WE'RE IN LUCK," SAID Larthaness, as the three ships leaped away. "The Raven isn't blocking our view. We'll get some action. Those poor folk from forty back are blocked, and the Raven's gunner will have all the fun."

"Multiple targets," said Gordrall, as he opened fire. Frank was stunned at the sheer number of enemy ships. It was impossible not to hit something and it soon became apparent that it was impossible to avoid being hit. Gordrall was a blur as he worked the controller and his eyes saw everything. It took Frank a while to realize the boy was picking his targets, trying to knock away missiles and to hit anything close to the ship. Frank was about to suggest a change over when the enemy seemed to disappear.

"Shift," barked Larthaness.

"I've got the screen," said Frank, as his hand hovered just above Gordrall's. "On three; one, two, three." At three Gordrall smoothly left the chair and Frank slid in just as the ship began her banking manoeuvre and return run.

"Not bad." Lathaness grinned as he slid into the right hand chair. "A bit more practice and you'll make decent gunners."

Frank started to ask a question, but there was no time. Suddenly the screen was alive with targets and weapons fire. It took him a moment to get the feel of the real thing, but he adapted swiftly. Once he hit his groove, Frank was almost having fun. He forgot this was real, he forgot that the enemy were living beings that wanted to kill all of them, he forgot everything but the screen.

Time seemed to stand still for Frank, as his mind focused in on the dance before him. He worked the control furiously and he was scoring well. Lost in the zone, it took a slap on his shoulder to draw him back. "Shift," barked Larthaness. "On three; one, two, three!" Frank slid easily to the left then sat back with a soft groan of protest. With a deep sigh he began to rub some of the stiffness from his shoulders. He stood and did a few twisting, turning stretches, then collapsed back into his seat.

"How long was I in the chair?"

"Too long, Frank," replied Gordrall, "but that's they way a battle goes. If we had more ships, we could share out the enemy a bit and get more breaks."

"It's not so bad now," said Larthaness, never pausing in his task nor taking his eyes from the screen. "We've got them scattered out pretty good, and the ships have broken formation. So tell me, how did I end up with the two of you anyway?" Frank was impressed at how easily the old warrior could work the guns and still carry on a conversation.

"That was my doing," said Gordrall.

"Oh?"

"I know who you are, Lathaness of Torvaless-Pem. When I was assigned to gunner duty, I checked the record of every available turret. When I found the greatest gunner in the fleet had an opening I grabbed it. Thordik told me to keep the chieftain's mate safe, so I brought Frank along."

"So, you're my babysitter?"

"No, Frank, not at all. At first I thought we would probably assign you to the healing bay, or to the great hall, but when I saw how swiftly you learned the guns, I wanted you with me. Thordik said I had to stay safe, so I chose the two best guardians I could find."

"So, you're saying that if I let anything happen to either of you two pets, Heather Mak-Kay-Hunter and Thordik will be after my head?"

"Yeah, that's about what it comes down to."

"It is a sad state I find myself in at this age. I should be lying on my back beside the red seas of Brialth, soaking up the suns, but instead I'm wet nurse to a pair of fluffies."

"It's a hard life indeed," said Frank, as Gordrall slapped Larthaness on the shoulder then took the controls.

"I hear that you broke the mind numbing without a blocker, and brought down a stealth ship from within, Frank," Larthaness said admiringly. "That was not the work of a fluffy, not by half."

"I had help. Actually, we were getting our heads pounded when Gordie came along and tore the ship apart."

"I know of Gordrall of Pull-Karr, now of Erikr-Dak as well. I'm quite pleased to have two such warriors to care for me in my old age." The friendly gentle banter continued along with the battle, and Frank soon realized that it was the way these folk kept the horror of their situation from overwhelming them.

"WHAT'S HAPPENING NOW?" demanded Thomas Mooreland impatiently.

"It is hard to tell, Mr. President. They seem to have stirred up a hornet's nest alright, but they are still moving closer. The Nymen are wreaking havoc with the enemy fleet, but there are just way too many. Some are bound to get through."

"Best estimate, how many?"

"Hard to tell at this point, sir," replied the soldier glued to the viewing screen. "The battle is slowly moving towards us. The Nymen are keeping them busy, but they're still coming. At this rate they will reach the asteroid belt in another few hours, and we already know the Nymen have a swarm of small fighters hiding there. Hopefully that will thin them out a bit more, but I'll bet at least a dozen or more reach us, and then there is that big fleet of enemy ships still way back and coming in."

"My god," sighed the president softly, "my dear sweet god."

"Mr. President, the vice-president has arrived."

"What?"

"The vice-president, sir? You asked for him to be brought in?"

"Oh yes, so I did. Where is he?"

"Right here, Tom," said a tall, thin man with a stiff military bearing.

"Cal, what is your assessment?"

"We're screwed. The world as we know it is about to end, and I just hope there are enough humans left alive on this planet to repopulate it."

"Never mind sugar coating it, Cal," grunted the president sarcastically, "tell us what you really think."

"I just did, Tom."

"So you don't think the Nyman fleet can stop them?"

"I doubt it, Tom. I'd say these folk are a true warrior society, and that they have come home to make a last stand beside all that is left of a kindred species. I believe that they know damned well how this will come out in the end, and, like a bunch of Klingons, they intend to go out in a blaze of glory."

"That's what I've always loved about you, Cal, your positive upbeat personality and your unbounded optimism. You can do the honourable Samurai all you want, but I think we can survive this. Yes, they've got a hundred ships, but there are billions of humans on this planet. We'll put up a fight, it's in our nature."

"Testing, testing, testing," came a soft voice from the background.

"What the hell is that thing?"

"Sorry sir. This is the prototype of that mind blocker thing the Nymen gave us the specs for."

"Is it working?"

"I guess so. It is on and generating some sort of weak energy pulse. The instruments can pick it up, but you can't hear it. I've got it positioned to protect the whole bunker, that is, if it really does anything at all."

"It does," came the voice of Jim Brady.

"What makes you so sure, Jim?"

"Heather wouldn't have given it to us if it was useless. That's not her style."

"Heather MacKay, how the hell did she gain control of that fleet anyway?" mused the vice-president.

"It doesn't really matter, Cal. Just remember what that girl did in Darfur. Now, imagine ten thousand soldiers like that on our side in this. Actually, I'm with Tom on this one. I'm liking our chances of survival, but there is one thing I would like to know for sure."

"What's that, Jim?"

"Government has known all along that those Grey things were here, isn't that right?"

"Yeah, Jim, we've known since the mid-nineteen hundreds."

"Then why the hell did everyone try so hard to deny it, and why work so hard to discredit people like Heather?"

"It was always felt best to avoid wide spread panic."

"You mean you wanted to see if you could grab an advantage with some alien technology."

"That's about it. We tried at Area 51, but the crashed ship we captured was just too far ahead of us. It is too alien for us to understand. Ah well, it's all too late now."

# The Battle Rages On

The Mjolnir was in the thick of it once again and Freydis was looking a bit ragged. "You need to rest, Captain," said Drass. "I'm fine."

"Freydis, you have not slept for the last two cycles."

"I know, but..."

"Shields down!" said Tessa. "Multiple scavs clamping on." Suddenly there was the strident blaring of the klaxon.

"Intruders. All decks," announced Tessa, her voice ringing out through the whole ship.

"Kett, get those damned shields back up," barked Freydis. "Elgess, get us out of here and shake off as many as you can."

The ship leaped away from the battle with dozens of small fighters clamped to her sides like alien parasites boring through her skin. The battle now raged hand-to-hand throughout the ship while Elgess tried to keep away from the pursuing enemy. She tore around Jupiter, then poured on the speed. In a matter of moments they shot right through the rings of Saturn. The icy rings managed to scrape off a few of the attackers, but not enough.

With an explosive sound, the door to the bridge burst open, and the room was suddenly filled with light and enemy fighters. Heather felt the familiar pull at her mind and nearly panicked, then Freydis slapped the blocker on Heather's tunic. Heather's mind cleared instantly, and she went on the attack.

The enemy she fought were a strange assortment of creatures. All were heavily armed, but all seemed to be painfully slow. All Heather's martial arts training was instantly put to use as she lashed out with murderous intent. The bridge crew needed to fly the ship, she had to protect them.

Horrified, Heather saw Freydis go down under a swarm of carrion fighters and Heather leaped to her aid. Freydis was back up in a heartbeat and in the fray once again. The room was slowly filling up with enemy soldiers and Heather was running out of room to fight. In a few moments their greater numbers would prevail. The Grey! There must be a Grey with them, she had to kill it.

Heather began to fight her way towards the shattered door. She was nearly there when a blow from the side sent her reeling to the floor. Lashing out with her boots she brought down three more before she regained her feet. Back on her feet, Heather caught a glimpse of a Grey just outside the doorway. It had some kind of apparatus strapped to its chest with an electrical harness connected to its head. She went for it.

The way was jammed by too many fighters and she was getting bogged down when Drass suddenly appeared by her side, helping to clear the way. He went down under their superior numbers, but he had given Heather the room she needed. Leaping over the body of a downed fighter she landed right at the feet of the Grey. He fired a hand weapon at her chest.

Heather had seen the weapon and dropped to the floor before the thing could fire. She swept the legs from under the Grey then crushed its skull with her heel when it fell. Instantly the enemy fighters on the bridge stopped in confusion. They became easy prey now, and soon were fighting to escape. There was nowhere to run as Heather was outside the door, a weapon in her hand, and another Nyman at her side. They were merciless. In moments the bridge was cleared of live enemy fighters.

Heather's new companion began dragging the bodies towards an air lock; she grabbed a corpse and followed suit. After they managed to clear away a number of them, the newcomer locked the door then blew the bodies out the hatch, and then they started again. Morness pitched in and soon it was done. Only then did Heather recognize her new companion. It was Clerisa, and she was wearing a blue sash.

"Well, my chieftain, how did I do?"

"Clerisa, why are you here?"

"I was assigned to the healing bay, I lost the draw of lots. I was part of the team searching for more intruders. I think we have them all now."

"Then you can help me here," grunted Freydis. They spun around to see Freydis holding a bleeding unconscious Drass. Freydis was bleeding from several wounds as well. Clerisa was instantly at her side helping to bear Drass's weight.

As they headed for the healing bay, Heather called out to them. "Clerisa, at first opportunity, change that sash to red." She turned back to the bridge then.

Heather didn't like what she found there. Everybody was nursing wounds and trying to work at the same time. "Is everyone all right? Does anyone need to get to the healing bay?"

"We'll survive, Chieftain," grunted Kett, as he lay on his back working on something under a control panel. "I'll have the shields back up in a moment, then we will need a few more minutes to charge them to max."

"Reports from all decks are pouring in now, Chieftain," declared Morness. "They are mopping up. This was a lot better than we had a right to expect. The scavs have been blasted off and the hull sealed. There are some wounds, and only three casualties. Apparently they threw most of what they had at the bridge."

"Ion cannon back at max, Chieftain," reported Kalla.

"There we are," said Kett, as he crawled out from under the control panel. "Shields back on line, Chieftain."

"We are just on the periphery of the battle, Chieftain," supplied Elgess. "I'm using just enough speed to keep them chasing us, so they don't reform into a solid formation."

"People, why are you reporting to me as though I am the captain?"

"The captain and her second are wounded, Heather," replied Kett. "That makes you the one in command until one of them returns."

"Me? I can't..."

"Shields back at max," he interrupted. "Orders, Chieftain."

Heather hit the pin on her tunic. "Freydis, we're ready to go up here."

"Then do something," was the reply ground out through clenched teeth as Skeezix sealed one of her deeper wounds.

"All right people, you know how this is done, so do it. Blow as many of those little bastards as you can straight to Andromeda."

"You're injured, Kett," Elgess said, as he tried to resume the pilot's seat. "Go get patched up first."

"I'm fine..."

"Kett, get to the healers, now," barked Heather. "Elgess, get us back in there, fast."

Kett just stared at Heather as Elgess swung the big ship around for another attack run. "Go, Kett," Heather said kindly. "We need you here, but we need you in one piece. Go on now, do like Mamma says."

Kett grinned and shook his head. "Yes, Captain, I hear and obey."

The others were still chuckling as he disappeared from the bridge. Heather returned her attention to the 3-D display to see the Raven getting swarmed. "Elgess, to the Raven. Kalla, see if you can clear away some of that mess from her sides."

"Yes, ma'am," replied Kalla, as she began working the smaller cannons. Heather was impressed with her skill as she cleared several of the scavs off the Raven's outer hull. The Mjolnir made a second pass, then the voice of Selian came through the speakers.

"Thank you, Freydis, your timing was impeccable as usual."

"This is Heather, Selian. Are you alright?"

"Heather? Are both Freydis and Drass down?"

"Drass was hurt badly. I don't think Freydis was though. She should soon be back. Are you all right, is your ship?"

"We've got a mess of them on board, but we managed to kill the two Greys. We just have to mop up a bit then get back to business."

"Selian, get your ship out of there."

"Yes, Chieftain. Freydis has left her ship in good hands, I see."

"Was there any doubt?" asked Freydis' voice, as she returned to the bridge. "Get out of there, Selian. Heather, report."

"Shields are at max and weapons fully functional, Captain. And may I say what a pleasure it is to have you back where you belong?"

"You may indeed, cousin. Now, get some rest."

"What???"

"Heather, Drass is down for a while, so it is up to you and I now. You fought like a true Valkyrie this day and you need to rest."

"So do you."

"Yes, and I will, Heather. In a long battle, all must rest in shifts. With Drass down, you and I will have to work that much harder. You rest now, then I will rest. Use my cabin, it's closer if I need you." Smiling she pointed at her cabin door. "Go."

"Aye, aye, Captain," Heather sighed, as she turned to the cabin door. Inside Freydis' sleeping cabin she found a rather homey, feminine space, and she smiled her delight. Heather collapsed on the bed and was instantly asleep. The next thing she heard was the klaxon.

THE BLARE OF THE KLAXON nearly brought Frank out of the chair. He had just slid aside for Larthness and was still trying to get the knots out of his shoulders. "Intruders. All decks," barked the speakers in the turret.

"Damn and double damn," growled Larthness. "I've got the guns, but don't take all day."

"Come on, Frank," said Gordrall, as he leaped towards the door, weapon in his hand. He touched a button on his uniform then the same one on Frank's. "Blockers on, shields on, and weapons ready. Let's go." He snapped the door open, but the corridor was empty.

"What are we looking for?" Frank asked softly as he peered all around.

"Anything that doesn't belong and moves. You see something that doesn't belong here move, you blow its buttocks to the next galaxy."

"Got it. So Gord, how do I work this weapon?"

"Point it at something then press that yellow stud right there. Make sure you don't point it at me, it will cut through almost anything, but it has only a short range. Never point it at the main hull unless you want a quick trip outside."

"Okay, got it. Look out!"

With that warning Frank knocked Gordrall aside and fired his weapon. The beam of light stopped short of the creature advancing down the corridor. Gordrall leaped ahead and dived into a forward roll. He came up firing and cut the lead creature in half. He brought down two more before they swarmed him and he went down.

As Gordrall went down, Frank waded into the fray. He took a few blows, but he gave as good as he got, and the shield protected him from major harm. Frank soon managed to use the weapon effectively. With a gunner's eye he saw the Grey controlling the beasts and he went for him. Gordrall was back on his feet now and right beside Frank.

"I see the Grey," shouted Frank.

"Get him. I'll try to keep them off you."

Frank was bobbing and weaving as best he could while trying to fight off his attackers. Through it all, he kept the Grey slave master in sight. With Gordrall beside him they managed to get close. The Grey broke and ran. "Go," barked Gordrall, as Frank was closer to the Grey.

Frank leaped after the fleeing creature while Gordrall went head to head with the carrion fighters left behind. It was a lot easier going without the Grey controlling their movements. As the confusion gripped them, he managed to bring his weapon to bear with great effect. Soon he was alone with a pile of enemy bodies.

While Gordrall battled the carrion fighters, Frank pursued the Grey. He chased it down two different corridors before he caught it trying to escape through a hole in the wall leading to one of its own ships. "You miserable little bastard, I remember what you did to me." Frank grabbed it by the leg and hauled it back. "It's payback time, sucker." Frank wrapped the wires from the device the creature wore, around its small neck then yanked hard. The head rolled away on the floor while the body lay twitching at his feet.

Another Grey poked its head through the opening and Frank shot it. There was a small explosion then a hissing noise. "Atmo leak," shouted Gordrall as he appeared and yanked Frank back from the opening. "Grab the rail." Frank obeyed just as much of the air was sucked out of the corridor through the hole. Suddenly a panel slammed down, and the leak stopped. The body of the Grey had been sucked out as its small fighter ship had fallen from the side of the Mjolnir.

"Come, Frank, our area is clear. We have to get back to the turret now."

"There might be more..."

"Another warrior's task, Frank. We have to get back before Larthaness falls asleep."

"Right, you hurt bad?"

"A few scratches only, they probably won't even scar. You?"

"I'm good. Let's get back. You go first."

"Me go first? Why?"

"I'm lost."

"This way," laughed Gordrall, as he led the way.

"Are you two done playing about?" grunted Larthaness, as they reached the turret.

"Shift." Gordrall leaned over the old man's shoulder.

The shift was smooth and Gordrall was instantly in the chair. Larthaness was rubbing his shoulders and trying to clear his eyes. "That took you long enough. You get them all?"

"All from our section," said Frank.

"Next time I get to play."

"When was the last time you slept, Larthaness?"

"It's been a while all right."

"Is this battle going to last much longer?"

"Oh yes, you can count on that."

"Okay, so here's the deal. You settle down there in the corner and sleep. When you wake up one of us will sleep, and then the other."

"Ullr's balls man, I knew you had the makings of a warrior. Damn few since old Erikr Rhode himself would think of going to sleep on a battlefield unless they had been there before."

"Frank's got the right of it," said Gordrall, never once pausing in his rapid fire of the guns. "Thordik has drilled us in this very thing for a full turn of the great wheel. Get some rest."

"How you expect an old man to sleep in the company of two such savages, I don't know." Larthaness promptly curled up in the corner and closed his eyes.

Frank smiled at him then leaned over Gordrall's shoulder for a moment. Once he had the screen he patted the young man on the shoulder. "Shift," he said softly.

# In the Midst of My Enemies

"Any news?" asked Thomas Mooreland, as he approached the young woman bent intently over her screen.

"It doesn't look too good, sir," she replied. "The Nyman ships are slowing them down and taking a toll, but there are just too many. It is really hard to follow because they move so fast."

"Are they drawing closer?"

"Yes, sir, they are. There are a number of them just passing the asteroid belt right now. We know the Nymen have their small fighters hidden there. I just don't understand why they haven't attacked yet."

"They're waiting to spring the trap." General Drake joined them. "They'll let a few pass then spring when the main body draws into range."

"I don't understand why the other Nyman ships are just hanging there," sighed Thomas. "They should be in the thick of it by now."

"I am sure they have their reasons, Sir. As I recall they said they only have three warships, the rest are just big transports. Maybe the others aren't equipped for this sort of thing."

"I doubt that. Cal said it best, they're a warrior society. I'll bet they are armed, alright."

"They're leaving, sir."

"What? Who is leaving?"

"The nearest Nyman ships, sir. They've just pulled out, rising well above the battle."

"Son of a..."

HEATHER CAME POUNDING out of the cabin to find the bridge defending itself once again. "Intruders, all decks," rang out a voice she didn't recognize. Heather wasted no time in joining the fray. This time she knew who she wanted and where to find him, but she was too late. Freydis had already killed the Grey and thrown the rest into confusion. Together they laid about with great vigour, Freydis with hand weapons and Heather with her fists.

"I really must teach you how to use a weapon," sighed Freydis, as the last of the carrion fighters sank to the deck.

"Frank does the guns," replied Heather. "They scare me." This brought a great bellowing laugh from Kett.

"And you are starting to scare me, cousin," chuckled Freydis. "Kett!"

"I can get the shields back, Captain, but we need a pilot."

"Shift," said Freydis, as she easily slid into the pilot's chair. "Heather, the ship is yours."

"Just keep them off us until the shields are back," replied Heather. "Brek, Selian, report."

"Alive and kicking," came Brek's terse report.

"The Raven is whole and sound, Chieftain."

"Brek?"

"Shields are going down."

"Kett, can we lock shields and bring everybody up to max?"

"We can if the Raven has power," he replied from under his control panel. "It would make my life a lot easier."

"Freydis?"

"I like it, Heather. It'll be tight in this bloody mess, but I like it."

"Selian, lock shields with Brek then come for us," shouted Heather, as Freydis made a tight roll to shake off several carrion fighter ships that were trying to close in.

"On my way, Heather," came Selian's smooth reply.

Heather watched the display as the Raven fought her way to the beleaguered Falcon and locked their shields together. A short while later they reached the Mjolnir. They moved along side and locked shields. "I have the board," declared Freydis, as control of all three ships came to her control panel. A few high speed manoeuvres later and they had shaken off most of the pursuit.

"Shields back up," declared Kett, as he righted himself then moved to take the controls from Freydis.

"The ship is yours, cousin," said Heather.

"Brek, Selian, report."

"The Raven is clear of intruders and shields at max," replied Selian.

"Shields are up, but have to charge," replied Brek. "We've still got a few unwanted passengers, but we're thinning them out now. A few more moments and we'll be ready to go."

"Kett?"

"Shields back at max, Captain."

"Dammit, we're getting our heads pounded," sighed Freydis. "We can't keep this up much longer."

"Shields back at max," came Brek's voice. "We're ready, Freydis."

"All right, here we go again. At least we'll soon reach the asteroid belt. Once the fighters join the battle we won't have so many damned scavs to worry about. Stay locked until we reach the centre of the cluster then break. Ready? Attack!" Once again the three locked ships swept down on their quarry.

"You need to rest, Freydis," said Heather. "You're nearly dead on your feet."

"When I waken I'd better still have a ship under me."

"Freydis, these folks know how this is done, and they won't let me falter. Rest now, we need you at your best."

"The ship is yours, Heather." Freydis sighed as she let her shoulders slump. Without another word she retired to her cabin.

All the while, Kett had been keeping the ships moving through the enemy like a shark through a herd of seals. "Break," barked Heather, as they reached the thickest part of the herd. The three warships split apart, wreaking havoc on the enemy once again.

FRANK AND GORDRALL had fallen into a pattern of shifting that was becoming automatic. Frank had no idea how much time had passed, all he knew was the endless supply of enemy targets. It was shoot, then rest, then shoot again; a never ending dance. It reminded him of the time he and his best friend had tried to set a world record for a video game. They had nearly burned their eyes out and gave up after thirty-six hours without sleep.

Gordrall was at the guns when the klaxon sounded again. Larthaness leaped instantly to his feet, weapons at the ready. "Gord's got the guns, come on, Frank," he bellowed as he fled the turret.

"Intruders, all decks," bawled the intercom, and they didn't have far to go to find them. They went on the attack, but things did not go as expected. Frank's weapon seemed to be useless against these new creatures.

"They've got shields," said Larthaness, as two long daggers leaped to his hands. "We'll just have to do this the hard way."

He waded in and the battle was on. Frank found himself going hand to hand with a tall creature intent on choking the life from him. Horrified, he recognized his assailant as a human female, or at least she had been once. He hesitated slightly, and it nearly cost him his life. He did not see her pull a weapon, but she died on Larthaness' blades before she could use it.

"She's not kin anymore, Frank," growled the old warrior, as he battled a new opponent. "She may have been once, but no longer. She is now just a carrion eater."

"Right." Frank snarled as he found the dagger in his own belt and drew it forth. He leaped into the melee beside Larthaness and they fought on. Frank was losing badly to a nightmarish creature when he saw Larthaness break free and go for the Grey. It squawked and fled, but the old fellow was fleet of foot and easily ran it down and killed it. As the Grey fell, the creature grappling with Frank let go and turned away in confusion. Frank drove his dagger deep into its side and it looked at the object in confusion as it fell lifeless to the floor.

"Well, that's our section," grunted Larthaness, as he returned to where Frank stood gazing down at what was once a tall beautiful woman.

"There but for fortune," he said, as his companion reached him.

"Easy, Frank, I know what's going through your head right now, but you can't give in to it. Once the battle is over there will be time for this, but not now. Now we fight to survive, and the enemy is the enemy, no matter who or what they once were."

"Wise words, my friend." Frank nodded his head. "Sorry about that lapse, Larthaness; it won't happen again."

"Yes it will," he grunted as he started dragging the bodies towards an air lock. "It happens to the best of us, Frank. You just have to recognize it for what it is, and put it aside until the right time. Now, let's go see if Gordrall has fallen asleep yet."

They found him leaning back in the chair, rubbing the knots from his shoulders. "Clear them out?" he asked as they entered.

"We did," replied Larthaness. "We blocked?"

"Blocked tight," replied Gordrall, as he allowed his arms to fall back to his sides. "When they locked shields the Raven covered us completely. I guess we've got a breather. Thordik is missing all the fun. I'll bet she's chewed off her gun ports by now."

"Gord is young and still has some life in him, Frank, looks like it is your turn for some sleep."

"I heard that." Frank slid gratefully onto the floor where he curled up and closed his eyes with a deep sigh of fatigue.

"THEY'RE GETTING CLOSER, everybody awake now," came a soft voice over the com. Thordik was instantly awake and at the controls of her fighter. "Thordik, hold your people back. Let the more experienced warriors go in first," came that voice, causing a snarl to cross her perfect features. "Once battle is joined, you and your people stay on the perimeter and pick off as many as you can." She did not respond at all.

"Thordik, did you hear me?"

"I heard you. All Erikr-Dak fighters to me. We will move aside for the more experienced warriors." Nearly a hundred fighter ships moved in behind her small scout ship. "All right people, hear my words and be ready."

There were a lot of snickers and chuckles through those hundred fighters, for they knew Thordik far better than that. Only Lord Freydis herself or Heather Mak-Kay Hunter would be able to hold her back now.

Each small fighter was crammed full of well armed warriors who had been training under her watchful eye for several turns. They knew her well, and they knew what was coming.

As the battle drew closer, Thordik moved her ships aside from the rest of the hidden fighters. Her eyes never left the screen before her, and like a hunting tigress, she waited.

BACK IN THE THICK OF the fray it was not going well. As the madness drifted slowly towards the asteroid belt, the three Nyman ships were still taking a pounding. True, they were wreaking havoc with the enemy, and had destroyed several ships, but there were dozens more, and they were slowly wearing down the three predators.

The three ships were quite far apart when they heard the rasp of Brek's voice. "Shields down, intruders all decks," he gasped.

"Brek!"

"Selian, my beloved, flee this madness," he rasped. "The Falcon is lost. Goodbye my love. Remember me." There was no more except the hiss and crackle of the ship's com and Selian's scream.

What happened next was pure madness. The Raven banked tightly and ploughed through the thickest mass of enemy ships, trying desperately to reach the stricken Falcon. She was instantly swarmed and her shields went down under the barrage. With no shields, the scavs were all over her.

"Kalla, clear them away from her," barked Heather.

"Yes, Chieftain," replied a deep male voice. as the guns turned and the Mjolnir banked into the melee. Heather turned to see a short thick set man at the guns. "Forgive me, Chieftain, but Kalla had to rest. I am Bjornfell."

"I'm Heather, Bjornfell. Now, see what you can do to take some of the pressure off the Raven."

"I work as we speak," he grinned as he worked the big guns.

Turning back Heather could see the Falcon covered in Scavs now and floating free, completely out of control. The Falcon had fallen. They could hear Selian trying to raise Brek, but to no avail. The ship could no longer respond. It was some time before Selian realized a voice was calling to her, insisting that she listen.

"Selian, hear me, Selian, it's Heather, listen to me."

"Forgive me, Chieftain," Selian replied at last, "but I go now to join my beloved in the Summerland."

"Selian, snap out of it. If you die then who will avenge Brek? Who, Selian? If not you, then who? Get your buttocks out of there and repair your shields. You've got work to do."

Somehow that seemed to have the proper effect. "Forgive me, Heather, but it may be too late."

"Selian, you have a ship full of people, and a clan to protect, now get to it. There will be time to mourn later," Heather responded harshly. "Get your ship out of there."

"Yes, Chieftain," came the curt reply. The Raven began to twist and turn violently as she tried to shake off those that clung to her sides. Suddenly there was a barrage of cannon fire from another quarter, clearing away much of what was on the Raven. With a lurch she broke free, leaped away, and fled the field of battle.

"Where did that come from?"

"It was I, Corfort."

"Corfort, what are you doing here? I thought you were supposed to attack their transports?"

"Yes, Chieftain, We are on our way to do that right now. Since we were just passing by, we couldn't resist taking a few pot shots."

"And we are thrilled that you did, Corfort," said Heather. "Your timing was impeccable. Thank you."

"Always a pleasure to serve," he replied as his six ships sped away towards the incoming transports.

Turning back to the display, Heather gave the order to lock shields with the Raven. Once they were locked, Kett was able to keep the enemy off them until Selian's ship was once again ready for battle. The Raven's shields were nearly fully charged once again, and her decks cleared of intruders, when another voice was heard over the command intercom.

"Thordik, what in the name of Skadi's teats are you doing? You were ordered to stay back."

"Stay back behind that rock if you fear death, Korvald, I care not."

"I gave you an order," shouted the first voice.

"And you will die for that once this battle has been fought. Only Heather Mak-Kay-Hunter or Freydis herself commands me. Right now Erikr-Dak has another task."

"Thordik, what are you doing?" It was Freydis who had just returned to the bridge.

"Reclaiming the Falcon."

"Thordik, get out of there, the Falcon is lost," replied Freydis, as she took in the display before her.

"Forgive me, Lord Freydis, I am having difficulty hearing your message? Did you say to reclaim the Falcon?"

"Thordik," came Heather's voice, in a cold commanding tone that cut through all other chatter.

"Yes, my chieftain?" Thordik's voice held a small hint of contrition.

"Fight hard, my sister. Come back to me."

"I will, my chieftain, and I will bring you the gift of a ship."

Helplessly they watched as a stream of small fighters shot out from the asteroid belt, and straight through the thickest part of the enemy fleet like an arrow through the heart. "This is her destiny, Freydis," said Heather. "We couldn't stop her, you know that."

"I know, Heather. It is better that she go in with our blessings than our censure. Fight hard child, this is what you were born to do."

# The Falcon Rises

It was a scene of madness and mayhem, a fool's attempt to outwit his own fate. This was no place for old men or tired women. Only the lightning swift reflexes of a well rested youth, could hope to evade the sheer number of enemy fighters in the immediate area of the stricken ship. Screaming her challenge, Thordik led her people into the jaws of death.

Like a spear from the hand of a god, the tight formation of small fighters drove through the melee. Twisting and turning they went, all but ignoring the attempts to stop them. It should not have been possible for these fighters to retain formation, or to manoeuvre at that speed, for they were moving far too fast to fight. It was now that all the time spent training under Thordik's direction served the young clan best. They reached the Falcon having lost only a single ship.

Like circling wolves, the Raven and the Mjolnir swept back and forth trying to keep as many enemy attackers as possible off Thordik's small ships. It was almost impossible at this speed, but they tried. They did manage to keep the enemy wallowing in confusion.

As she reached the Falcon, Thordik began bawling orders. She and ten other ships swept through the Falcon's launch bay doors that were partially open. The rest of her fighters began swarming around the ship, knocking off as many Scavs as possible. It was an impossible task at that speed, but it was the speed that was keeping them alive. They did what they could, leaving the rest for Thordik and her crew.

Once inside, the Nyman warriors swiftly donned atmo suits, while the gunners laid down cover fire. Trying to avoid blowing the sides off the Falcon, the gunners nonetheless managed to keep the enemy pinned down until the fighters had suited up and were ready for combat. On Thordik's barked command the guns fell silent, and the doors opened to release the warriors. Like charging wolves they sprang from the small fighter ships and attacked.

The Falcon was full of carrion fighters, and a surprising number of Greys. They were trying to gain control of the superior ship themselves. "Kill the Greys," shouted Thordik, as she waded into the fray. Like a ravening bear, she moved through those who opposed her, leaving a trail of dead and dying behind her. Ten companions followed closely behind, the rest having spread out through the ship. Each group headed for a vital section, with orders to regain control and begin repairs.

"Hausenfoss here," came a voice in Thordik's ear. "Engineering recovered and secure. Life support back on to all decks, launch bay doors closed."

"Well done, Hausenfoss." Thordik snarled as she fought on, making her way towards the bridge several decks above. "I'm proud of you, my brother. See what you can do about getting her some shields."

"Already working on it."

"Kleese here, Great Hall recovered and secured."

"Helgess here, Healing Bay recovered and secured."

"Gudress here, we're pinned down at the armoury. There are just too many, and we're being pushed back."

"Hausenfoss, Kleese, Helgess, send three each to Gudress," commanded Thordik, as she fought on.

In truth, the going was a lot tougher than even Thordik had imagined. She, too, was getting bogged down, and it was making her angry. She had managed to get within two decks of the bridge, but no further. Thordik paused for only a moment then grinned.

"Hausenfoss, can you cut the gravity on decks two, three, and the bridge?"

"Just give me a moment, Thordik," came his thoughtful voice. "There, how's that?"

"Perfect." Thordik and everyone else free-floated from the floor. The enemy was suddenly thrown into confusion as the gravity disappeared. Before the Greys could right themselves and regain control, Thordik and her troops were on them. Several gave thanks as they fought, that Thordik had made them practice this as well.

Terrified by the attackers who could fight as well in zero gravity as they could under normal, the Greys in the corridor tried to flee. As the carrion fighters fell into confusion, it was easier for Thordik to get to the fleeing Greys. Leaving the carrion fighters to her comrades, Thordik swept down on her prey.

Through decks three and two they went until they reached the bridge. It was blocked by a solid wall of carrion fighters with heavy weapons.

Once again Thordik was pinned down and swearing as she hovered just around the corner from the one place she wanted to be, stripping off the atmo suit as she cursed. All crews had reported in now, and Hausenfoss had the shields back online.

"Leave the shields down for now," said Thordik. "I don't want to let the rest of them know we're back until we're ready to fight. Now, bring the gravity back to decks two and three and bring the bridge to twice normal gravity."

"With extreme pleasure," chuckled Hausenfoss as he worked the controls.

With a grunt of surprise Thordik fell to the floor and was nearly crushed. "Get up. We have work to do." She grunted as she levered herself back to her feet. Her troops were also upright once again, for they had practised this as well. The horrified Greys lying on the floor began to chitter in fear.

As they neared the door to the bridge, they realized that the wall of carrion fighters were all there were. The bridge itself was crawling with Greys, literally. The carrion fighters were trying to regain their feet in confusion, as there was no direction coming to their befogged minds, only fear. They tried to flee, but they were cut down.

Now came a scene of carnage as Thordik and her troops entered the bridge and began the work of slaughter. Each and every Grey was killed and piled near the door. Not until it was done did Thordik speak. "Bridge recovered. Hausenfoss, cut the damned gravity back to norm would you?" A moment later a great weight was lifted from her shoulders, and she sighed deeply in relief.

"Gurdess here Thordik, armoury recovered and secure."

"Shields at max," came Hausenfoss' voice, "weapons and helm control are back online."

"Alright people, we've got control back, now let's clear the scum out of the rest of her. Don't flush anything out just yet, I want them to think she's still a derelict. Colorthen, how are you doing out there?"

"We're getting our heads pounded, Thordik. We've lost six ships. We're holding our own for now, but they're starting to wear us down."

"Get inside, now. Hausenfoss, open the launch bay doors, let them in then throw up the shields. Once they're inside, switch engineering to the bridge and get your buttocks up here."

"Doors open," came his terse reply. The rest of Thordik's small fighters swept into the belly of the ship then the doors were slammed shut. While Hausenfoss raced to the bridge, Thordik herself took the helm, righting the ship. One of the others manned the guns and began firing a barrage right in front of their path.

"We're coming out," barked Thordik, as she opened up the engines.

It took some tight twists and turns, but she got free of the melee and shot into open space with half the remaining enemy fleet on her trail. The Mjolnir and the Raven swept in from the sides and cleared away some of her pursuit. Soon the three predators were circling the herd once again.

By now the battle was even more confusing than before, as the remaining few thousand small fighters had struck just as Thordik fled. The melee was buzzing with small fighters and the scav ships were fleeing back to the larger ships for protection. The three warships now had one less thing to worry about, but it was harder for the gunners now, as they had to avoid hitting their own small ships.

"Lord Freydis, I Thordik of Erikr-Dak claim this ship in the name of my clan, by right of salvage," came Thordik's voice over the intercom. "We're clearing away the debris now, and the Falcon will soon be ready for battle."

"Thordik, that was a might deed, my girl," replied Freydis admiringly. "You bring great honour to yourself and your clan."

"Thordik," came Selian's voice. "Are there any survivors?"

"None, Selian." There was true regret in Thordik's voice. "I found him on the bridge, buried under a pile of dead enemies. I do grieve with you, Selian, for I too have lost someone precious to me this day. We shall avenge him together, I promise you."

"I would ask a favour of you, Thordik."

"Name it, Selian my sister, and it shall be yours."

"Give that ship a new name, Thordik. Let the Falcon remain in the past with him, so he will always have a ship to fly."

"It shall be as you desire, Selian. Heather Mak-Kay Hunter, Chieftain of Clan Erikr-Dak, I bring a ship of war to your service. She is called the Valkyrie, and she is yours to command."

"Thordik my sister, I am so proud of you I could just split," said Heather. "Remain aboard the Valkyrie as captain, and place your ship at the service of Lord Freydis."

"It shall be as you require, my chieftain," replied Thordik, merriment clear in her voice.

"Thordik, just what kind of shape is the Valkyrie in?"

"She's taken a pounding alright, Freydis, and the damned Greys were trying to strip her out, but they didn't have time to do a lot of damage. She will need a serious refit once this is over, but she can fight. Give us a few more moments to clear off the last of the scavs, blow a few more carcasses out the air locks, and we're ready to go."

"Can you do that in flight?"

"We can."

"A dozen or more ships have gotten past us, Thordik. Don't waste any time fighting them, just catch up and scatter them around a bit. Hit them once just to keep them guessing, then get back here ready to fight."

"Be right back," sang Thordik, as the Valkyrie suddenly leaped away from the battle with alarming speed.

It took a span of time, but the Valkyrie caught her quarry about halfway between Earth and Mars. Like the goddess whose name she carried, the Valkyrie swept down on the prey at speed. She struck with all guns blazing and blasted right through the cluster of ships scattering them in all directions. A swift tight banking turn and she came around for a fast run at the larger fleet.

WHILE THORDIK WAS STILL in the asteroid belt, Corfort had led the transports against the bulk of the enemy transport ships. His ships were faster and better armed, but he was not a match for the nine remaining Raiders who were escorting them in. As he neared his quarry, all six of the Nyman ships fired their point singularity cannon. Three more Raiders and seven transports vanished instantly.

Like an axe streaking towards the block, the Nyman ships locked shields and drove in, creating havoc. Unlike a warship, a transport cannot manoeuvre so easily. It wasn't long before they were bogging down and the Raiders were all over them. Before Thordik gave her fateful order and led her troops into battle, Corfort had lost one and was near losing three more.

"Freydis, Corfort calling," came a voice over the com.

"Go ahead, Corfort," Heather replied, never taking her eyes from the display before her.

"We're getting our heads pounded, and it looks like you aren't doing a lot better. We've lost one and three are in trouble."

"We've lost the Falcon and it doesn't look good, Corfort. Get your ships out of there and make a run for it. Find some place to hide and rebuild the clans. May the gods smile on your journey."

"Farewell, Heather, Freydis, you will be remembered," came Corfort's voice, as they watched his remaining five ships make a break for it. Only four managed to escape. They shook off their attackers then went super-light speed, vanishing into the darkness of deep space.

"Farewell old friend," Freydis breathed softly as she reappeared on the bridge. There was a moment of silence as the reality of their situation began to sink in. This would be the last stand of the Nymen. And then Thordik attacked.

"THIS DOESN'T LOOK GOOD, sir," sighed the tired voice of the young woman at the screen.

"What now?" asked Thomas Mooreland.

"The Nymen have lost a warship and the other Nyman transport ships have fled into deep space. They just went past light speed. Over a dozen of the enemy ships have made it past the asteroid belt and are on their way here."

"Then the battle will soon begin on the ground. Warn the Icelanders."

"There's no need, sir. We've had a call from them telling us the same thing. They wished us luck."

"And we're going to need a lot of it," he sighed more to himself than to anyone in particular.

# The Battle Draws Nearer

Frank and his companions had worked the guns furiously as the Mjolnir tried to keep the scavs off Thordik and her crew. "She's not going to make it," breathed Frank.

"You don't know Thordik, Frank. She'll have the Falcon back in action before you know it."

"You could be right," grunted Larthaness, as he shifted into the gunner's seat. "If anyone can reclaim her in this mess, it will be Thordik."

They fell silent then, all eyes on the screen, and no one tried to sleep. They gave a ragged cheer, then held their breath as Thordik's troops disappeared inside the stricken ship. It was a long while of hard fighting before the big ship righted herself. Frank had taken the guns just as she fled the battle, half the enemy fleet in hot pursuit. "Well I'll be damned." He grinned as he began picking off some of those who pursued the Falcon.

"I told you so." Gordrall sighed deeply as he spoke, the relief easy to hear in his voice.

"It's alright, son." Larthaness gripped the young man shoulder, "She made it. We'll have a bit of rest now, while she tidies the Falcon up a bit."

"NYMAN WARSHIP INCOMING!" shouted the young woman at the screen. The president and the rest leaned forward to see what was happening. They were able to see as Thordik struck the near ships from behind and scattered them to the winds. There was a ragged cheer at that.

"They're regrouping, sir," said the voice softly. They all watched as the enemy ships drew together once again and continued their approach to Earth.

"Your best guess?"

"Maybe six hours at this speed sir, eight at the most."

"Then everybody should get some rest, for there will be little enough once the enemy arrives."

The folk in the bunker did try, but there was too much apprehension in the air, not to mention fear. All across the planet it was the same. The fearful hid in fear, the devout prayed, the pragmatic armed themselves and dug in as best they could. The president just kept pacing, trying to keep the despair at bay. He needed to be strong for his people.

"How close now?" asked Thomas Mooreland, as he continued his pacing.

"They're here, Sir, and the Nyman warships have abandoned the field."

All eyes returned to the screen just in time to see one of the ships explode. There was an exclamation as another ship was blasted apart and the rest fled. Another was shot down before they circled the planet out of sight of the big guns.

"What was that? What the hell was that? Somebody just shot down three of them. How the hell did they do that? Who was it?"

"It was the Icelanders, Sir. At least the weapons fire came from that direction. We know there are Nyman people there. They must have brought some heavy artillery with them."

"My god," sighed Thomas. "Now what is going on???"

"EMP, Sir. The enemy has used the pulse like we were warned. They've knocked out all out satellites and the space station is gone."

"Thank god we brought our people down in time."

"They'll be landing now, Sir," said General Drake. "I'm willing to bet they will steer pretty clear of Iceland until their reinforcements arrive. That means the rest of us are going to take the brunt of it."

"Coms back up," shouted a voice. "We've got audio only for now, but we're coming....shit. Coms down again, sir."

"Keep trying to get communications back up," sighed Thomas Mooreland, as his shoulders slumped. "All we can do now is wait, and hope that our people can do what they need to do. May god help us all."

FREYDIS WAS PACING like a caged tigress. It was not going well and the rest of the enemy fleet would soon catch them from behind. Even a slow bulky transport had weapons, and the more weapons trained on her, the poorer their chances of survival.

"Freydis, they're getting pretty close," said Kett.

"I know. Suggestions?"

"If we're going to survive we'd better do something fast."

"I have a suggestion," said Heather, as she returned to the bridge from Freydis' cabin.

"Let's hear it."

"We have always known we could not stop them all. Our deaths in a futile battle will not help our brothers on the planet. I suggest we get out of here and lick our wounds."

"You mean run away," came a snort of derision from the gun station.

"If you doubt my courage, friend," said Heather, in a cold deadly voice.

"Easy, Heather," soothed Freydis. "No one here doubts your courage. Continue with your idea."

"Our ships need time to effect repairs, and our crews need to rest. I suggest we get out of here, make what repairs we can, catch a

short sleep cycle, then come at them from behind. Right now we are
between a rock and a hard place. She who fights and runs away, lives
to fight another day."

This brought another snort from the gunner who was not known
to Heather. In a heartbeat she was at him, but Freydis got between
them. "Tell me, friend," snarled Heather, as she glared past Freydis'
shoulder, "just how much help can our glorious deaths be to my
people down on that planet?"

"Easy, Heather, easy," soothed Freydis. "I am of a similar mind
as you on this. Kaifeld means no harm, for if he did I would spill
his guts myself." The man blanched at that for he knew she meant it.
"Kaifeld, find yourself another assignment." Swiftly the man left the
bridge.

"Selian, Thordik."

"Here Freydis."

"Call in your fighters, lock shields and release the board, we're
getting out of here. We'll lick our wounds for a bit then come back
for more."

The two big warships closed in and locked shields, but it was
nearly too late. The bulk of the enemy fleet was in range and they
opened fire. Suddenly a ship dropped sub-light and opened fire on
the enemy from behind, causing them to scatter in confusion. With
her arms around her companions, the Mjolnir made good her escape.
They called, but there was no answer, the newcomer had gone
super-light once again.

"Corfort, you damned fool," muttered Freydis. "I owe you one."

WELL OUT PAST THE ORBIT of Uranus, the three battered
ships hung in space. The crews worked frantically to make repairs,
while the captains all met on the bridge of the Mjolnir. They watched
helplessly as the enemy fleet moved inexorably towards the planet

where their own people had taken refuge; the planet of their origin. Most of the remaining fighter ships had dropped back to keep between the Nymen and the planet. Suddenly another ship dropped sub-light. It swiftly located the Mjolnir and approached.

"How goes the battle?" asked a voice over the ship to ship com.

"Badly, Corfort, and thanks for the rescue," replied Freydis. "What the nine hellions of Porapix are you doing here anyway?"

"Minimal crew only, Freydis, bridge crew and gunners only. Everything else is on auto. I'll keep my distance, but..."

"Where are they, Corfort?"

"Nearest star, there's a likely planet there. The air isn't great, but they're already working on it."

"That's awfully close, old friend. I expected you to hide them better than that."

"Yes, well, they wouldn't go, Freydis. They're gutting the old North Wind. They're making a warship out of her. Tornan will be here with another battleship in about three sleep cycles, can you hold out that long?"

"Tell that damned fool to use the ship to defend the last of the clans."

"Tell him yourself when he gets here." Her reply was lost as he went super-light once again.

"Damned fools." Freydis sighed as she let her shoulders slump. "Ah well, there's nothing I can do about them now. We have other things to deal with. Selian, how's the Raven?"

"She's been better, Freydis, but with a few repairs she will have lots of life left in her."

"Thordik?"

"The Valkyrie is pretty battered, but she can still fight. We need a bit of time to patch the holes they put in her. The shields are back to max, the engines are at full, and all guns are working once again."

"Suggestions?"

"We could join Corfort," said a new voice.

"Drass, what the hell are you doing back here?"

"Reporting for duty, Captain."

"Are you fit?"

"I'll manage."

"So, you think we should run?"

"We must discuss all options."

"Very well, I won't run, and I won't abandon those people we left on that planet. Give me other options."

"I have one." That was Heather's voice.

"You want to rest up a bit then you want to take that savage clan of yours and land them on the planet. Am I right, Heather?"

"You're starting to scare me, cousin. That is indeed what I want to do."

"I don't like it, Heather, but I have to agree. We have little choice. Does anyone else have a better plan?"

"None," sighed Selian. "Heather has the right of it. We have to face them on the ground now, and she is the most familiar with both our allies and the terrain."

"Decided then," Freydis declared with a note of finality in her voice. "Heather, go to your ship..."

"You mean Thordik's ship..."

"If at all possible, a ship should have a clan chieftain at the helm, Heather," said Thordik. "Come back with me. Together we will make the Valkyrie the terror of the skies."

"Alright, my sister, lead on."

"You might want to take along a few more gunners," suggested Drass.

"Splendid idea, Master Drass," grinned Thordik. "Do you know where I might find such folk?"

"Turret thirty-seven, Thordik. You might want to take their partner along as well. I hear they've become quite an efficient team."

"Well then, gather them up and meet us in the great hall," said Freydis. "We'll all share a meal together before we return to battle."

"THERE'S TOO MANY INCOMING," said Larthaness, as he worked the controls. "We'd better get out of here before..." His voice trailed off as the three ships locked shields and fled the field of battle. "Screen's clear." He sighed as the Mjolnir shook off the pursuit. "It's time to lick our wounds. Let's set this turret back in order then find out what in the name of Thor's goat is going on."

Frank and Gordrall agreed and set to work. They were just finishing up when a voice came over the com. "Clean up and repair stations, then head for the Great Hall. All designated repair crews to the main hull."

"So, we get a bite to eat," grunted Larthaness. "If we're lucky we might even get a small sleep cycle as well."

"You three report to the Great Hall now," said a woman, as she poked her head in the door. "You've just been reassigned to the Valkyrie."

"The Valkyrie? Never heard of that ship. Where did she come from?"

"Thordik reclaimed the Falcon after she was downed, Larthaness. She has been renamed the Valkyrie. Heather Mak-Kay-Hunter herself is taking command. Good luck, and I wish I was going with you."

"Be glad you're not," sighed Frank. "If Heather is leaving the Mjolnir, that means that she is planning to go back to Earth. We're going to be the Marines on this one."

"You really think we're going planet side, Frank?" asked Gordrall, as all three left the turret and headed for their first full meal in days.

"I know Heather, she'll take the fight to the Greys alright."

"I now see why Thordik made her chieftain. They think alike."

"Now that's a sobering thought," chuckled Larthaness.

As they entered the hall, there was a squeal of delight as Heather flew into Frank's arms. "Are you alright, Frank?"

"I am now. This is my babysitter, Gordrall, and this is Larthaness."

"It is good to meet the new Chieftain of Erikr-Dak," grinned Larthaness, as he gripped her forearm in the warrior's grip. "Tell me you aren't really going to make me go down to the planet's surface."

"Actually, we have another plan for you," said Thordik, as they reached her in the food line. "The Valkyrie needs a chief gunner."

"Bridge gunner. It has been a while since I was on a bridge."

"I know that you were still at the guns when the Hagalaz was shot out from under you," said Thordik. "Brek often told me of how they had to drag you away."

"What do you say, warrior?" asked Heather, as she linked her arm through his. "Be our gunner?"

"Love to. Can I have Frank as second gun?"

"Thanks, Larthaness, but I can't be babysat anymore. I know the lay of the land down there better than anyone else up here. It is time for me to earn my keep."

"You earned your bread, Frank, never doubt that," grunted Larthaness. "I asked for you as second gunner because I think you're the most likely to keep the ship in the air. You've got a good eye, and damned fast hands."

"He's right, Frank," agreed Gordrall, who had Thordik draped over his shoulder. "By the time we were halfway in, you were the better gunner. The simulator is one thing, and the turret is another. I'd put you on the bridge any day."

"That's good enough for me," said Thordik, as she gave Gordrall another bone cracking squeeze then released him.

They reached the table where Freydis and the others were sitting. "We were just talking about you, Heather," smiled Selian.

"Oh?"

"It has been a long time since our people were taken from this place," said Freydis. "We didn't know what to expect. I will admit, I could have flattened Thordik when she made you chieftain. I had hoped to convince you to be the ambassador, but the last thing I wanted was an unknown on the bridge of my ship during a battle. I'm delighted to report that we all agree you're a fine chieftain, and that you bring great honour to your clan. I will trust my fleet to you any day."

"Thank you, cousin." Heather blushed shyly. "I did very little. Your people did everything. I just took up space."

"You took command of the whole damned fleet," said Kett. "I've served many captains, Heather, but, excluding Freydis, I have served none better than you. Had you been at Freydis' side at the Battle of Xtak Prime, we would have come out with a lot more ships than we did."

"Agreed," said Drass. "With the two of you, plus Selian, how can we lose?"

"Why thank you, Drass," smiled Selian. "You place me in high company."

"It is only just. I too grieve at the loss of so great a warrior and friend as Brek, Selian. There will come a time to mourn him."

"We will find the graves in Erikr's Fjord," said Thordik. "Brek will be laid to rest beside his ancestor. He has earned that much, and more."

"First we avenge him," replied Selian, "and then we will take the time to mourn him. For now we must rejoice in the arrival of the Valkyrie, with such an elite crew of fighters."

"Speaking of that," interjected Freydis, "we need to supply the Valkyrie with as many fighter ships, weapons, and warriors as she can carry. Drass, I hope you're well rested. I want a ship to come back to."

"Freydis?"

"I'm going down with you, Heather. You and Thordik take half the warriors and I will take the rest."

"Then I guess I'm in your party."

"Frank?"

"As much as I'd like to be Larthaness's back up, Freydis will need someone with some knowledge of Earth and her peoples. I'm no expert, but I can function, and I've been all over the world a few times."

"You're right, Frank," agreed Heather. "You guide Freydis, she will need you."

"Are you certain, Heather?"

"Behave yourself, cousin," laughed Heather. "You will need him, Freydis."

"Agreed. All right people, get some rest. One half sleep cycle, then we go back in."

# Into The Trenches

It wasn't going to be as easy as all that. While they made repairs and caught some much needed rest, the enemy was busy. The great transport ships were nearing their quarry, and the remaining fighter ships were taking up defensive stations just outside Earth's orbit. They were preparing for the Nyman attack should it ever come. Come it surely would.

While the remaining thirty or so fighters took up their defensive positions, the transport ships began landing. They were staying well out of range of the Icelander's guns, but Iceland wasn't of that much interest to them anyway. They wanted captives and they wanted plenty of them.

The monstrous ships landed near many of the major cities of the globe, the first fighter ships having already destroyed the defences. As soon as they landed, the huge doors opened and carrion fighters began fanning out through the population centres. All electricity would fail, internal combustion engines would fail, great lights would appear, and the harvest began, as millions of helpless people were herded into the transport ships for processing.

Some people were able to resist the mind control and tried to hide, or fought back. These folk had to face the carrion fighters, and few were successful, but some were. In the days that followed the first landings, those who managed to escape and fight back began to find each other and unite into a more cohesive resistance. Of those who resisted, they swiftly learned that stealth, rage, and primitive weapons were most effective.

—————— ✝✝ ✝✝✝ ——————

"WHAT THE HELL IS GOING on up there? Can somebody tell me what the hell is happening?"

"We've got some land lines back up, Mr. President. Intel is sketchy at best, but we are getting some information. The enemy has knocked out most electricity all over the globe. They are landing the big ships now. They seem to be landing near the major population centres. We've got three in North America, one in New York, one in LA, and one at Mexico City. I guess there aren't enough Canadians to bother with right now."

"Can we contact the Canadians? Can they help us?"

"Already done, sir," supplied General Drake. "Canadian troops are already on American soil. I have no idea how long it will take them to reach New York, or how effective they'll be, but they're coming. Apparently our own troops aren't having much success. All attempts to use missiles have failed. The entire Air Force has been destroyed, as has the Navy. The enemy has knocked out all transportation, and they have some sort of personal defences that render all modern weapons relatively ineffective.

"On a brighter note those mind control blockers work quite well, and that's helping some, but this is going to be hand to hand in the trenches."

"Heather MacKay was right, and I wish to god right now that I had ten thousand troops like she had with her that day."

"They'll get here, Tom," came the voice of Jim Brady. "We just have to hold out until they arrive."

"What makes you so damned sure, Jim?"

"I know Heather well," he replied with a hint of a smile. "She'll be back, and she'll bring friends. Tell me, General, what would you do if you were outnumbered twenty to one and about to be caught in a crossfire?"

"I'd withdraw, regroup, re-supply, and then attack using guerrilla tactics. So you think the Nymen will come back."

"They knew all along they couldn't stop them all, General. They gave it a hell of a shot, but now they have to lick their wounds a bit before they come down here."

"You're convinced they will return?"

"Tom, I know Heather well. She showed us what that girl could do, then she arranged for a demonstration that was up front and personal. She warned us we would have to fight them on the ground, but she took some of the arrogance out of us, and showed us what our allies were capable of at the same time. She'll be back."

"My god, I hope you're right."

SEVERAL HOURS LATER a young man's shout rang through the bunker. "Sir, sir, you have to hear this."

"What, what is it?"

"Listen, listen..."

There was a lot of hissing and crackling from the speaker, but an excited voice could be understood. "It's leaving, the ship is leaving," shouted the voice. Wild cheering could be heard from behind. "We nearly had them, but the bastards got away from us."

"Who is that? Can we talk to them?"

"I'll try, sir, just a moment. This is the office of the president of the United States here, who is on the line please?" He tried twice before he was understood.

"General Sanchez, speaking from Los Angeles. We have driven off the intruder."

"Sanchez, Thomas Mooreland here. How the hell did you manage this wonder?"

"It was the Vikings, sir."

"The Vikings?"

"Yes sir, one of our captains is a member of a Viking society, or something like that. When the standard weapons didn't work, he gathered some people he knew. I guess he already had them waiting or something.

"Anyway, they came charging over the hill on horseback with armour and lances and shit like that. God, it was something out of the Middle Ages, but it worked. One look at the horses and the enemy took flight. Between the horsemen and the guys on foot with swords, we drove them right back into the ship. A few more minutes and we would have captured the damned thing."

"Did the mind blockers work?"

"Most of them didn't have one. They say they're berserkers and the battle rage is all they needed. We lost quite a few, but we won the day."

"Well I'll be damned. Good work, Sanchez. Stay sharp."

"Vikings," grunted General Drake. "Jesus Christ, only in California."

"Don't knock it," chuckled Jim Brady. "At least it worked."

"Amen to that, brother, amen to that."

JUST AS FREYDIS AND group were leaving the great hall they heard some of the warriors talking. "I say we apply for adoption into Erikr-Dak. Ever since Heather Mak-Kay Hunter showed up and took over, that clan has risen fast. With Thordik backing her, Heather will be earl before this is finished." Several others chuckled at that.

Freydis did not even acknowledge that she had heard, but Heather did. She stepped up behind the speaker and gripped his shoulder tightly as she spoke. "Hear me clearly, friend, Erikr-Dak is not accepting any more adoptees at this time. Furthermore, as long as I'm chieftain of Erikr-Dak, the clan will honour its agreement with, and its commitment to Pull-Karr. Lord Freydis is Earl, and Erikr-Dak means to see she stays that way."

"Well spoken, my sister," rang out Thordik's voice. "Heather Mak-Kay Hunter is chieftain of Erikr-Dak, and I mean to see that she stays that way. Heather leads the clan and Freydis leads the Nyman folk. If there are any who object to this arrangement, they can discuss it with me at any time at all."

"Gods, I hate politics," muttered Heather, as she released the man's shoulder and joined Freydis at the door.

"Thank you for that vote of confidence, cousin," Freydis smiled, as they headed for the air lock where the Valkyrie was joined to the Mjolnir. "It was well done and I thank you for it, but this kind of talk is always rife in such times. The folk need to know a strong leader is at hand if the earl should fall. Morale is high now, as both you and Thordik are here as well as Selian. The prospects of at least one of us surviving are pretty good."

"Now that is an encouraging thought," grunted Larthaness.

As they reached the air lock Thordik turned to Gordrall and smiled. "We shall meet again, soon," she said softly. She gently squeezed his shoulder then started to turn away.

Gordrall grabbed her and spun her around quickly, a move that surely would have gotten anyone else killed immediately. "Don't do this to me, Thordik," he said, as he went nose to nose with her. "I'm not some pet Seekeet for you to keep on the shelf out of harms way. Make no mistake here, my heart is set for you if you want that, but if I'm to be your companion, I must prove myself worthy of you, in your eyes as well as my own."

"Is it so wrong for me to want to keep you safe, Gordie?" she asked, as she squeezed his shoulders gently.

"No, I guess not, but I meant what I said, Thordik. Look at the chieftain, her companion is a proven warrior, and here he is, going back into the battle beside her. Shouldn't you be following your sister's example?"

"Alright, Gordie, but if you get yourself killed I'll never speak to you again."

"I'll watch him for you, Thordik," grinned Frank.

"So who will watch out for you, my fine husband?"

"I will," said Gordrall. "Frank and I work well together."

"Please don't tell me I have to babysit the both of you," Freydis sighed elaborately. "If I let anything happen to either of you I may as well not come back."

They were laughing as the crossed to the Valkyrie, where they found Skeezix dragging his healing chamber along a corridor. "Skeezix, what in the name of Thor's goat are you doing?" asked Freydis.

"This one did as you asked, Lord Freydis," he replied, as he stopped to rest.

"Explain."

"Lord Freydis asked if this one could make a learning crystal to teach the language of Heather's people. This has been done. Lord Freydis asked if this one could make it work through the whole ship during sleep cycle. This one can. Since Skeezix's clan now has a ship of their own, and since this is the ship that will take all warriors to the surface, this one assumed that Lord Freydis would want this one to do this here. Was Skeezix wrong?"

"You are quite right, Skeezix. In the heat of battle, I forgot about our conversation. I am glad that you didn't. We'll help you, then you must hurry, for we have time for a half sleep cycle only."

She grabbed one end of the chamber while everybody else stepped in to help. "No, Lord Freydis," grunted Skeezix as he tried to steer the now moving chamber, "a full cycle is needed."

"Sorry, no time, Skeezix, no time."

"Heather, my chieftain, you must make her listen," urged Skeezix, much agitated now. "A full cycle is needed, or disaster will follow."

"Explain," said Freydis as she stopped pulling.

"If folk awaken too soon, they will have only a mix of languages in their minds," replied Skeezix. "It will be different for each, and no one will be able to understand anyone else. The crystal needs time to impart the knowledge, and then to organize it properly."

"So it is a full cycle or no language."

"Exactly."

"Blast it, that knowledge would be useful. Suggestions people?"

"Which language did you program, Skeezix?"

"The one you and Heather speak, Frank Hunter. There are very many more, but yours seems to be the most wide spread."

"You've done your homework all right," said Frank. "It looks like we get Europe, Freydis. Heather only has English, but I can manage in French, Italian, and Spanish as well."

"I suggest you take the time, Lord Freydis," Larthaness said. "Erikr-Dak is a young clan and can go without rest well enough, but not all your warriors are as young, and we have been in a long battle already."

"As badly as I hate to admit it, Freydis, I have to say he is right," sighed Heather. "A few extra hours rest might just be the difference between life and death on the planet. The battle on the ground won't be ended quickly. Perhaps we should rest now while we can."

"Agreed, Heather, agreed. I was almost afraid to suggest it myself, with all of you so eager to get back into the thick of it, but I do agree. So be it, a full sleep cycle then. We can put the ships on auto while our shields are locked, so we can all sleep before we return."

"Splendid idea," said another voice, as Hausenfoss appeared with three others. "Let us deal with the healing chamber, Lord Freydis. Thordik can show you to the booths."

"Are all the warriors on board now?"

"They're settling in nicely. We're a bit cramped in a few places, but some are sleeping in the small fighters, so it is all working out well."

"Alright then, Thordik, lead on, and don't sound that damned klaxon until after a full sleep cycle. I don't want to wake up wondering who I am."

Thordik chuckled as she spoke to Skeezix in his own language, then led the way to the cabins. Heather made a mental note to ask Thordik what she had said when time permitted.

# Once More into the Breech

Heather awakened slowly. Exhausted, she had fallen asleep in Frank's arms, and she was still there. She listened to his deep rhythmic breathing and smiled. For a moment she had forgotten where she was. Eventually, awareness and memory penetrated. She opened her eyes, wondering why the klaxon had not sounded. Right on cue...

Frank nearly jumped out of his skin as the loud offensive clanging rang out in the cabin. Together they leaped up and pulled on their clothes. A quick visit to the facilities and they left the cabin to find themselves in the meeting room right off the bridge. Another door and they found themselves on the bridge, where Thordik and Freydis were conferring with Larthaness.

"Are we ready, family?" asked Heather, as they entered.

"Ready and willing," replied Freydis, speaking in perfect English.

"I see the crystal worked, cousin."

"Yes, it did, and you can tell that little blue bugger that he didn't fool me for a minute with that tale of mixed languages."

Thordik burst out laughing at that. "I told him you weren't fooled."

"We did need the rest," sighed Freydis, reverting to her own language. "I knew that as well as he did, but he knew I wouldn't take it unless forced, so he provided me with the excuse."

"So you put up just enough resistance to make it look good?" asked Frank.

"Yes."

"I see now why you're the earl. A true leader also knows when to be led. I believe I'm in good hands."

"So what is the plan?" asked Heather.

"We make an attack run," said Freydis. "The Mjolnir and the Raven keep them busy while we slip through and drop the Valkyrie's fighters down over Iceland. Once we are on the surface we will all confer with the Icelanders and make further plans from there."

"That sounds good to me."

"Then let's be about the business. Drass, Selian, can you hear me?"

"You are heard, Freydis," replied Selian.

"Clearly, my chieftain," said Drass. "We are down to one gunner to a turret, Freydis. With all the fighters on the Valkyrie, the Mjolnir and the Raven can't fight a sustained battle up here. What is your plan?"

"We all make an attack run, Drass. They're guarding the planet now, but they're avoiding the area around Iceland. This is creating a hole in their defences. As we attack, the Mjolnir and the Raven draw their fire, while the Valkyrie drops her cargo over Iceland. Once we're on the surface, all three ships pull back."

"Pull back? Freydis?" That was Selian's voice.

"Just come at them enough to keep them busy, Selian, but you no longer have the numbers aboard to fight a pitched battle, as Drass has already pointed out. Your main purpose, once we are on the surface, is to make certain none escape."

"Now that sounds better. What say you, Drass my friend, shall we be the hunters this time?"

"It will be my great pleasure to accompany you, Selian. So, who is to be our companion? Who will be commanding the Valkyrie?"

"A good question," said Freydis. "Heather, who will be left in command of your ship?"

"Me? How should I know who... I know, I know, chieftain and all that. Thordik, who would you recommend?"

"When I was a small child, I heard of a great captain who lost his ship guarding the safe retreat of the whole fleet. He was still at the guns when the ship was blown out from under him. His second had to drag him away to the fighter and their eventual escape. That man is now our chief bridge gunner."

"Larthaness it is," said Heather. "Listen you," she said, as she turned to him, "I expect a ship to come back to once this is done."

"I did lose the last one," he grinned. "Are you certain about this?"

"Thordik, Frank, Freydis, Drass, Selian, your opinions please."

"You have made a wise choice, Heather," said Freydis. "Agreed," chimed in the rest.

"Larthaness, I won't compel you, but I do need you," said Heather. "No false modesty now, can you do it?"

"It has been a while, but of those you're leaving on board, I am the only one with experience. I'll do my best."

"I will ask no more of you, Larthaness, the bridge is yours. Shall we ready ourselves, family?"

"Agreed," said Freydis, as she turned on her heel and headed for the door. "Selian, I leave the fleet to you, make sure I get one back."

"Trust me, Freydis," purred Selian, but Freydis and companions were already gone from the bridge.

"They're headed for the launch bay, Selian."

"Then prepare."

"Battle stations," roared Larthaness, and several young people leaped to their stations as the klaxon sounded once again. "Bring her alongside the Raven."

"Yes, Captain," grinned Hausenfoss, for it was he who was at the helm.

"Are you my second?"

"I am, Captain. I'm Hausenfoss."

"Were you one of the number who reclaimed her?"

"I was."

"That was well done. How much can she take?"

"We're pretty battered, but we can fight," grinned the young warrior. "I would recommend a strike and fly approach, a sustained battle would be hard to survive in this shape, and with a reduced crew."

"Good advice, and I'll heed it. Ready, Selian."

"Ready," called Drass.

"Lock shields. Good, I have the board. We will split just as we reach them. Drass and I will try to draw them off while you drop your cargo, Larthaness."

"Understood, Chieftain."

"We go," declared Selian, and the three locked ships leaped away towards Earth and the enemy ships defending her.

This was to be a different battle now, and one more suited to the faster ships of the Nymen. Before they were trying to stop the massive tide headed for the planet, now they were the raiders, the wolves circling the herd of sheep.

"Well, we're on our way," sighed Freydis, as she felt the sudden acceleration of the ships. "It's been a long time since I went into battle without being on the bridge of the Mjolnir."

"There was no reason to come with us, Freydis," replied Heather, as they reached the far overcrowded launch bay. "No one expected you to do this."

"I will not send my people to a place I won't go myself, Heather. The battle is on the ground now, and that is the earl's rightful place."

"I understand. So Drass was left on the ship because he is not fully recovered?"

"Yes. I am quite pleased to have him there actually, but had he been fully recovered I could never have made him stay."

"And Selian?"

"The fleet needs a chieftain, and she is the only one left available. This is your planet, so you must lead your clan to battle, and I must lead the Nymen as I'm the earl. Life is what it is, and Selian knows that. She's one of the best, the fleet is in good hands."

"So, do we have any battle plans for when we arrive on the surface?"

"Frank said something about us getting Europe?"

"He's right. As badly as I hate to split us up, I think we should. If we are all clustered together it will be easier for them to attack us."

"I'm ready for any and all suggestions, Heather."

"I suggest I take my clan to North America, and you take the rest to Europe. By now there'll be resistance movements forming. We need to find them and support them."

"That's sound reasoning. We'll do it. Frank Hunter, will you be my advisor?"

"It will be an honour to serve so great and beautiful a chieftain," he grinned, drawing a slap on the arm from Heather, and a round of laughter from all those who were near.

"What else, Heather?"

"Well, does anyone know how many fighters each of those ships carries?"

"It is unlikely that each ship would have more than a thousand, with less than a hundred and fifty Greys. After all, they want as much space as possible for the captives."

"So we can split up our forces a bit. How many are we taking?"

"Six thousand. Alright, I suggest that once we split up we each connect with a resistance movement then choose an advisor from among them. We then assign that advisor to a group of six hundred warriors. That means that we can divide into ten battle groups."

"That makes perfect sense to me," said Heather, as she climbed into a small fighter ship with Freydis, Frank, Thordik, and Gordrall, who was already at the controls.

"All are ready, Thordik," he grinned, as they entered. Four more warriors followed. The ship was only built to carry a maximum of six so it was a bit crowded, but they made the best of it.

"Everyone try to sleep until you hear the klaxon," said Freydis, as she leaned back and closed her eyes. "There will be little enough once we hear that call."

LIKE AVENGING ANGELS the three Nyman ships swept down on the enemy guarding the planet. They split apart at the last second, but there were just too many defenders and so they had to withdraw. "What's happening up there," demanded Freydis, as she slapped at the button on her tunic.

"We're a little busy up here," came Larthaness's terse reply. Freydis sighed and relaxed back again. It was a long time before Larthaness came back on. "We're about to make a second run, but there is a lot of them, and they are concentrating on the weakest ship, me. We're going to find a hole through this time, so be ready. This will not be pretty, and you'll come out into a Varn's nest." With that he was gone again, and the ship suddenly accelerated.

This time the Raven and the Mjolnir shot in first with the Valkyrie close behind. As they split apart the Valkyrie dropped low at high speed. This manoeuvre nearly dropped her into the atmosphere. Still twisting and turning, she made her run for Iceland. "Ready doors," bawled Larthaness. Everyone grabbed on to something. "Launch!" he roared, as the ship made a twisting barrel roll just above Iceland, spewing out fighter ships as she went.

The thousand small ships spilled out of the huge ship's belly and into complete mayhem. There were enemy fighters, small scav ships, and weapons fire from both as well as return fire from the Nyman ships and the ground battery on Iceland. Ducking and dodging, they all ignored every enemy and shot straight for the ground as fast as they dared.

As soon as her cargo was launched the Valkyrie leaped away and shot straight out past Mars before she swung around and came back in, all guns blazing. She struck again then withdrew with the Raven and the Mjolnir. "Well, they're on the ground now," said Larthaness, as he spoke over the ship to ship. "Now what?"

"Now we keep them entertained, but no more," replied Selian. "Anything that tries to leave the surface is our main target. I don't really care if one or two raiders escape, but I swear, not one transport will carry away a captive."

"Agreed," came Drass's voice. "Better dead than a slave to the Greys."

"GREETINGS, HEATHER," called the President of Iceland as he hurried towards the small ships settling down on the tarmac of Reykjavik's airport.

"Hello, Ragnar, how goes the battle?"

"Badly, I fear," he replied, as he reached them. "So, you must be Lord Freydis," he smiled as he extended his hand to her.

"Freydis, please," she replied, as she seized his forearm in the warrior's greeting. "You are Ragnar."

"Yes, I am he, and may I say what a thrill it is to meet you? Especially since you have so many fine fighters with you."

"You may indeed, Ragnar. Now, you say it goes badly. Tell me."

"We on Iceland are fine so far, Lord Freydis, but not so the rest of the world."

"Are we having no success at all?" asked Heather.

"Little," he sighed. "Some Americans did manage to drive off a ship using horse cavalry and footmen with swords, but the enemy returned with air support and levelled the city. The horse troops and foot soldiers escaped into the hills, but the city is destroyed. Over half of the cities in North America have been emptied out, Europe the same. Apparently each of those ships will hold millions of captives."

"They will," said Freydis. "Frank."

"Here, Freydis."

"You're the guide now, lead us to Europe. All assigned fighters and Erikr-Dak report to your chieftain. Let's go, Frank."

Freydis leaped back aboard the small fighter, and Frank gave Heather a peck on the cheek as he followed. "Soon, my love," he called, as he leaped aboard the ship and the door closed behind him.

"Soon," she breathed, as the small ship leaped into the air, followed by five hundred more.

"She is a woman of few words," said Ragnar.

"Freydis doesn't waste a lot of time when there is work to be done," agreed Heather. "Okay, I guess we should make ourselves scarce. If we stick around it will only make you a more enticing target. Would you call the President of the United States and tell him I am on my way?"

"Of course, Heather, and he will be thrilled to hear it."

Heather turned to see Thordik standing beside a different fighter ship. She waved Heather on then stepped aboard. As soon as Heather was aboard, the small ship leaped skywards followed by the rest of the fighter craft.

"Are we returning to the same place, Heather?" asked Thordik, who was now at the controls.

"No, but go in that general direction. As soon as we sight land, start scanning for the enemy ships."

"Already scanning, my chieftain," sang a cheerful voice. Heather turned to see Clerisa smiling at her.

"Let me know when you find one. Thordik, don't attack instantly, just find a place where we can observe for a moment."

"Observe?"

"I don't want to go in blind, Thordik. They already know we're here, and they may try to set a trap for us. Besides, we need to find those who are resisting."

"As you desire, my chieftain," Thordik replied softly, "so shall it be."

"MR. PRESIDENT, MR. President, Iceland is on the line for you."

"What? Here, give me that phone. Hello? Ragnar?"

"Thomas, I wanted to give you some good news."

"Good news is rare these days, Ragnar. Your call is most welcome."

"I have called to tell you that an old friend is about to visit you, and she has brought more friends."

"What are you talking about, Ragnar?"

"Heather MacKay-Hunter has landed with thousands of seasoned warriors, Thomas. They are headed your way. I thought you might want to know."

"Ragnar, that is the best news I have had since I was elected. Thank you, my friend."

"You are welcome, Thomas. I must now return to duty. Be well."

"Be well, Ragnar," Thomas Mooreland sighed, as he passed the phone receiver back to the young woman who hung it back up.

"Sir?" asked General Drake.

"She's here."

"She?"

"Heather MacKay, and she's brought thousands of those warriors of hers with her."

"I told you so," said Jim Brady. "I told you she'd come back."

# Down and Dirty

It didn't take Thordik long to find a ship. As soon as they reached the shores of North America a ship rose slowly into the sky. "Go to ground, now," commanded Heather, and every small ship sank swiftly to the ground behind a mountain.

"Heather?"

"I didn't expect to find them this far north. The lands to the south are much more populous. This one must be cleaning out the smaller cities up here. If I'm right, that was Sidney Nova Scotia."

"What are your commands, my chieftain?"

"Easy, Thordik my sister, easy. If we shoot them down right now we kill everyone on board. Let's see where they are going, and hit them once they are on the ground with the doors open. The arrogant little bastards, they didn't even notice that we're here."

"They're heading off, Heather," said Clerisa.

"Follow them, but stay close to the ground. I don't want them to spot us just yet."

Slowly, ponderously, the gigantic ship made its way south. Either the Greys didn't know that they were being followed, or they didn't care. "I don't understand why they haven't fired on us," mused Clerisa.

"They must think we are surface vehicles, and they know those can't harm them," said Thordik. "They will soon learn the error of that line of reasoning."

"They're settling down again," declared Clerisa.

"Halifax. This is a much larger city. Land on that hill for a moment, I want to see this firsthand."

"As you desire, my sister, so shall it be," replied Thordik as she set the small ship on the ground. All the rest followed suit.

The doors opened and Heather stepped out to watch. As the huge doors of the giant ship opened a bright light shone from within. A horde of fighters on small speeders came out of the light followed by several scav fighters. The sudden roar of jet engines split the air as the Air Force attacked, but the jets were no match for the scavs and had to retreat. The scavs followed and destroyed every one.

On the ground the military attacked with tanks and artillery, but all to no avail for the scavs quickly stopped the heavy vehicles. As the ground troops closed in they opened fire with smaller weapons, but had similar results. "Heather..."

"Patience, Thordik, patience. A moment more..." Silently they watched as the ground troops fell back, then they saw the ruse. As the troops fell back, thousands of fighters with hand weapons attacked from hiding. They could have no effect on the scavs, but they were having a bit of success against the carrion fighters on the ground.

The problem was that they had no personal shields, or mind control shields, so the Greys slowed them down and the carrion fighters used their hand weapons to great effect. Still they were putting up a good fight.

Once the surprise had been sprung the military troops dropped their rifles and whipped out long knives then charged back in. Again they seemed to have an effect, but it would not be enough.

"Heather..."

"Now. Thordik, knock down those scavs, then get us through those doors. I don't want that ship getting off the ground again."

They were barely back on the ship when it leaped skyward. The scav fighters scattered as the Nyman ships attacked, but it did them little good. Half the fighter ships attacked the scavs while a number of the rest flew straight through the giant doors, guns blazing.

The light was strong inside, and even with the blockers on full, Heather still felt the resolve draining from her. "Bastards," she swore as she slapped at the button on her tunic. "Rage, my kinsfolk, rage is your best weapon now. Let's show them what the children of Erik Rhode are made of."

With screams of challenge the Nymen poured into the belly of the ship, slaughtering all before them. Even as they fought they felt the great ship begin to rise. "The bridge, Thordik," bawled Heather. "Find the damned bridge."

Like an avenging Valkyrie, Thordik raged through the ship. It was well into the air when she fought her way to the control centre, but she found it. Heather caught up to her a moment later. They waded into the carrion fighters side by side, and gained the bridge. Fortunately, most of the carrion fighters had been outside the ship when they attacked so the resistance wasn't as strong as it could have been.

Thordik suddenly burst past the fighters in her way and gained the control centre. With screams of pure rage and madness she attacked, with Heather close behind. While Heather fought anything close enough to kill, Thordik went for anything that was near a control panel. The great ship began to wobble, then crashed back to the ground, not so very far from its first landing site. Once the control room was cleared of Greys, they began to hunt through the rest of the ship for more. There were some, but not many. As each Grey fell, the mind control over the carrion Fighters lessened, throwing them into complete confusion.

Back on the ground, the Nymen had brought down all the scav ships except one which had fled. With the enemy thrown into confusion, the human warriors renewed their attack and were having much more success. Suddenly the Nyman ships landed, spilling out thousands of warriors into the field. With these new reinforcements, the humans soon had the last of the carrion fighters on the run.

"Kill them all," bawled one of the newcomers in perfect English. "Leave none alive, for they would do worse to you." The humans needed no further encouragement as they began to hunt down and slaughter any enemy fighters who tried to run from the field. The task was made easier once the Greys lost control and the creatures began to stumble about in confusion.

A wild cheer rang out as the ship crashed back to the ground and the big doors were blasted open from the inside. Dozens of Nyman fighter ships poured from that gaping wound and settled to the ground. A steady stream of dazed and confused people began to emerge from the belly of the ship with some of the Nyman warriors guiding them.

A human soldier asked who was in charge and was directed to Heather who stood leaning against Thordik. She looked exhausted and was spattered from head to toe with gore. "Are you the commander here?" he asked politely.

"I am," replied Heather as she straightened up. "Are you in charge of the human forces?"

"Yes. Major Billy Strong, at your service, ma'am."

"Heather MacKay-Hunter, it's a pleasure to meet you, Billy."

"Believe me, Heather, the pleasure is all mine," he grinned. "We were getting our asses kicked until you showed up."

"You were doing fine, Major," said Thordik. "It is no easy task to fight these things without the blockers."

"You mean the mind control blockers?"

"Yes, weren't you able to construct some? We sent the instructions."

"I know, Ma'am, however, there was only time to build a few, and they were held back to protect the political leaders and generals. We poor grunts have to make do with what we can."

"I can see that the phrase, 'military intelligence' is still an oxymoron," sighed Heather.

"I've heard that before. Ma'am, this is truly your victory here. What do you want us to do?"

"See what you can do for those captives, see to the wounded, Billy," replied Heather. "Make certain there are no more enemies left alive. Clerisa, bring this man some of those personal blockers that we brought." Clerisa hurried away to fetch the blockers. "We brought extra blockers with us, Billy. We'll give you a few. Here's another hint. If you face those things again, shoot at their feet. Those damned personal shields are weakest where they touch the ground. Also, every blasted one of them is controlled by one of those little grey bastards. Kill the Grey and the fighters fall into confusion."

"Now that is useful intel, Ma'am, and I'll pass that along."

"I hate to leave so soon, Billy, but I have another appointment. Thordik, how are we doing?"

"The ship is down, and the opposition destroyed."

"Okay then, mount up folks, we have more work to do. Billy, as soon as you get all the captives off that ship, bring up the artillery and blow it to Mars."

"Yes, ma'am."

"I mean it, Billy. I know you probably have orders to capture one to study, but I'm telling you, that is a seriously bad idea. Blow it up. Once this is over we'll share some technology, but if I come back and find that damned thing's still here..."

He just grinned as he took the microphone from the clip on his shoulder. "Captain Harrington, train your guns on that ship. As soon as I sound the all-clear, blow it to hell and back."

"Yes, sir," came the voice over the radio. The Major waved as the small ships rose into the air and streaked away to the south.

———

FRANK HAD TEARS IN his eyes as they passed over what was left of Ireland. It had been completely decimated. A few survivors could be seen foraging through the rubble, but they fled at first sight of the small ships. Britain was much the same. London itself was just a big pile of rubble, nothing more. "Frank?"

"Sorry, Freydis," he sighed as he got a grip on his emotions. "It's just that there were millions of people down there, and I knew some of them very well. There will be a reckoning for this. I swear it."

"As do I, Frank Hunter. Gordrall, find me an enemy ship to destroy."

"Yes, ma'am," grinned Gordrall, as he guided the small craft over the English channel, barely feet above the waves. France had been destroyed as well, but they found their prey in the Netherlands.

"Ship ahead," declared Gordrall, as they topped a low rise, nearly crashing into the partially hidden ship.

The great doors were open and thousands of captives were being herded in. "Karall, get the scavs," shouted Freydis. "The rest follow. Inside, Gordrall, now."

Like an arrow through the heart, the small ships shot through the open doors. The great bay was suddenly filled with weapons fire and screaming captives. The Nymen poured from their crafts and carried the battle to the enemy. Freydis had fought this foe before, and she knew just where she wanted to be.

Frank and Gordrall were having trouble keeping up with her, but they managed. Suddenly a glancing blow tore the mind control blocker from her tunic, and Freydis paused in confusion. What was going on? She had something important to do, what was it?

Remember, she had to remember, but it was too much trouble. Just let the masters deal with it. She would just wait here until one of them came to get her. A sudden pain in her side caught her attention. As she turned slowly a hand slapped her hard across the face. Rage leaped to her eyes and she lashed out at her attacker, knocking Frank against a wall.

"What in the nine hells are you doing?" she snarled, as her mind suddenly cleared.

"Has anyone ever told you that you are beautiful when you're angry," he grinned as he picked himself up again. "You lost your blocker, Freydis, you have to use the rage now. Get mad, girl, and stay that way."

"Follow," she snarled, as she waded into the enemy, "and try to keep up." Both Gordrall and Frank were grinning as they fought their way to her side. A few moments later they reached the control centre. Like a bear in a sheep pen, Freydis attacked the large group of Greys cowering there. Her fighters streamed in behind her and it was soon over. The ship had not even gotten off the ground.

Outside, the Nymen were mopping up the remains of the carrion fighters, with the help of a large group of humans. As Freydis emerged from the ship, the battle outside was about over and the human/Nyman allies were facing each other in silent mistrust. "Alright, Frank, talk to these people."

"Yes, ma'am." Frank grinned as he approached the nearest human, a tall blonde fellow holding a long sword with blood and gore dripping from the blade. "Hey there, do you speak English?"

"Ya," he grinned, "I speak English."

"You fool," laughed Freydis as she hit Frank on the shoulder knocking him sideways, "I could have done that myself. All right, my friend, who is in command here?"

"By all appearances, you are in charge, ma'am," smiled the tall fellow. "May I say that your green skin suit is extremely attractive? Does it act as armour as well?"

"My skin suit?"

"Allow me," said Frank. "My good man, this is Lord Freydis, chieftain of Pull-Karr clan, and Earl of all Nyman folk. That is not a suit of armour, sir. It is her scales."

"Scales? My god, they are so beautiful." He smiled as he reached out his hand. "I am deeply honoured to meet you, my lord. I am Peter Van De Velde." As she reached to shake his hand he brought her fingers to his lips. "Exquisite," he smiled as he stroked the back of her hand lightly before allowing it to fall from his grasp.

"Are you the leader of these people?" asked Freydis, a knowing smile playing at her lips.

"I am, Lady. We are the resistance, such as it is. This is our third encounter with the enemy, and we are getting better, but we are a long way from successful."

"You need blockers to shut off the mind control, Peter. Gordrall, give Peter as many as you can, weapons as well. Leave him two ships and a dozen warriors also. The warriors will help you learn how to defeat this enemy, Peter."

"We are all in your debt, Great Lady."

"I shall return to this place one day, Peter Van De Velde," she smiled wickedly, as she turned to go. "You had better still be here when I do, for I shall want another ration of that delightful charm when I arrive."

"I will practice daily until your return, my Lady." He grinned as she turned to gather her troops and take to the ships once again. "What an exquisite woman," he sighed as the small ships leaped skywards again.

"My chieftain has no equal, that is true," said a Nyman warrior who was standing close enough to hear. "I'm Karleness of Pull-Karr. I will now show you the method of using these weapons, as well as the mind blockers. Once you've gained some proficiency we will go hunting."

"Need we wait?"

"We do," replied the tall Nyman. "Freydis would have my hide if I let you go into battle unprepared. Beware, my friend, Lord Freydis is not a woman to trifle with."

"I will bear that in mind, my friend, for I sense that it is good advice."

On the ship Frank felt Freydis' eyes on him. "What?"

"Thank you, Frank Hunter, that was well done, and it surely saved my life." Frank just smiled shyly. "Frank."

"Yes, Freydis?"

"Don't ever do that again." Frank was still chuckling when they found the next ship. This one escaped into space before they could bring it down.

# The War Drags On

"Incoming!" shouted a female voice, a shout which brought Thomas Mooreland running.

"Where? What? Is it the Nymen?"

"Negative, sir. It's the enemy. They've just landed in Washington."

"Drake, Drake? Where the hell is General Drake?"

"He's gone topside, sir," supplied another voice.

"Are we locked down?"

"We are, sir. If the enemy wants us they will have to dig us out."

"I doubt they give a damn about us at all," said the voice of Jim Brady.

"You're probably right there, Jim. All they want is captives. Christ, they've cleaned out over half the Earth's population and they're still at it."

"It gets worse, sir," sighed a male voice.

"Worse? How the hell could it be worse?"

"After they clean out an area, they destroy it utterly," replied the young officer. "We got intel while you were resting. I didn't think it was worth waking you for."

"I guess you're right about that, there's not a damn thing I can do about it. What's the situation topside?"

"I have General Drake for you, sir."

"Harvey, what is your status?"

"We're getting our asses kicked, Tom," crackled the voice that came over the intercom. "The mind control blockers are working pretty well, but we still don't have effective weapons. The Air Force got clobbered and so did the heavy ground forces. The Viking style attack seems to be best, but they have personal shielding of some sort, so it is hard to get past their hand weapons to close with them. The bullet proof vests are helping, but this is not going well...Yeee Hawww!"

"Harvey, what the hell happened?"

"The cavalry is here, Tom. Hundreds of Nyman fighter craft just appeared out of nowhere and went at them. My god, they're inside the ship tearing it apart right now."

The battle raged long and hard for hours. Twice the ship tried to rise, but was forced down again. Inside, the Nymen found a new enemy tactic that they did not like at all. The carrion raiders were using human captives as shields, and the Greys were hiding behind that. It was extremely slow going and the Nymen were starting to get pushed back.

━━━━━━╫╫╲╲╞╪━━━━━━

SLOWLY THE NYMEN GAVE ground away from the control centre. As they took shelter around the corner of a passageway Thordik turned and hugged Heather tightly to her. "My beloved sister," she whispered, "as badly as it grieves us both, you know what must be done. We cannot allow the ship to rise. We must stop them."

"I know," replied Heather, as she returned the embrace then stepped back, "I know." She slapped at the pin on her tunic then spoke. Tears streamed down her face, and her voice choked, as she gave the fateful order. "This is Heather. Hear me, my people. Destroy all in your path, the Greys must be killed at any cost. Let nothing dissuade you in your resolve."

With that order ringing in their ears, the Nymen attacked again. This time they cut down the human shields as well as those who hid behind them. The tide of battle turned swiftly then, and soon Thordik was on the bridge, terrible in her battle fury.

Heather was at her side and even more savage. Her hatred for the Greys was only increased by what she had been forced to do. In short order the carrion fighters were milling around in confusion, and had become easy prey.

Outside the ship, all was frenzied hand to hand combat. As the Greys lost control of their slave fighters, the humans redoubled their attack, led by the Nyman warriors. It took some time, but as the prison bays of the great ship began to empty, the Nymen and humans were starting to mop up through the streets where many of the confused carrion fighters had fled. As the maze of streets became too confusing for the Nymen they returned to their ships, leaving the remaining carrion fighters to the humans.

General Drake swallowed hard as he approached the open doors of the gigantic alien space vessel. There was a steady flow of dazed and confused human captives streaming out into the square now. He stood gazing in amazement as they stumbled past him. "Are you in command here?" demanded a tall, young Nyman, as he confronted the general.

"I am."

"Then start moving. Organize your people to help these captives that we have released. Our chieftain will want to see that in motion when she emerges from the ship." With that he stalked away.

Bristling at the tone with which the youth had spoken, the general was nonetheless shocked into motion. He called an officer to him and soon the effort to organize the refugees was put in action. Most were South American and could speak no English, that was hindering things a bit. He was reporting to the president when Heather and Thordik emerged from the ship.

"Ambassador, you are a welcome sight indeed," he declared as he hurried towards her. He skidded to a halt as he saw the look in her eyes. "I'll take you straight to the president."

Turning to lead the way, he began barking orders for the bunker to be relieved from lockdown. Heather followed behind as he led her to a vehicle which took them to the bunker. It was a bit of a ride, and neither Heather nor Thordik spoke, but remained lost in their own thoughts. Once they arrived, a swift ride on an elevator brought them into the war room so far below the surface. "Ambassador Hunter," smiled the president as he advanced to greet her. He too stopped at the look in her eyes.

"I need to contact my people in Europe, and I don't want to put a ship high enough in the air to do it. It would be too easy a target. Can you use land lines from here? Are they working?"

"We can connect you with Iceland, but I don't know if we can raise anyone in Europe," he replied as he stepped aside and indicated that she should enter further into the room.

"Heather," exclaimed a voice and she turned to catch Laura Brady in her arms. Jim swiftly joined the hug.

"It is so very good to see you both safe and sound," she breathed, as she hugged them tightly, tears streaming down her face. "Please forgive me, I'm somewhat of a mess. Come, I want to introduce you to someone. This is Thordik, my sister from across the stars. Thordik, this is Laura and Jim Brady. They are very dear friends of mine."

"It is a great pleasure to meet the friends of my sister," smiled Thordik, pouring on the charm. The radiance of her smile lifted the spirits of everyone in the room, and they suddenly forgot that she was covered in the blood and gore of both enemy and human alike.

"I want to thank you for the timely rescue, Mrs. Hunter," said the president smoothly.

"Save it for later, Mr. President," sighed Heather, as she turned back to him. Her eyes had gone cold once again. "We're not out of the woods yet."

"I have Iceland for you, ma'am," said a young woman in uniform as she indicated the big screen on the wall.

"Ragnar here, Heather, how can I help?" It was voice only, but it was clear.

"I need to talk to Freydis. Can you make a connection?"

"I believe we can," he replied as his face suddenly appeared on the large screen. "Just one moment. Alright now, go ahead, Heather."

"Heather here, can you hear me, Freydis?" Her voice was now coming over the room speakers as well.

"I am somewhat busy at the moment, Heather," came the terse reply amid the hiss and rattle of weapons fire.

"Freydis, there is something you should know..."

"The enemy is using the captives as shields, and you have to cut your way through your own people to reach the enemy?"

"Yes. I see that things are the same with you."

"Yes. Heather, forget our previous battle plan, keep your people together."

"Already done. Fight hard, Freydis."

"Fight hard, cousin," came the reply then the connection was broken.

"And so to war," sighed Heather, as the line went dead. "Please forgive my manners folks. This one is my sister, Thordik. Thordik, this is the President of the United States of America, commander-in-chief of my people."

"A pleasure..." started Thomas Mooreland, but Thordik's snort of disgust cut him off.

"This? No, Heather, my sister, that woman you just spoke with is the commander-in-chief of your people. She leads them in battle, as a commander should. This one hides here in the ground like an aging Arcanian Sleen while his people fight and die on the surface above." She stepped aside and Thomas cringed under her baleful gaze.

"Look at this woman," she said, as she indicated Heather. "See her tunic spattered with the blood of her enemies. See the pain in her eyes at what she has had to do to defend you all. This is a leader worth following. That is not."

"Easy, Thordik."

"No, Heather, I will not. This snivelling coward hides here in the ground while his entire species fights for its very existence. It disgusts me. It is unworthy."

Thordik's rant was suddenly interrupted as Heather's shoulder pin began to speak. "Heather, we have incoming."

"What? Where? How many?"

"Two carrion ships from space and another transport."

"Get out of there. Everyone mount up and scatter in all directions. I'll contact you soon." She spun towards the elevator doors. "Quick, get me back to the surface," she barked at the young soldier standing guard there.

"As I said," grinned Thordik, as she entered the elevator, "a commander worth following."

Thordik was on the coms even as the elevator rose swiftly to the surface. As they emerged into the sunlight, a fighter ship was waiting for them. Clerisa was at the controls and she gave way to Thordik instantly. "Is it ready?" asked Heather.

"Ready, Heather," grinned Helgess, as she rubbed her thumb on the button of a remote device.

"Not yet," said Heather. "Thordik, can you get us close?"

"I can and I will," grinned Thordik, as she sent the ship into the air at an alarming rate. Soon she was twisting and turning as she dodged scav fighters as well as fire from the big ships. "We certainly got their attention," she muttered, as she swept out of the way of another burst of enemy fire.

"So it would seem. Yes, they're all bunched up. Are we safe at this distance?"

"Only just."

"Do it, Helgess." Helgess punched the button just as Thordik made a tight turn and zoomed away from the blast. The first ship suddenly exploded, taking one of the carrion fighter ships with it, and badly crippling the second transport. The third Raider fled.

"Regroup," barked Heather and Thordik turned back towards the scene of destruction. From all directions the Nymen fighter ships swept back into Washington. The square was gone as well as a few square blocks around it. There were a number of scav ships about, as well as the damaged transport. Once again the Nymen attacked. The day passed and the dawn was near before the mopping up began. It was left to the humans while Heather sought a place of refuge for her people to rest.

"SHIPS RISING," DECLARED the man at the sensors.

"Withdraw," commanded Selian. The three Nyman warships pulled away and retreated back to Mars then regrouped. "I see you," said Selian, as she gazed at the display before her. "You can try to run, but you cannot hide."

"I make it four transports," came Drass's voice.

"As do I," agreed Larthaness.

"And I as well. Drass, make a wide circle about the planet. Let's make sure they do not have more on the far side away from our view."

"Ships going down," announced the warrior at the sensors.

"So I see. It appears that the earl has attracted their attention. This makes our task a bit easier. Larthaness, are you still battle ready?"

"Valkyrie ready."

"As soon as Drass returns we shall attack. The Raven and Mjolnir will try to pull away the guards while your task is to knock down one of those transports."

"Understood, Chieftain." Larthaness sighed deeply as he turned from the display to face his bridge crew. "People, I have to say, I have never fought beside finer warriors than you. You've done your chieftain proud. Now I ask you, can we do this? No false bravado now, can we do it?"

"One moment, Captain," grinned Hausenfoss as his hands flew across his instrument panel. "Captain, we are ready to go. In fact, we are not in such bad shape as we thought. Heather left us a few extra hands, and they've been busy making repairs. We can do it, Captain."

"Now that does please me. Heather will skin me alive if I lose her ship."

"Incoming ship," bawled both ships' sensor readers at once. "Just dropped sub-light."

"Whose is it?" demanded Selian.

"Ours. Incoming message."

"Selian, where is the Mjolnir?"

"Freydis is on the surface, and Drass is making a pass on the dark side of the planet, Tornan," replied Selian. "I've been left in command of the fleet."

"Brek, what do you think of that?" laughed the voice.

"Brek has fallen, Tornan. The Falcon was lost with all aboard, but Thordik managed to recover her. She has been renamed the Valkyrie, under Erikr-Dak ownership, Larthaness is currently commanding."

"I grieve at your loss, Selian. This ship is the Slepnir, Tornan commanding, Chieftain. May we join your fleet."

"You are most welcome, Tornan. What is your status?"

"We've gutted two other ships to make her battle worthy, Chieftain. We have three light-plus engines, three sets of shields and we added two extra sets of ion cannon. It took a bit to get used to the handling of three engines, but she is surprisingly agile."

"Excellent, Tornan. The plan is thus, as soon as Drass returns we will attack. Our objective is to knock down at least one transport ship. We three will try to keep the fighting ships entertained while Larthaness goes for the soft underbelly."

"I am yours to command, Selian. I like the plan. Those damned transports must never be allowed to escape."

"Chieftain, the Mjolnir returns."

"What news, Drass?"

"All enemy ships are in view, Chieftain," replied Drass. "They're going to be very protective of their loaded transports. I'd wager they'll just sit there waiting until they're all loaded, then try to escape under the protection of the raiders."

"We shall afford them no such luxury. Drass, the newest ship to the fleet is the Slepnir, Tornan commanding."

"Welcome aboard, Tornan."

"Thank you, Drass. We're ready, Chieftain."

"Lock shields," barked Selian, and all four ships moved closer together.

As soon as she had control they all leaped towards the cluster of ships orbiting above Earth. Selian held them together until they made contact. The locked ships with enhanced shields struck like a hammer, all guns blazing, and then they split. Three ships rolled to one side and right through the defenders.

The Valkyrie turned away and dove under the ponderous transport ships. Like a striking shark, she rolled beneath one gigantic ship and opened fire. Her guns raked along the belly of the huge ship, gutting it like a fish. The Valkyrie finished her run then banked hard before a fast return to her position near Mars. The others swiftly joined her there. Together they watched as the giant ship slowly rolled on her side then crashed back to Earth.

"That was just a taste," Selian's voice purred over the ship to ship. She was unaware that her musings were being broadcast to all. "Just a small taste, my enemy, but there will be more. The death of my beloved Brek will cost you dearly, for I will hunt you all to the death.

I will destroy your entire species, even as you have tried to destroy mine."

As she spoke a young warrior reached over to close the channel.

# To the Death

While Selian prepared for another run, Freydis was being pushed back. They'd made their way to Germany, and destroyed another ship in the process, but it went to hell from there. They found still another ship, but this one was bait.

As Freydis attacked, three carrion fighter ships dropped swiftly from space and attacked her from behind. "Scatter," shouted Freydis as they spotted the ships moving in. The Nyman battle cruisers were far superior in space, but the smaller carrion ships and the Grey Raiders were superior in an atmosphere.

All her forces scattered at her command, but Freydis' small ship almost seemed to be singled out for special attention. Sliding behind the controls herself, Freydis saw only one means of escape and she took it. With a diving left roll, Freydis' fighter swept behind the gigantic transport ship.

The others could not get to her while she was so close, but the broadcast mind control devices were extremely powerful at this range. It was difficult to keep your thoughts clear, even with the aid of the blockers.

Suddenly, Freydis began to curse as the carrion fighters found her. Dozens of scav fighters appeared and surrounded her scout. Freydis fought like a trapped tigress, and both Frank and Gordrall were working the small guns as best they could, but all to no avail. They felt the ship shudder and begin to spiral down as her engines were hit.

Somehow, Freydis managed to get the small fighter on the ground in one piece. They leaped out and made a run for cover, just as the scavs opened fire and destroyed the small ship.

"We're outgunned here, and I'm down," shouted Freydis, as she slapped the pin on her tunic. "I doubt I can survive. Hear me my people, abandon this place and find Heather to the west. She will make a fine earl, may you serve her well."

"We will not abandon you, Freydis..."

"I am lost, do as you are bid, go to Heather." She had time to say little else, as the building she had taken refuge in was suddenly swarmed by carrion foot soldiers. Finding herself alone, with her back to the wall, Freydis sent a silent prayer to her ancestor, and to Thor, then she leaped at the massed troops before her, determined to sell her life as dearly as possible.

As she fought, Freydis became aware of another fighting at her side. It was Frank Hunter, and Gordrall was near also. Somehow they had found each other, then her. It was beginning to go badly, when suddenly there was the sound of human weapons. The carrion fighters began to falter in confusion. The Nymen redoubled their efforts and finally met their human and Nyman rescuers over the bodies of the slain enemies.

"Lord Freydis, it is a rare pleasure to see you again," smiled the tall man as he approached.

"Peter Van de Velde," laughed Freydis. "What are you doing here, and how did you get here?"

"In order, beautiful lady, I am here returning the favour you did for me earlier, and I got here in the small ships you so graciously left for me. You have managed to keep them busy enough, that we got some ground transports running again as well. It was hard going, but we managed to find you."

"And just how did you manage that?"

"We followed all the excitement. I knew that wherever there was excitement, you would be at the centre of it."

"I owe you my life, Peter. One day I hope to repay the kindness."

"We are allies in a war to the death, Freydis. There is no debt between us. All I want is your friendship."

"Oh really?" she asked, arching an eyebrow at him. "Are you certain that is all you want?"

"Well, perhaps not all, dear lady, but it will do for a start."

"This is all very sweet folks, but we have other issues to attend to," growled Frank, as he grabbed a machine gun and opened fire at the oncoming enemy. "There are more ground troops coming."

"Get angry, Peter," said Freydis, as her smile faded, "rage is your best weapon against the mind control. Hide your people there and there. We will lure them into the trap. Frank, Gordrall, with me now."

A short while and a hard battle later, they were once more alone. Peter had acquired a German guide who led them deep into the city. A game of cat and mouse followed that went on for two days until they were finally cornered.

"INCOMING FIGHTERS," shouted a voice on Heather's shoulder.

"Whose?" she asked, as she fought on towards the control centre of yet another transport ship.

"Ours," supplied the voice. "They say that Freydis has been shot down and has declared you the earl, Heather. They're here to help."

"Put them to work then, swiftly now, let none escape." She fought on and soon she reached Thordik who had already gained the bridge. The carnage was swift and merciless as they cut down the enemy.

"Thordik," gasped Heather, as they stood searching for signs of an enemy.

"I heard, my sister."

"Thordik..."

"Gordrall and Frank Hunter were on that ship with her. I know, my sister."

"Do you think they're dead?"

"I don't know, Heather. What do you want to do?"

"First, let's empty this pig and blow it to hell. Then we're going to Europe."

"It shall be as you desire, my chieftain." Thordik began bawling orders.

Heather soon found herself back in the sunlight, as millions of captives stumbled from the downed ship. "Hurry, keep them moving," shouted Heather, as the fear of a surprise attack, and her impatience to rush to Frank's aid, overcame her. It took far longer than she wanted, and eventually she gave up waiting. The sun was beginning to set.

"Thordik, leave as many as necessary here to complete the task. We're moving out. Tell those left behind to finish up here then beat a retreat to Iceland and await further instructions there. Bring me someone who saw Freydis ship fall."

It a very few moments the small Nyman fleet of fighter scouts was ready to take off. A woman Heather did not know was brought to her. "You saw Freydis go down?"

"I did, Lord Heather."

"I am Heather, nothing more. Freydis is Earl, and it stays that way until I see her cold dead body. Now, what is your name?"

"I am Gudrir of Pull-Karr, Heather," grinned the battle-scarred woman.

"Gudrir, take me to the place where Freydis' ship went down. Hear me people, follow this ship and stay alert."

Without further ado, the Nyman fleet leaped into the air and shot away to the east at terrifying speed. The thunderous crack as so many small ships broke through the sound barrier was deafening.

All was in darkness as they reached the place. There were several downed Nyman fighters as well as dozens of scavs and one transport ship. The Greys had set down one their own to bait Freydis in, but it would not rise again. Somehow they must have known she was the leader and focused on destroying her.

Silently they settled to the ground, then Heather touched the pin at her shoulder and called softly. "Freydis, can you hear me?" Nothing but silence responded to her call. She tried a few more times, but to no avail. She tried Frank and Thordik tried to reach Gordrall, but no answer.

"Nothing," sighed Heather as she leaned back against the wall of her ship. "Thordik, if they are still alive, what are the reasons they would not answer?"

"If they survive, their communicators must either be blocked or damaged, or they may have been captured and stripped of their clothing."

"I don't like it at all. We will rest here, then try again as soon as it becomes light." With that she settled down and promptly fell asleep against Thordik's shoulder.

"We will avenge them, my sister," Thordik whispered softly into Heather's hair as she put her arms around her chieftain, and allowed her own fatigue to claim her. The rest of the small fleet put their own ships on automatic sensors, then settled down to rest.

Dawn found Heather pacing restlessly. There was still no response from Freydis. "Clerisa, take a ship and rise up as far as you dare. See if you can locate them. If you can, give me their location. If you are threatened, go straight to the Valkyrie or to Iceland, do not try to return."

"Understood, my chieftain," declared Clerisa, as she and two others leaped aboard a scout ship which shot skyward. It made one swift circle then returned. Heather and Thordik were waiting as it touched down. "There is another transport ship under attack Heather. It is not so far away. Freydis is there with human troops, but they are getting their heads pounded."

"Mount up!" Heather leaped aboard Clerisa's ship with Thordik right on her heels.

FREYDIS DUCKED BEHIND a wall then ran to avoid enemy laser fire. The wall was sliced to pieces where she had been standing. "There has to be a better way."

"Fire in the hole," bawled Frank, as he opened fire with a small rocket launcher. The missiles exploded in the street right in front of advancing carrion fighters. The burst pavement, tossed up like shrapnel, managed to get past several personal shields and do some damage, but not nearly enough. Slowly but surely they were getting pushed back, herded into a corner like trapped animals.

"May I say it has been an honour to meet so beautiful a woman," Peter grinned, as he fired his rifle at the feet of the oncoming enemy, catching a few with the ricocheting bullets. "My one regret is that I did not get the opportunity to take you dancing."

"Well, we're not dead yet. You may yet get your chance. Everybody get down!"

Freydis had heard the squawked warning from her battered com device. She did not completely understand the words, but Gordrall had. "Everybody down," he bawled as well. "We've got incoming fighters."

Like a swarm of angry hornets, the Nyman fighter fleet swept down on the gigantic transport ship. They spread out to attack the carrion fighters while Heather led fifty ships right inside the huge bay doors. Freydis and companions stayed down and caught a breather as the Nyman fleet took over the battle. A while later the carrion fighters on the ground began to mill about in confusion. Freydis then led her new troops into the fray.

Freydis stood leaning against Peter's shoulder, as a gore bespattered Heather approached. As Heather neared, Freydis pointed to her left. Heather looked and saw Frank resting against a wall. With a squeal of delight, she flew into his arms. "Oh Frank, when they said Freydis was shot down, I…"

"None of that now," soothed Frank as he held her tightly. "None of that, we're alright, all of us. Your timing is impeccable as usual though, my darling, much longer and we would have been fried chicken."

"I did promise to keep him safe for you, cousin." Freydis smiled as she approached. "I have kept my word."

"Heather is earl now?" Heather arched an eyebrow at Freydis. "I am so very sorry, cousin, but if I am not allowed to run off with my lover, then neither are you. I am very much afraid that you are still the earl."

"When I gave that order, Heather, I was certain we would perish within moments. We were badly outgunned, and rather than see my entire clan fall in a futile effort to save me, I sent them to you."

"I am a bit overwhelmed at your faith in me, Freydis. Are you sure you weren't just trying to slip away for a few days?"

"What?" Heather just grinned and nodded at Peter.

"You must be Heather MacKay-Hunter." Peter poured on the charm as he reached for her hand. "I had thought that there could be only one woman so beautiful, but Frank did assure me there are two."

"A pleasure, Peter, but you must stop distracting my cousin from her duties. We have a war to fight, and it is she who must lead us."

"Ah well, if I must. Heather, see what you can do to outfit Peter's troops with mind blockers and small arms."

"I'm on it," said Gordrall, as he squeezed Thordik's arm before racing away to see what he could scrounge for their new allies.

"Ships rising," called a voice. They turned to look at the sky and saw several transport ships rising into the air.

"They're leaving." Freydis leaped towards a small ship.

"Mount up," bawled Thordik as they all raced to their ships.

As the Nyman fleet of fighter ships leaped into the sky, Peter Van de Velde's shoulder suddenly spoke to him in Freydis' voice, startling him almost into shock. There was a small pin attached to his shirt that he had not seen before. "I will return, Peter," she purred, mischief clear in her voice. "Make certain you are still there when I do."

"I will be waiting," he called to the ships vanishing into the morning sun.

# Desperate Measures

"**S**omething big is going on down below." Selian had barely left the bridge for days, and it was showing.

"Selian, you must rest..."

"Not now, something is afoot. Prepare for another run. Ready?"

"Ready, Chieftain," came three voices at once.

"Lock shields. This time we break them up completely."

As she gained full control, Selian sent them in hard. They struck like a hammer right at the thickest cluster of fighter ships, ignoring the transports. "Break!" They sent the enemy scattering and she released control of the three other ships. They split apart and shot in different directions.

As usual, the Valkyrie went for the transports and again she was successful. Larthaness took her back to his post near Mars orbit, but only the Slepnir and the Mjolnir returned to him. Suddenly they heard Selian's voice as her small fighter ships emptied from the Raven and fled to the rest of the fleet.

"I will join you in the Summerland soon, my beloved Brek. My engines are gone, and my shields have failed. I am drifting out of control and being pulled down to the surface. Once the enemy realizes I am crippled, they will come.

"You will come to me, my enemy, and I will have a surprise for you. Even as the Valkyries come to take me home, I will strike at you. Even in death I will destroy you. With my last breath I will curse you, and lash out from the shores of death. I will not go gently from this realm, but kicking, biting, and tearing at your throat."

"Selian, get the out of there."

"Lead my people well, Drass," replied Selian as the enemy sensed her distress and began to close in, "the fleet is yours now."

"Selian! Dammit. Larthaness, what in hell's name are you doing?"

"Tornan, Drass, keep them off my back." The Valkyrie shot toward the stricken Raven.

"Go," barked Drass, as the Slepnir and the Mjolnir leaped forward. They shot past the Valkyrie and the Mjolnir struck the enemy like a hammer. With manoeuvres that her bulk would belie, the Slepnir joined the fray. Startled at the sudden attack, the enemy split apart yet again.

"Get out of here, Drass," shouted Selian, "the Raven is lost. I am too low into the atmosphere and starting to burn. Get out."

"Hang on, Selian, we're coming." The Valkyrie, streaming flames from her burning shields, swept under the Raven.

"Larthaness, you cursed fool, you'll kill yourself..." Her protest was lost, as she was thrown to the deck when the ships struck together. The Valkyrie locked her shields around the Raven. They were deep into the atmosphere now, and the shields were struggling to hold up against the heat and weapons fire from the enemy. Slowly, like a leviathan rising from the deep, they struggled up out of the atmosphere and into a swarm of enemy ships.

Just as the Valkyrie rose with her cargo, the Mjolnir struck again, scattering the enemy and giving Larthaness the pathway to freedom that he needed. Once free of the atmosphere, the Valkyrie shot straight out to her post near Mars and released the Raven. "Selian, I'm sending scouts for you. How many are there aboard?"

"Only I am left aboard," she replied softly. "Keep your ships for now, Larthaness. I am safe enough, for I still have life support."

"Can she be repaired?" came the voice of Drass, as the Valkyrie leaped back towards the battle.

"Not in time, old friend. Fight hard." Selian sank back onto her seat, and glanced about at the eerily silent ship that had been her home for most of her life. "I fear you must wait a bit longer, my darling Brek, for they have cheated me of my death once again.

"It is possible Thordik was right. Perhaps there is still something for me to do in this realm yet. Ah Brek, how can I go on without you, my beloved? How can I continue on alone?"

Alone and exhausted, Selian finally gave in to the well of sorrow that had been trying to claim her. She sank to the floor and wept bitter tears as she mourned the death of her life long companion.

As the tears finally subsided, Selian drifted off to sleep. It was many hours later that they found her there on the floor of the bridge. Her second covered her with a blanket, then silently slipped away to inspect the damage to the ship.

"It's no good, Drass," sighed the voice on the ship to ship. "It will take months to repair the damage and make her fit once again."

"Very well, bring your people and whatever supplies you can to the Mjolnir. Once Selian awakens, bring her here as well. She belongs on the bridge of the Mjolnir now."

"It shall be as you say, Drass."

"Drass, what do you think?" asked another voice.

"I'm starting to like our chances, Tornan," replied Drass, as he focused on the display before him. "They're down to barely a dozen fighting ships and we've knocked down several transports as well. We're pretty battered, but I'm starting to like our chances."

"Now is when they will try something desperate," said Larthaness.

"I agree," said Drass. "Stay alert for something nasty."

"Mjolnir, Mjolnir, can you hear?"

"I hear," replied Drass as he motioned for Morness to clear up the signal. They had indeed been successful, if they were getting communication with the planet back.

"This is Kassoth on Iceland," crackled the voice. "I have word that Freydis is down, and that Heather of Erikr-Dak is now earl, but I cannot confirm."

"Acknowledged," Drass replied softly, in shock at what he had heard. "How goes the battle down there?"

"Sorry, Drass," said Morness, "I've lost the signal."

With a deep breath, Drass shook off the shock and straightened up. "Larthaness, did you hear?"

"I heard, Drass."

"The Valkyrie is flagship now, Larthaness. What are your orders?"

"My orders are to stop mourning the dead until we see the bodies," replied Larthaness. "Kassoth could not confirm, so the Mjolnir is still flagship, and once Selian awakens, she will be brought aboard your ship. We'll take our orders from her Drass, until we can confirm otherwise."

"Wise words, old friend," agreed Drass. "As soon as Selian awakens, bring her aboard."

"I am already on the way, Drass," came Selian's voice, as a small ship dropped from the belly of the derelict Raven and shot towards the Mjolnir. A short time later Selian stepped onto the bridge.

"The ship and fleet are yours, Chieftain."

"All captains report." She smiled as she squeezed Drass's huge shoulder.

"The Valkyrie is fit and ready for action, Chieftain."

"The Slepnir is fit and ready, Chieftain."

"All the remaining weapons and supplies from the Raven have been distributed to the rest of the fleet, Chieftain," reported Drass. "All personnel have had a short rest and are ready at your command."

"Very good, Drass. So, let's see what our enemy is up to now..."

Before she could finish there was a shout from the man at the sensors. "Ships rising."

"Whose?"

"Theirs. It looks like they are getting ready to make a run for it. More ships rising. Our scout fighters are returning."

"Close in, give them covering fire," commanded Selian, as the three ships leaped forward.

With a barrage of fire from the warships to distract the enemy, the small fighters made their way to open space and freedom. As the last of them broke through, the big ships backed off and took them on board. A short time later Freydis strode onto the bridge of the Mjolnir.

"Freydis, it is so good to see you alive," said Selian. "We heard that you had fallen, and that Heather was now earl."

"The report of my death was a bit premature," grinned Freydis. "I was indeed shot down and facing my doom. I gave the order to raise Heather, but she refused, and so I had to return."

"Now that is a tale for another time, and I do want to hear all of it," said Drass.

"As do I," agreed Selian. "Lord Freydis, the ship and fleet are yours."

"Report."

"The Raven is lost and has been stripped. She can be repaired with time, but not right now. The Mjolnir, Valkyrie, and Slepnir are fit and ready for battle."

"Thank you, Selian."

"Lord Freydis."

"Yes, Tornan?"

"Both the Mjolnir and Valkyrie have their chieftains on the bridge, but the Slepnir has none. I believe the battle is about to come down to the final, and most desperate encounter. We would be honoured if Selian could take the bridge of the Slepnir."

"You have no need of me, Tornan," said Selian. "Do not give up your ship so lightly."

"I do nothing lightly, Chieftain," he replied. "In time you will want to reclaim the Raven, but for now we need you on the Slepnir. The battle is about to come down to it, and the entire fleet should face this with a chieftain on the bridge. You know this to be true. You have led the fleet well, Selian. We would feel a lot better if you were here with us."

"He's right, Selian. Go now, for I suspect there is little time left to us."

"It shall be as you command, Freydis." Selian fled the bridge of the Mjolnir. A short time later she was on the bridge of the Slepnir, just as the enemy fleet formed up and began to move away from the planet.

"THEY'RE COMING OUT," declared Gordrall, who was now at the sensors of the Valkyrie. With Thordik peering over her shoulder, Heather fastened her gaze on the display before her. She could see the enemy ships form up with the last dozen or so fighter ships leading the transports. The Nymen had dealt a terrible blow, for there were less than thirty transport ships left to the Greys. Slowly they began to advance on the remnants of the Nyman fleet floating just outside the orbit of Mars.

"Suggestions people?" asked Freydis, over the ship-to-ship.

"Shall we back off a bit and let them come out to us?" asked Selian. "If we let them get far enough out, we can use the point singularity cannon again."

"Good possibilities there. Heather?"

"Sounds good to me."

"I don't like the smell of this," muttered Larthaness.

"Talk to me, Larthaness."

"Well, it just seems too easy to me, Freydis. We've pounded their heads, and cut their numbers to less than a quarter of where they started. Why would they just come out to their doom?"

"I agree, old friend," said Freydis. "I expect they will engage us with the fighter ships, then the transports will scatter in all directions. We cannot let a single one of them escape, for if they do, they can rebuild their fleet and return to finish us off. We can't go another prolonged battle against such odds. We've lost too many warriors and too many ships for that. We must end this here."

"Then I suggest we adopt other tactics," interjected Heather.

"You mean we keep them bunched up and pick them off one by one?"

"Yes, I can see that you are one step ahead of me as usual, cousin."

"Here they come," declared the man at the sensors of the Mjolnir.

"Back off and let them come out a bit," commanded Freydis. "Heather, lock shields with the Raven and bring her out with us. I want them to think we're still at full strength."

Hausenfoss was at the controls, and he easily slid the Valkyrie up beside the Raven and locked shields with her. Together all four vessels backed off as the enemy advanced.

"THEY'RE GONE, I BELIEVE," sighed the old battle-scared warrior sitting in Ragnar's office. "At least they seem to have for now. We've got all our coms back, and the air is quiet. We'll give it a while, then send those ships Heather gave us to check things out."

"That is indeed good news, Kassoth, my friend." Ragnar sighed as he sank back into his chair. "If it is indeed true. If they truly are gone, then Iceland has escaped unscathed. You are a warrior of vast experience, do you think they are truly gone?" Ragnar eventually had to prompt the old fellow who would not meet his eyes. "Kassoth?"

"I have a bad feeling, Ragnar. This is too easy. Our ships have cut them apart, and we've held our own on the ground. They had time to fill most of their transports, but I don't see how they expect to escape with them intact."

"You suspect a trick?"

"I think they'll get them ready to go, get as far out as they can to draw the fleet away from the planet, and then send some of their fighting ships back here."

"To draw your fleet away from the transport ships and allowing them to escape?"

"Yes, but Freydis will never fall for that, so we will be on our own until she can finish them off and return to help us."

"Can we survive, Kassoth?"

"With the addition of Heather's eight ships, I believe we can, but it will not be easy. The rest of the planet will be on their own."

"Then I must warn as many of them as I can. Hope for the best, but prepare for the worst. What should I tell them?"

"Get out of the cities. If they come, they'll destroy the cities and all signs of industry. That way they can expect to return in a few generations for another harvest without facing newly advanced weapons. They'll try to drive you back into barbarism by destroying as much industry and technology as possible."

"You believe they will try to return?"

"If a single transport escapes with its millions of captives, they can rebuild their fleet and return. If that happens, I doubt we can do a lot about it. I expect our fleet is pretty battered by now. Great Thor's beard, they've actually destroyed a fleet twenty times their size. They can't have come away unscathed."

"You paint a very bleak picture of the future, my friend."

"Shall I lie to you?"

"Please do."

"Call your friends, Ragnar," chuckled Kassoth as he rose slowly to his feet. "Tell them to scatter to the hills. We can worry about rebuilding after the enemy is gone."

With that, he left the office and Ragnar reached for his phone. "Inga, see if you can raise Thomas Mooreland for me, would you please?"

# The Final Battle

As the Nyman fleet backed off, the enemy continued to fly straight at them. "We can't wait much longer, Freydis," muttered Drass, as they reached the asteroid belt.

"I want to get them a bit further out, Drass," she replied, never taking her eyes off the 3-D display before her. "They're too damned big to hide in the asteroid belt, and I want a bit more room to manoeuvre."

"Yes, but they're picking up speed. They'll make a break for it any moment."

He was right. Just as the enemy fleet passed the asteroid belt, eight of the twelve remaining enemy fighter ships suddenly turned back towards the planet while the rest of their fleet broke formation. "Split starboard." Kett threw the Mjolnir into a tight turn. "Hem them in, use all the speed you can, but hem them in. Heather, what are you doing?"

"I'm going after the ones who turned back," replied Heather, as the Valkyrie began to give chase.

"No Heather..."

"I have to. My people..."

"Are here, Heather," said Thordik, as she pulled Heather into a hug and held her tightly. At a signal from Thordik's hand, Hausenfoss turned the Valkyrie around once again.

"Heather Mak-Kay Hunter, chieftain of Erikr-Dak, I, Freydis, Earl of Nyman now demand the loyalty and obedience that you swore to me. Return and help stop these transports from escaping."

The harsh command in Freydis' voice cut through some of Heather's near panic.

"It's a ruse to draw us away, Heather," Freydis went on more gently as she saw the Valkyrie turn. "If even a single transport escapes us, they can rebuild their fleet and come back to finish us off."

"Forgive me, Freydis." Heather sighed, as she disentangled herself from Thordik's arms. She gave Thordik a friendly squeeze on the arm, then returned to her display.

By now the battle was joined. The Nyman ships tried their best to encircle the fleeing enemy, but it wasn't all that easy in three dimensions. On another note, without the fighter ships to defend them, the transports were easy pickings. The Nymen ignored the carrion fighter and three Raiders who tried desperately to engage them. Instead they hunted and shot down the transport ships.

The sheer number of enemy ships was the biggest worry, and several did manage to escape temporarily, but the Valkyrie chased them down. The Mjolnir and the Slepnir with her great agility, stayed to harry the remainder as best they could.

Heather would just knock down one ship when Gordrall would point out the next farthest away. Slowly but surely, by killing the farthest away first they managed to drive most of them back into the tighter area where Freydis and Selian could get at them.

It was a long hard battle for very tired warriors, but they slowly cut down the numbers of enemy ships. Finally Freydis looked up from her display and sighed. "Dammit it all, three got away. See, Drass, Heather is too far away to get them all. She is running one down now, but the last two will elude her, and we are also out of reach."

"Incoming ship, just went sub-light."

"Who? Where?"

"It is the Wanderer, Chieftain," said Tessa. "She dropped sub-light right into the path of an enemy ship. That one is down. Only one escaped us."

"That was one too many. Heather, can you hear me?"

"I hear you, cousin. Again, I beg forgiveness for my poor judgment."

"A moment's lapse only, Heather, and we've all had more than one. Come to me now, and we'll return to the planet and finish the task."

"On my way."

"THAT'S ABOUT WHERE we stand now, Thomas," said the face of Ragnar Thorvaldsson on the big screen. "We cannot be certain of this, but it's the best guess of my Nyman advisors. They have fought these things before, and the home planet of one of their founding species suffered this fate. Unfortunately, they were unable to recover. We are perhaps in a better position."

"A better position? How do you figure that?"

"Our Nyman allies have cut them to ribbons, Thomas, albeit at great cost to themselves. We will face far fewer enemy ships than our predecessors did. We also have our Nyman allies here on the ground as well as in space. We just have to hold out until they return."

"That's pretty easy for you to say, Ragnar, you've got Nyman warriors and Nyman weapons to defend yourself with. We have nothing left."

"Have you nothing at all, Thomas?"

"Our entire military machine was pretty much wiped out in the first attack. Forgive me, Ragnar, is there any advice you can give us that will help?"

"Head for the hills, Thomas, and hide what you can from sight. I am told they will attack the cities, and anything that looks like industry. They want to drive us back to the stone age. With luck this will not happen, but I believe it best to prepare."

"Agreed, and thanks for the warning, Ragnar. Will you folk be all right?"

"I believe they will raze the rest of the planet first, then concentrate their efforts on Iceland. We will be the last, but without the return of the Nyman ships, we will surely fall. Good luck, Thomas. I must call as many others as I can now."

"May God be with you, Ragnar," replied Thomas Mooreland, but he was already talking to a blank screen. "Get me General Drake."

"INCOMING ENEMY SHIPS, eight in all," bellowed the man at the sensors.

"Ion cannon at the ready," roared Kassoth, as he came pounding out of the hanger where he had been conferring with the small fighting force Heather had sent to him. Just as he reached the base of the cannon mounts, the big guns opened fire. The enemy ships scattered out of range, but one had fallen. A cheer went up as it spiralled down into the North Atlantic Ocean.

"Well, that's one," he sighed, as he turned back to the hanger. "Don't waste your time," he growled as he found the ships loaded and ready for take off. "They'll come back to us soon enough. Once they do, it will be your task to lure them into range of the ion cannon. There are not enough of you to bring down half dozen or more Raiders."

"The place seems empty and quiet, now that all our people have scattered into the hills," commented one of the fighters.

"I know," he replied. "I was becoming accustomed to the hustle and bustle of Reykjavik, and now the whole city is empty."

"Have the President and Prime Minister withdrawn yet?"

"Ragnar won't go, neither will the Prime Minister. They're made of the right stuff alright. Ragnar will do what he can for the rest of this world, then he will come here to stand with us at the end."

"That is as it should be."

FOR TWO DAYS THE GREYS pounded a helpless Earth. The great cities were swept from existence as was all signs of industry. Broken pipelines spewed oil onto the dessert sands, where it slowly returned to the ground from which it sprang. Great factories lay in ruins, no longer able to make consumer goods for a population that no longer existed.

The destruction was quite methodical. After inadvertently stumbling into range of the Icelandic guns, they swiftly retreated to the southern hemisphere where they began to obliterate any and all signs of life they could find. Large bands of human refugees were found and destroyed. Nothing was left standing as they slowly worked their way back northwards.

All through Europe and North America people went into hiding. They spread out as best they could, hiding weapons and food and whatever else they could carry. Many large bands were found, but some others eluded the attacks.

In North Central Canada a large number of farmers managed to disguise their machinery, as well as their own whereabouts. In the days to come this would catapult them into high standing world wide.

It took a couple of days, but the destroyers worked themselves back towards Iceland once again. This time they came in from all sides at once. The big guns took down three before they were destroyed, along with a portion of Reykjavik. The Raiders were having a bit of a time trying to bat aside the small fighters that kept buzzing around them.

The combined fire of the scout fighters even managed to knock down one of the larger ships. As soon as it hit the ground, the Icelandic ground troops and Nyman warriors were all over it. The Icelanders were well trained by the Nymen, and all were equipped with mind control blockers as well as effective small arms and personal shields. They soon fought their way inside and a short while later they fled, followed by an explosion that tore the Raider apart.

Even that was not going to be enough. There were only three Raiders left, but without the ion cannon, Iceland was doomed. Ignoring the swarm of annoying scouts buzzing around them, the Raiders began their final deadly pass.

As they opened fire there was the scream of tortured metal as a ship twisted and burned with the speed of entering the atmosphere. Like her namesake, the Valkyrie swept from the skies and struck deep into the atmosphere. She had come so fast that the Raiders had no way to escape her. Two went crashing to the ground as the third fled. The Valkyrie banked and swept back into space, but there was no enemy there for her to kill. The ship that fled ran straight into the Mjolnir, with predictable results.

"Are you completely bloody mad, Heather Mak-Kay Hunter?" sighed Freydis' voice, as the three ships hung in close orbit, maintaining position over Iceland. "Who in their right mind takes a wounded ship deep into atmosphere and opens fire?"

"They have killed my entire planet," replied Heather, her voice so cold it made Freydis shiver, "but they did not escape me. They will not escape me. Ready this damned ship, we're going after the one that got away."

"Easy, my sister, easy," soothed Thordik, as she held Heather tightly. "Frank Hunter, come take her now. We beg pardon, Freydis, but our chieftain has collapsed from exhaustion, and the rest of us are not far from it."

"As are we all," replied Freydis. "Put everything on auto, Captains. Let your people rest. We will meet in my cabin to confer after a full sleep cycle and a meal."

HEATHER HAD LAIN IN Frank's arms and cried herself to sleep. She awakened to his smiling face, and for a moment she forgot all that had happened. The world had been changed forever, but they had survived it. She laid her head on his shoulder and sighed deeply. "Good morning, my beautiful bride," he whispered softly as he lightly kissed her hair. "Care to share a shower?"

"Oh dear gods, yes." She sat up to beam her most winning smile at him. "How long has it been since we had a chance to get cleaned up?"

"Far too long." He grinned as he wedged himself into the small enclosure with her.

They emerged and dried their hair under the blower, then re-entered the cabin to find fresh clothing laid out for them. "You know, this having a chieftain for a wife has advantages."

"Oh yeah? Like what?" she asked, mischief in her voice.

"Well, it is a lot easier to get a good cabin on the chieftain's ship. Now, shall we see if we can get some food?"

"Oh gods yes, you have to feed me, Frank."

FREYDIS, TORNAN, SELIAN, Corfort, and Drass were already waiting as Heather and Thordik entered. All were smiling and well rested. "Freydis, I owe you an apology for my actions during the final battle," said Heather, her eyes downcast.

"Thor's beard woman, if those weakened shields of yours had buckled, you would have burned alive," said Selian. "Freydis has chosen her successor well, I believe."

"That was worthy of a certain earl I know when she was younger," said Drass.

"Heather, you surely must have the blood of the first Freydis in you alright," laughed Freydis.

"You're not angry with me?"

"Well, you could have saved a few for the rest of us. Heather, it was well done, if a bit reckless. In future you will have to be a bit more dispassionate and thoughtful, as an earl should be."

"What are you saying, Freydis?" Heather sank into a chair, not sure if she were fully understanding what was going on.

"Heather, as Earl, I am bound to make certain that the people have a good leader at hand should anything happen to me. I have no surviving children, and my mate was killed long before we set out to find Greenland.

"As chieftain of the next strongest clan, you're the most natural choice. You've proven yourself in battle, you've proven yourself an exceptional leader, and you have proven yourself a trustworthy ally.

"I've chosen you as my successor. I made that choice under fire on the surface of the planet, and since that time you have proven over and over again that it was the right choice."

"But Selian..."

"No, Heather. I lost my love and my spirit in this battle. I have no heart for the task. As soon as things settle down a bit, I intend to retire and let another lead my clan. I need time to mourn Brek, and I need to find a new purpose in life. You are the right choice, Heather."

"But I was going to retire and make Thordik chieftain..."

"No, my sister. At one time, before you came to us, I did think myself ready, but now I know better. There is so much I will learn about leadership from your example, so much you can share with me that will help me in the future. My time as chieftain is a long way off as yet."

"I don't quite know what to say..."

"You could start by saying yes," grinned Drass.

"All right. Yes, if this is what you all want. I'll do what I can for you all, but right now I need a scout ship, Thordik as pilot, and Freydis as passenger."

"What??? What are you up to, Heather Mak-Kay Hunter?"

"Come along and see." Smiling with delight, she rose from her chair and led the way. As the small scout ship dropped from the Mjolnir she called the Valkyrie. "Frank honey, we girls are going into town, can you keep an eye on the ship for me?"

"Gordrall and I are going to play video games, lover," came Frank's voice, full of mischief. "Larthaness is babysitting."

"Works for me. Thordik, take us to Erik's Fjord but do not land."

"Yes, my sister, it shall be as you desire."

A short while later they were hovering above the snow covered valley where Erik Rhode once built his farm. Darkness lay on the silent land, and the new fallen snow glittered in the moonlight. "Now, go westward as we did before, but not so far."

Thordik sent the small craft speeding out over the Atlantic. As soon as they hit the coast Heather turned them north. "Where are we going Heather?" asked Freydis.

"I have a surprise for you cousin. I just hope it still exists. That way Thordik. All right, follow this coastline northwards. Okay, it should be hereabouts somewhere...there, over that way. Yes, land by those houses."

Thordik set the craft down beside some houses that looked like something out of the past. "These look like the drawings of the houses our ancestors once built," mused Freydis.

"They are," replied Heather as she led the way into cold air and the open field. "Come."

"Heather, what is going on?"

"This is the place, Freydis," said Heather. "This is the place where First Freydis fought the Scraelings. That is a replica of her house there. This is where the smithy was located, and that would be where the men fled, leaving her behind. Here she fought them, and here she drove them into the sea, just as you have faced another fleet of Scraeling and destroyed them. I thought you would like to see the place."

With tears running freely down her face, Freydis sank to the ground in the gathering sunset. "All my life I have heard the tale of how she cried out to Freya and turned to fight. Since I was a small child I have heard of how, with broken sword, she drove her enemies from the lands, never to return. Ever have I looked to her for inspiration when the odds against survival were bleak. The battle is never lost as long as you draw breath, that is what she was reputed to have said once the enemy had fled and the men returned.

"Heather, I can never thank you enough for bringing me here. You say that is a replica of her house? They have made a proper monument to her here?"

"No Freydis, to the people here she was a murderess and a villain."

"But this is truly the place."

"Yes, she probably turned at bay right where you sit. This is the place."

"Ah well," sighed Freydis as she regained her feet, "I will not mourn battles lost so long ago. It is enough that you have brought me here, Heather. This is truly a gift I will cherish for the rest of my days."

"I have another reason to bring you here, Freydis."

"Oh? What might that be?"

"You must remember that First Freydis won the battle for the survival of her people, but she lost the political battle that followed. It is a new kind of battle you will face now."

"Then I shall take a page from the Book of Erikr-Dak. As ambassador to this planet, and my heir, I will put you in charge of all our dealings with the people of this world."

"I'll do my best for us all, Freydis, but I'll make no commitments without your approval first. Come now, we should return to the ships."

"You're right, Ambassador," sighed Freydis as she rose to her feet and gazed out to the heaving sea. "Promise you will bring me back here one day."

"We will return, Freydis. We will return, I promise you."

# From the Ashes

"Recall the captains to my cabin," commanded Freydis, as they returned to the Mjolnir. By the time she reached the room they were waiting for her. "Alright people, now we get down to it. First, I want a full report on what has happened at the next system."

"We've found a suitable planet, Freydis," replied Corfort. "It's teeming with life, but it shows signs of being cleaned out by the Greys long ago."

"Have you found any intelligent beings?"

"A few wandering tribes only, but we have begun to trade with them. The air is vile, but harmless, and with a bit of time you get used to it. We believe it is left over pollution from a former industrial age. We're cleaning it up now. A few more turns and it will be good as new.

"We've ravaged what ships survived to make the Slepnir and some shelters on the surface. I managed to get the old Wanderer back into service with one old three times light engine, that's how I managed to get here. Tornan was gone so long we feared the worst, so I came to see what was what."

"Have the folk there encountered any resistance?"

"None. We have named the planet New Greenland. I hope that meets with your approval."

"It surely does, Corfort."

"Drass, give me the bad news."

"We have three functional battle ships, but all need extensive repairs. We have one functioning transport, but she needs repairs as well. The Raven hangs in orbit out past the asteroid belt, and we believe she can be salvaged. There is a lot of debris floating about this system now, and we can also salvage some of that for our needs.

"As for people, our elders, children, infirm, and young mothers, as well as the pregnant, have all survived unscathed. Our warriors have not fared so well. We've lost nearly half of those who came here with us. We can field barely three thousand warriors at this time. We need to rebuild the clans as quickly as possible. I also recommend developing some sort of cloaking device such as the Grey stealth ships use, for both the new home planet and for our ships."

"Agreed. Our supplies?"

"Well down, but I believe we can recover the food from New Greenland, and there is a small planet orbiting the gas giant in this system that contains a wealth of the minerals we will need to create the rest."

"How is the gravity and climate on the New Greenland?"

"The climate is temperate for the most part. The gravity is a bit light for us, but we will adjust easily enough according to my Xtak healer."

"Speaking of healers, if there is a spare healer available, I need him on the Mjolnir. Heather stole my last one."

"I have two on the Wanderer, Freydis. You'll have one aboard in less than a turn."

"Heather, I need Skeezix over here as well, to confer with my new healer."

"Sure, but what are you up to?"

"If that gravity is a bit light for us, maybe it will be tolerable for the humans. If that is so, perhaps we can recruit a few folks from the planet to bring up our numbers a bit. In a generation or two all would be easily adapted to the gravity of New Greenland and our people would be as one."

"That makes good sense to me. Thordik..."

"Skeezix is already on his way, Heather."

"Alright then, here's what we shall do," declared Freydis. "We'll take a few days to rest, then we will get down to work. Selian, it will be your task to take the Slepnir and salvage what you need to revive the Raven. Once she is battle ready, take her to New Greenland in case they might need you there.

"Tornan, once Selian is on her way you continue to salvage as much useful material from this system as you can. The Mjolnir will assist you. When the salvage operation is finished, we begin the mining."

"Shall I search for mineral deposits in the new system?" asked Selian.

"Of course, but your primary mission will be the defence of our people there. Corfort, as soon as the Raven is ready, you will transport all our folk from the surface and carry them to New Greenland.

"Heather, your task is to create ties with a new world government on the planet below. You also need to get as many recruits for us as you can. They will accompany our folk on the Wanderer, for the internal gravity of the warships will be too great for them to bear. We can damp it down a bit on the transport. Use whatever means you feel necessary to get this done."

"Freydis, the folks on Earth will want to hold some sort of celebration in our honour, and you will be expected to attend."

"I believe I would like that, Heather. Will you need the Valkyrie close at hand, or can she help us with the salvage operation?"

"If I may, Freydis, I would like to tow the Raven in close so the people on the planet can see the ship hanging above Iceland. Those on the ground need not know the ship is damaged. This way I have a ship at hand, and the Valkyrie can assist with the salvage operation."

"All right, but we'll put a crew on the Raven just in case you need to make another demonstration."

"I like it," laughed Heather. "Selian, may I borrow your ship for a while?"

"I would be honoured, Heather."

"Then let's be about the business, people," said Freydis as she rose to her feet. "We'll meet right here in three days for an update."

"Thordik, I'll need a scout to take me down to Iceland," said Heather as they made their way to the docking bay of the Mjolnir. "You take the Valkyrie out and retrieve the Raven. Put whoever you need on her then send Larthaness out with the Valkyrie to help with the salvage."

"It shall be as you require, my sister." Thordik led the way to their scout ship. Skeezix was waiting for them there.

"Skeezix, what's the good word?" asked Heather as they climbed aboard.

"The new healer on Lord Freydis' ship is a very pretty girl," purred Skeezix.

"Oh really? What about the gravity thing?"

"The new planet has good gravity for humans and Nyman folk. Both can survive there, but is best of all for Xtak folk."

"That is good news indeed." Heather smiled as her small scout rose up into the belly of the Valkyrie.

Thordik grinned as they arrived in the docking bay. "Wait right here, Heather, Frank will be right along."

"Good thinking, my sister. I'll need his advice on all matters political, as well as other duties."

"Other duties?" asked Thordik, arching an eyebrow at Heather.

"Well, Freydis did say we had to repopulate the clans, didn't she?"

"Indeed she did." Thordik grinned as she touched the pin on her shoulder. "Gordie, send Frank Hunter down to the launch bay, he has a lot of work to do."

FOR THE NEXT SEVERAL days Heather toured the planet in her small scout ship with Thordik at the controls. Frank had stayed in Iceland to help organize a meeting of the world leaders, or at least whatever was left of them.

Ragnar had insisted that Heather occupy the residence of the American ambassador which had been abandoned as soon as the second fleet had arrived in the solar system. Each night she returned there and first conferred with Frank and Ragnar, then reported to Freydis.

For a nearly destroyed planet there were actually quite a few people left, scattered about the world. With the help of the Nyman scout ships, many of the leaders were transported to Reykjavik for the summit meeting. Ragnar knew what was coming, but he had not prepared any of the others at Heather's request.

The big day arrived, and as soon as everyone was seated in the meeting room, Heather entered and stepped to the podium. She sighed to see only thirty people assembled there. Only thirty from the hundreds she had addressed at the United Nations not so very long ago.

"Good morning ladies and gentlemen," she began, "I am Heather MacKay-Hunter, ambassador to Earth from the Nyman fleet. Not so very long ago I had the unhappy task to warn you that a deadly enemy was at your door. This time I am here to tell you that enemy has been defeated, but not completely destroyed."

There was a round of applause at that and she waited for it to subside before continuing. "Against all odds, the Nyman fleet was able to destroy the enemy ships, all but one. Unfortunately, that one most likely was filled with human captives, many millions of them. With those captives, the enemy will be able to reassemble their fighting forces and fleet in less than a single generation. They may, or may not, decide to return and wipe us out, but we believe it is best to err on the side of caution. I have asked you here to assign your tasks to you."

There was a loud outcry at that, and she waited for order to be restored. "I know you don't want to hear this, but you must, my brothers and sisters. The old ways are gone and will not return. You must forget all your past differences and work together if our species is going to survive. No longer do you have the luxury of a few people being able to hoard the resources, or the power over the many. The days of self service are past. Now is the time when all people must work towards the safety and well being of the entire species. From now on a man's wealth will be judged by his accomplishments on behalf of the many. The Nyman folk will help guide you in the new ways.

"Hear me well people, you can work with us, or you can be swept aside. It's for you to decide. Know this, the rebuilding of Earth's defences has already begun. The few remaining Irish have, by their own request, been annexed by Iceland. They will begin by growing the food for a more industrialized Iceland. This is an example of what must be done.

"America, Germany, and Russia have managed to retain a few of their top minds, if not their industries and infrastructure. I believe a pact of mutual benefit is already in the works there. Canada has somehow managed to retain a large portion of its arable land, as well as the means to farm it. She will be needing workers as well as fuels for her machines. Iceland has already pledged to help. Can you see where this is going? You know what you have to do, so stop squabbling among yourselves and get it done.

"Now for the one you really won't like. In the past, all attempts at forming a true world government were futile, as the major nations, my own especially, refused to share power. Those days are past, for you no longer have the luxury, or the time, for petty rivalries. A new Nyman style of world government will be established. Earth will now be governed from Reykjavik..." Heather had to pause again as she was shouted down once more.

"As I was saying," she went on relentlessly, once order had been restored, "Earth will be governed from Reykjavik, and the Nyman Alliance will give Iceland the means to enforce this. You can get on board, or you will be swept aside like so much dirt on the sidewalk."

Only silence greeted this statement, so she continued. "We would surely have preferred another approach, people, but there is no time for playing politics. We must rebuild earth's industries, and create a planetary defence system that is effective, and we have precious little time in which to get it done.

"Under the Nyman style of government, no one is allowed to hoard resources, no person and no group or organization. All work for the common good. There is also a strong emphasis on education, as well as combat training, and that will be implemented here as well.

"Now, I have cruised the planet with the Prime Minister of Iceland at my side. She has seen the devastation first hand, and has devised a plan of action. Each major geographic area will be appointed a governor, and through that governor food and supplies will be distributed. I will go into no further detail, for that is the task for the new world President, Ragnar Thorvaldsson. Ragnar, the floor is yours." With that Heather stepped down from the podium.

It took the rest of the day for Ragnar to hand out the laurels and assign the Governors their territories. Thomas Mooreland buried his face in his hands as all that was left of North America was placed under the authority of a retired Canadian General who had reappeared to organize a resistance movement. Europe and Russia went under the Norwegian king who also had fought the enemy hand to hand. The Nymen had little use for a leader who hid underground.

The Germans and the Americans were to spend their efforts on trying to rebuild some industry, while the Canadians and the Russians were given the task of rebuilding the world's agriculture. It went on and on until well past dark.

The next day was much more fun for everyone as there was to be a grand ball, something that would be almost impossible anywhere on Earth except Iceland. The Nymen arrived in a different kind of clothing. There were many bright colours, and the shimmering clothes were snug to the body. The women were in mid length dresses with billowing sleeves and the men were in one-piece suits with flared legs.

After the feast there was music and dancing. Freydis herself had arrived for the party and had been duly feted. As the dancing began she was approached by a familiar figure. "Lord Freydis," smiled Ragnar as the tall man approached, "this is Peter of Orange, king of the Nederlands."

"Thank you for the introduction, Ragnar, but Lord Freydis and I have met before. I do believe I owe you a dance, my lady."

"Indeed you do, sir, but I am quite unfamiliar with the steps of this dance."

"Fear not, fair lady, for I shall be your guide." He smiled as he took her hand and led her onto the dance floor. "Put your hand here, and this one here, now, I will steer us about and all you have to do is come with me." With that he gently started them off.

"So, you're a king, are you?" she asked as he swept her about the floor.

"A king of a destroyed land and a vanished people, Freydis." He smiled sadly. "Our cities are gone, our dykes broken, and the lands submerged, our industry is gone, and most of our people have been killed or captured.

"Without our industries, our few remaining engineers will not be able to rebuild, or maintain, the remaining dykes, and so the sea will soon fully reclaim my poor battered country. I have been assigned a German overseer, a fact that rankles me somewhat, but that is an old wound that should not be reopened. No, my dear Freydis, I am no longer a king, just a man from a vanishing people."

"Perhaps there is no need for them to vanish, Peter." The music stopped and they applauded politely with the others.

"What do you mean, Freydis?"

"Ah, ah, ah, not unless you dance with me again."

"It will be my very great pleasure to do so, fair lady." It was odd for him to be gazing directly into her eyes, for indeed she was fully as tall as he, and if possible, her eyes were bluer.

He smiled as the music started and he swept her into another dance. "What were you saying about my people?"

"My own people are colonizing a planet that orbits the nearest star, Peter. You say your folk are engineers and farmers. I know them to be courageous fighters as well. You are welcome among the Nyman folk if you wish to come."

Peter nearly stumbled and fell at that, but he recovered nicely. "That is a truly tempting offer, Freydis, and I am so very intrigued. Tell me, what is the catch?"

She laughed with delight as they twirled about the floor. "All right, I'll confess, Peter. First, the gravity is heavier than you're accustomed to. It will take a while to adjust, but I have been assured by our healers that you can do it. Also, there is no trace of the slave religions among us and we intend to keep it this way."

"Slave religions?"

"One form of it was brought to Greenland by Erik Rhode's son, and I have seen how they have almost destroyed the planet and made it ripe for the pickings, by keeping everyone at each other's throats. We believe they may have been started by the Greys, but who can say for sure?

"Among the Nyman folk each clan is dedicated to a god or goddess from the tales of our ancestors. Each clan has a chieftain, and a second to take his or her place should they fall. The clans elect an earl to lead all the people, and that one is usually the chieftain of the strongest clan.

"In times of war, the earl names a successor so the transition is instant. All the clans work toward the common good and survival of the people. This is how we live, and this is how you would have to live as well."

"I am not a religious man, Freydis, nor are most of my people. I was planning to ask Ragnar to absorb us, but you present me with an enticing option. When do you need an answer?"

"In a few days from now, the Wanderer will be transporting most of our folk to New Greenland. Any of your people who wish to go, are welcome. Heather can arrange it for you."

"I will consult as many of my folk as I can find, Freydis. I'm sure that many will take advantage of your generous offer."

"What about you, Peter? Will you come?"

"I have no useful skills, Freydis. I would be of little use to you."

"Oh, I believe I can find something useful for you to do, Peter," she purred in reply. His laughter was full and rich, and something he had thought he would never do again. "Peter, you're a natural leader, and those of your people who join with us will need you there. They will look to you for guidance."

"Alright, Freydis, but only if you promise to dance with me from time to time."

"Peter, I have no surviving children, and my companion was killed in battle long before we set sail for this system. I'm still young enough to bear children, but I am getting a bit old for games. I like you and believe we could do well together."

"Are you proposing to me, Freydis?" he asked, mischief in his voice.

"Yes I am, so what are you going to do about it?"

"Freydis," he replied softly, as he pulled her closer to him, "I will do my best here for I, too, am aware of the attraction between us. I have not been alone so very long, but this war has caused many years to pass in a number of weeks. If you are serious, I will accept your proposal."

"I am serious, Peter, but we will have little time together in the near future. Once the situation here is stabilized, I will take the Mjolnir and join you on New Greenland. Now we must escape this affair, for I want this night with you before you are spirited away. Come."

She took his hand and led him off the dance floor. Soon they were inside a scout ship. "Kett, are you on the bridge?" she asked, as she guided the small ship into the air.

"Here, Chieftain."

"I have vanished into the depths of space and cannot be found, Kett. I care not if Thor himself comes looking for me. I cannot be found."

"Understood, Chieftain," laughed the voice.

"Now then, I believe I may just be able to find the place again," she mused, as the small speeder shot out over the ocean.

"What place is that, Freydis?"

"The place where my ancestor, whose name I bear, fought and defeated her enemies. There is an empty house there, and I think we shall occupy it for a short time."

# New Beginning

Weeks had gone by and things on Earth were beginning to settle into a routine. It was still winter in the northern hemisphere, but, with the help of the Nymen, the Canadian farmers had a solid crop going in South America. As soon as that was harvested it would be planting time in the north. The salvage operation was complete and the repairs to the warships were finished.

Selian had handed the Raven over to her eldest daughter, Breklass, the new chieftain of her clan. There had been a few Nylass among the carrion fighter they had fought, and so Selian and Drass had built a super scout ship from salvaged parts, equipping it with a fifteen times engine. They planned to go looking for them. Somewhere out there were surviving Nylass, and they hoped to find them and bring them back.

Freydis had taken the Mjolnir to New Greenland to join her new mate and the two thousand or more Dutch people he had recruited to join them. Now only the ship assigned to the Governor of Sol System and the Ambassador, hung above the Earth. The Valkyrie floated in the sky above while her scouts ferried folk about the planet, as well as to and from the mining sites throughout the system. Only now were Earth engineers beginning to understand that the metals needed to build such ships could only be produced in zero gravity.

On the planet, the scattered remains of a once vast population was beginning to be brought together in several centres for easier distribution of services and education, and the efforts to educate were intense. The old world was gone. Ragnarok had come, and the survivors were now trying to rebuild by working together.

"Well, Governor, what do you think of it all?" asked Heather, as Frank held her gently in his arms. They were snuggled down in the cabin of the Valkyrie.

"Actually, I think we are getting somewhere. A lot more humans survived than we first thought. It will take them some time to completely let go of the old ways and embrace the Nyman system, but we're getting there."

"Ragnar says you're a natural diplomat. He says you're very persuasive."

"I just tell folks that if they aren't willing to be reasonable, I'll hand the situation over to the Chieftain of Erikr-Dak, or the Captain of the Valkyrie. The threat of having to deal with the dreaded Heather, or the terrifying Thordik, is all it takes to make them see reason."

"Frank, did all this really happen? Sometimes it seems like it was just yesterday that you spotted the Mjolnir out in space, and other times it seems like that life was just a dream."

"I know, lover, I know. So tell me, did you really give Thordik the directions to the hideout in Denver?"

"They need a place to get away once in a while, honey, you know that. I'm still amazed that it survived the devastation."

"Yeah, me too, sweetheart. Have they finished building the monuments to Erik Rhode in Greenland?"

"Yes, that's what they are celebrating tonight. Frank, honey?"

"Mmmm?"

"Remember when I said I'd marry you and bear your children if you could find those little Grey buggers?"

"Ah-huh, and I remember I said I wanted six kids too," he replied as he lightly kissed her hair.

"Only five more to go, husband."

"Heather?"

"Yup, we've got incoming, Frank."

## The End

And now for a peek into another world:

### Rise of the Queen

by

**Prudence MacLeod**

**Book one of the Elvish Chronicles**

(second edition)

Copyright June / 2016

## The Chronicles

Herein I will endeavor to record the events which brought the Elves back from the gates of extinction to rule the vast forests of Elendor. Through several twists of fate, and the rediscovery of their ancient magics they were returned, and now they inhabit and control the vast forests of northern Elendor.

It all began with the sudden appearance of the assassin...

## Shadow Assassin

IN THE CITY OF MAGDAN, as ruled by the Geni Overlord, Ocra, the night had fallen strangely silent. It was one of those odd silences that sometimes falls for no reason, and vanishes a moment later. However, it was enough. Ariel, newly promoted to the City Watch, arose from her bed with liquid grace, stepping into her soft boots and silently sliding her sword from the scabbard hanging at her bedside.

Ariel, descended from the High Born Elves of Elendor, had managed to earn her freedom from slavery and rise to a post in the Watch. Few Elves ever managed to earn freedom; none had ever been trusted to carry a sword.

With silent steps she slipped from the building and cast her gaze about for anything that was amiss. She found it on the rooftop, a shadow in the moonlight that did not belong. A few swift and silent strides carried Ariel to the dark figure. "Stand and surrender." She spoke in a clear ringing voice as she laid the tip of her blade against the intruder's neck.

"Not tonight, little sister. Go back to your warm bed and your dreams of glory. Live to fight another day." Ariel was shocked. First, the voice was low pitched, yet feminine, and gentle, almost loving, caressing her senses. Second, the intruder had spoken in High Elvish, a language that was forbidden on pain of death. Few remained who could actually speak it.

Ariel didn't realize the figure had moved until a strong arm encircled her neck and a silvery blade caressed her cheek. Again that gentle loving voice spoke. "Go back, little sister. I've come here this night to take a life; I'd prefer it not be yours. Return to your warm bed and sweet dreams." The arm left her neck and a strong hand deftly relieved her of the sword. She barely noticed it happen.

Ariel felt the intruder step away and she turned to face her opponent. The moon broke from behind a cloud to show her a tall Elf with elaborate tattoos on her left cheek. Ariel swallowed and stepped back. "You're one of the ancient Borni tribe. You can't be real. Your people died out centuries ago."

The woman's eyes danced with merriment and her smile was radiant. "No, little sister, we did not vanish from the realms, but we did withdraw from this one for a time. Now we're returning." That voice was still soft and gentle, almost hypnotic. "I must be about the business now. I beg you, do not follow me or sound the alarm. It would grieve me to have to harm you."

The woman tossed Ariel her sword, then leaped from the roof top to vanish into the shadows of an alley below.

Without a second thought, Ariel followed as best she could. This Borni was like a wisp of smoke in the breeze. Somehow Ariel managed to catch sight of her quarry often enough to keep up yet stay back out of sight.

Her heart froze in her chest, the woman had slipped into Ocra's house, the most heavily guarded palace in the entire region.

Ariel knew she should sound the alarm. She knew it would mean her death if it was discovered that she had known of the intruder but done nothing. She swallowed hard, but before she could make a decision, the Borni slipped out of the house, carrying a sack. There had been no alarm.

"A common thief," mused Ariel, disappointed, and not knowing why. And then she saw the blood dripping from the bag. The Borni had said she'd come to take a life. By all the gods, what had she done? Ariel followed as the assassin headed for the wall that surrounded the town. With a cat-like grace the woman leaped to the top and disappeared over it, vanishing into the darkness below.

Ariel climbed swiftly to the wall and peered over as well. The assassin was sitting on a horse below, waiting for her with a huge smile. "Well? Are you coming or not?"

Without a second thought, Ariel slipped over the wall and landed beside the horse. A hand was extended and she grabbed it, swinging up behind the Borni as the horse leaped away. She could hear the alarm sounding back in the town.

As she clung to the rider, Ariel's heart beat wildly with the sudden and intoxicating rush of true freedom.

# Don't miss out!

Visit the website below and you can sign up to receive emails whenever Prudence MacLeod publishes a new book. There's no charge and no obligation.

https://books2read.com/r/B-A-ZKBBB-LJEBD

**BOOKS 2 READ**

Connecting independent readers to independent writers.

# Also by Prudence MacLeod

**Children of the Goddess**
Lady Blue
Fallen Angel
Lady Justice
Lady Shadow
Lady Seeker
Watcher and Warrior
Shadow Ascending

**Children of the Wild**
Immortal Tigress
Children of the Wolf
Vampire's Lair
The Hawk and the Wolf
The Oregon Incident
Race the Wind
Heir to the Throne

**Elvish Chronicles**
Rise of the Queen

The Road Home
A Winter Seige

**Forgotten Worlds**
Suvi
Echo of the Past
Survivors
Ship
Fleet
Unite
IGEN
T.E.N.

**Nova series**
Novan Witch
Novan Witch
Assassin of Nova
Beyond Nova
Claimstake
Red Nova

**Standalone**
The Second
Hell Comes Home
Incoming

Watch for more at https://www.prudencemacleod.com/.

Telling a story is like knitting a sweater. Start with a ball of possibilities, pull out one small thread and begin. With luck and patience you will create something quite wonderful.

## About the Author

On a far off windswept island Jennifer Crandall sits with her dogs and cats creating fantastic stories for all to enjoy. She publishes as JL Crandall, Prudence MacLeod, and Jenni Leigh.

Read more at https://www.prudencemacleod.com/.

www.ingramcontent.com/pod-product-compliance
Lightning Source LLC
Chambersburg PA
CBHW020734250626
47155CB00003B/757